James,
All the best!
L.B. Sisk

www.lbsisk.com

PANTERIA CHRONICLES
DAMNED

L.B. SISK

Copyright @ 2016 by L.B. Sisk

ISBN-13: 978-1540399007
ISBN-10: 1540399001

All rights Reserved

No part of this publication may be reproduced in any form or stored in information storage or retrieval systems, or transmitted by any electronic and mechanical means or otherwise, without the prior permission of the author. A reviewer is authorized to quote short excerpts for this book's review.

This is a work of fiction. Names, characters, places, and incidents either are productions of the author's imagination or are used fictitiously. Any resemblance to actual events, locales or persons, living or dead, is entirely coincidental.

Cover design and Artwork by Ron Sacdalan
Interior design by L.B. Sisk

ACKNOWLEDGEMENTS

Once again, to my family, who were just normal enough for me to be the *weird* one.

To my friends, who have put up with my antics, and have yet to send me on the Long Walk.
(The comic book reference with judges, not King's novel ...).

To my friends who have provided extra eyes on my work, and having to edit the product created by my deranged mind.

To Ron Scadalan for the beautiful cover and the help. If you are an author who needs incredible cover art, please contact him at PageBacon, www.pagebacon.com.

You the readers, thank you.

<><><><>

CONTENTS

PREFACE	9
CHAPTER ONE	27
CHAPTER TWO	68
CHAPTER THREE	91
CHAPTER FOUR	121
CHAPTER FIVE	194
CHAPTER SIX	215
CHAPTER SEVEN	223
CHAPTER EIGHT	262
EPILOGUE	287

PREFACE

Memories and dreams sometimes can seem indistinguishable from one another. Sanity provides the edges.

(About the Neo-Holocaust)

—Harker Garvey, Controversial Televised Therapist, Refugee Trauma Center (2157 A.D.)

The van lurched. Jennifer screamed and watched the missiles pelt her house and the surrounding neighborhood.

"No, no," she yelled, trying to see Max, see if he was still strapped down—No, where he should have been was a hole with scorched edges. *What the fuck?* "Max? Max?"

She heard screams from across the street, and she looked over in time to see people incinerated by heavy lasers. More rockets slammed into the street, and a wave of dust spread everywhere.

"Sir, I think I found someone," a man's voice shouted through the explosions.

Jennifer held her breath. She could see his shadow coming toward her. She tried not to make a sound, not sure if the voice was really talking about her.

"Over in the van?" another voice asked and Jen's heart started pounding.

The shadow came closer. An armored helmet peered into the van's wreckage and looked Jennifer's way. "It's okay, young lady," he seemed to say calmly. "It will be over soon."

Jen began to calm down when she saw military fatigues and insignia, but she gasped when the soldier raised and pointed his gun at her. "I'm sorry, but my orders are clear."

"Oh my God," Jen screamed and—

"Jennifer? Jennifer?" a warm voice asked. Gentle hands grasped her shoulders, even though she tried to fight them off. "Jennifer, it's okay. It's me, Rebecca. Remember?"

Hendricksen opened her eyes and blinked back tears that so desperately wanted to come out. She looked around and found Max safe on a doggie bed. Then she focused on a tall woman, face showing concern, standing over her.

Where are we? She noticed a PDL in another woman's hands near the door. That woman wore a caduceus on the left breast pocket. *A hospital?*

Right. Right. She fought down the realness of the nightmare, and remembered that she was staying with a group of people called *Crystalians*. Their leader Jim St. John had rescued her from a mutated gorilla named Gridlock, who had been a captain in a military organization called Infiltration. *That* was a group even the President of Panteria didn't know about.

The woman gently holding her was Rebecca Anita Alexander. She had been helping her cope with her parents' deaths and new life.

That was an understatement. Hillmount Estates, Jen's former home, had been wiped out by a band of rebels/vigilantes in reaction to a horde of escaped criminals who had taken refuge there. Then, on her way to try to find her uncle in California, she had nearly been abducted and raped by Gridlock, only to be saved by Jim. Then, upon her arrival to Crystal Mountain, she had learned that rebels hadn't been involved at all. In reality, the sub-rosa government, the Puppeteer Government and controlled by the Panterian Guard, had ordered the strike. One of its organizations had gotten a bit overzealous and had killed everyone—innocent or otherwise. Yet, regardless of that cluster fuck, the resulting cover-up had pointed to a group of "merciless" rebels, which simply ignited an even greater "anti-rebel sentiment" by the general population. All in all, it was a "Win-Win" for the Guard.

"Jennifer?"

"Uh, yeah, sorry." She shook her head and smiled at Rebecca. The woman was tall, about six-foot-two, and strong and beautiful. She also had long platinum blonde hair, the bluest eyes Jen had ever seen, and her body would probably make any swimsuit model want to hide in shame.

Alexander had been born via a government project known as FEMET, which had created super soldiers for the Puppeteer Government. Since Alexander's own parents had been murdered because of governmental cover ups, Jim must have thought that Jen and Becca had something in common. Needless-to-say, despite being a government-trained assassin and being able to press fifty or sixty tons or more, Rebecca was very sweet.

Jennifer smiled timidly and grasped her friend's hand. "Rebecca, sorry, I just had an awful dream. It took me a moment to calm down."

She remembered the actual events at Hillmount. Unlike the recent dream, when she had woken up in the van, it had been covered by debris. The subdivision had been completely leveled and no one else had survived within a five mile radius. She never found her parents, since her house had taken direct missile strikes.

Tears began to well up again and she felt Rebecca's arms encompass her. "It's okay, Jen. Trust me. It's going to take time to get over, but I'll be here. You understand, don't you?"

Jennifer held back the tears though, not letting them pass, not ready to grieve the loss of her parents just yet. She couldn't help thinking about them, and then couldn't help thinking about how she'd been thrown into this!

Unbelievably, this rebel group, these people the media was branding as terrorists and vigilantes, had taken her in, clothed her and offered her a home if she wanted it.

Am I still dreaming? She just nodded her head, hugged Rebecca tightly and willed herself back to sleep.

<><><><><><><>

The Panzer armor spun, leapt fifty feet up into the air, and then did a summersault before it landed quietly. Inside the four-foot diameter, diterium-polymer ball, Logan eyed the five, match-head-sized targets at the other end of Hanger Bay Two.

"I'm going to show off now," he laughed to the glee of elementary-school kids, who were all behind thick electromagnetic barriers.

"And when would that be any different than ... *ever*?" Ecie teased.

"OK, you got me!" Logan immediately did a single-armed handstand in the armor, picked up five needles from a stand and tossed all of them at the targets. Each needle sank halfway into a match head.

The crowd cheered as they watched it happen on giant 3D projections above them.

Logan pushed off with the armor's fingers—propelling him forty feet up. As he fell, his cape extended and billowed and his gas jets hissed as a cloud of smoke and chaff blasted around him as he landed. He'd added the "smoke screen" years ago, which had helped during various hostage situations. Sometimes a ten-foot-tall, robotic monster walking out of smoke was more impressive than a cloaking field being deactivated.

"Drug Czar Burnett"—Logan increased the volume of his speakers so he could be heard over the screams of glee—"had ridiculously small security bots that swarmed potential intruders. I took out scores of them like I did with those match heads. They were a real bitc—pain in the butt!"

The kids giggled at his sudden shift of descriptors. And of course his use of "butt."

"However," he laughed. "Fire is a good resolution to most things." He tapped on the case—labeled ROASTER—that rested on the lower half of the ball of his armor, which was where the flame thrower was. He'd use *that* piece of hot awesome on the rest of the security bots, the building and good percentage of the personnel.

Instead of pulling that out though, he pulled the fifty cals, which were holstered on the armor's hips, and proceeded to shoot zombie-shaped targets positioned away from the crowd. The zombies made squawks and other weird, zombie-dying sounds as they were blown apart. Logan had seen someone making those on some old show for fun, and he figured the kids would enjoy that. They did. Who doesn't like killing zombies? Especially Zombie Flanders?

Logan laughed to himself. He liked the classics—well, not what *most* people considered classics. Growing up in war-torn California had left him with limited entertainment options as a kid… until he'd found a collector's treasure trove of literature and history.

Being a kid ... and later a big kid ... he'd found a good chunk of shows and books in the 20th, 21st and 22nd centuries as particularly entertaining. Naturally, he still kept up with the current stuff—he was a junky. However, his obscure references of one-thousand-year-old fiction often got blank stares ...

Occasionally, he'd bump into someone that managed to have stumbled onto entertainment or various artifacts from the Old World. It was always nice to meet someone that shared your guilty pleasures. Well, without having to recruit a newb ... So, now, he only needed to find a single lady with the same interests.

Ha. Like anyone would put up with my baggage, he joked but his smile faded briefly, thinking about what *that* baggage was. Wanting to think of something else, he turned and faced the crowd. "You must remember that the Executioners only hurt people when necessary. Your parents have taught you the value of life. But some people are very bad. In the end, they have ultimately harmed themselves."

Hmmm ... Logan chewed his lower lip on that one.

"Ah, the 'Look at what you made me do to you' analogy," Ecie chuckled over their private channel. "Isn't that what a comic-book villain would say?"

"Muah ha ha ha," Logan laughed maniacally. "Nah. It was what my brother used to ..." He paused, thinking about his brother Eli. How many years had it been since he died? Was his mother still alive? Did this vendetta he had against people like Burnett even matter? How many people would he put into the ground by the time he was done?

Jim's scrutiny echoed in Logan's head as he walked over to a stage. It was weird that a Kurgon Beast seemed to have such a laissez-faire attitude toward recreational drug use, especially considering how much they had affected St. John's life. Sure, Logan, conceded, it wasn't Jim's choice, but still. Needless-to-say, that was the ideological difference though between Jim and Logan.

And Logan still believed that if they could "wake some people up" the public might start questioning what the government was doing in California, why some businesses had private armies better equipped than what the Marines had ...

Fuck, Logan cursed to himself. *The Panterian Guard and the rest of the Puppeteer Government have operated in secret long enough!*

He moved over to the stage, which was about five-feet tall. He popped the armor's hatch, removed the control helmet and pulled himself out. He jumped onto the stage, quickly threw on some coveralls and addressed the crowd, "Okay, everyone, thanks for watching me make a spectacle out of myself. I hope you enjoyed the show."

The kids, teachers and chaperones clapped and cheered in response.

"I know you all are going to get lunch in a bit, but you'll all get a chance to take a look at the Panzer armor as you walk out. So have fun. I'll be around to answer quick questions, but make sure everyone gets a chance to see it."

"Umm ... remember the message," Ecie reminded him.

"Oh ... right ... and don't do drugs!"

"Hi, Dad," Rebecca said in the holographic theater.

Her father's image suddenly materialized beside her. "Hi, Daughter," he said stoically in a computer-like voice ...

They both laughed and she gave him a hug. They were talking daily now. The program her father had left for her—a personal assistant to help her sort through and access his research—was very much like him. She suspected that he had had access to some type of brain-scanning tech, which might have allowed him to copy over some of his personality traits and experiences.

Naturally, she didn't ask, nor did the holographic image ever offer any clues. Ecie could have looked at the code if she asked, but the Executioner Computer Console, an organic sentient computer, told her that *that* would be a bit "creepy."

"You did something new with your hair," he said.

"Yes." She nodded. "The platinum blonde look is fun. Not that I have any choice. But I figured some pink highlights would spice it up some."

"I'm sure 'he' thought it was cute?" he teased.

She blushed. She'd had lunch with Jim after her salon appointment. "He was. He doesn't stutter very often."

"You are going to give that poor boy a heart attack, child," her father laughed. "You should..."

She was giving him that *warning* look, which meant to drop it. It was fun to talk about the innocent flirting, but Jon Alexander knew when to bite his holographic tongue.

"He's a good friend, Dad," she offered carefully. "That's what we *both* need right now."

"I know, sweetie. You know that I just want what's best for you. Even though *some* dads might object to their daughter dating a Kurgon Beast ..." He father smiled. "Hmm ... okay ... I think it's best that you guys are *just* friends."

"R-i-g-h-t." She allowed herself a "girlish" giggle—soon realizing that she had been allowing more of those out than usual lately.

"Anyhoo." He shrugged. "Why are we meeting in the holo-theater today?"

"I wanted to go on a walk with you."

"Ah. You know that I don't need exercise, right? I'll be *thirty-nine* forever."

"You've been hacking into Logan's collection again, eh?"

"Moi? I was an investigator, not a spy," he laughed, feigning shock at such an accusation. "Besides, Logan told me that I should watch the *Jack Benny Show*. I can actually digitally put myself into the audience. I look good in black and white."

"You are such a dork," she teased and laughed when he gave her his *sad* face. "Anyway, you want to take a walk in the moonlight?"

"Sure, that sounds peaceful."

"Great." She waved her hand and the room disappeared and was replaced by an actual moonscape, with the United States' Apollo 17 moon landing in the background.

"Ooooo! Pretty." He looked around quickly, not even giving Rebecca the satisfaction of ridiculing his choice of words. "This should be fun!"

Her father was—or *had* been, she had to try to keep telling herself now days—an ancient astronaut junky. He always used to say that people had it way too easy these days. Hell, parents were taking their kids to mining operations in the Kuiper Belt and Oort cloud.

Rebecca had never made it out that far. She had led a team to the main asteroid belt to expose a group of stigs to vacuum a couple of years ago. Those dumbshits had planned to drop a rock just outside Tamorami—and one on it—if their demands weren't met. *That* was the last time terrorists traveled out into space for nefarious dealings.

Fighting in space sucks ass, she thought, remembering the three month trip there and back, with much of *that* time spent tracking those bastards down. Apparently, most people agreed with that bit of wisdom. Wars with the colonies on Mars and in the Venus atmosphere centuries ago had had very high mortality rates. And those were the reasons why there were no longer any colonies out in space—just mining operations or research stations. Most fighting just happened on Panteria ever since.

"Yep." She grinned, tears starting to form in her eyes as she looked his way. "I thought you'd enjoy it. Happy ... umm ... happy birthday!"

He blinked. His eyes began to glisten too. "You ... you remembered?"

"I will never forget again. I'm sorry, Dad."

"Thank you, Rebecca. That means everything to me."

For the rest of the day, Rebecca and her father toured the landing sites of an ancient civilization. The monuments were still up there on the real moon. She and her father had never actually gotten to visit them when he was still alive, even though he had always promised that he'd take her one day.

He was like a kid at an amusement park as they toured each landing site. She even watched while he hopped into one of the lunar rovers, which he almost immediately drove over a cliff ... and almost rolled it over twice. Of course, he was pretty damned proud of that, especially since the fastest recorded speed for one of those things had been 11.2 miles per hour.

Rebecca promptly asked Ecie to create a holographic trophy for that honor. However, the award presentation later, in the middle of ancient Wrigley Field, which had been somewhere in Toldeclevchikee, seemed to be a bit over the top.

"No," Arthor said to Terry Dupree, who was the representative of Delphi, the Tunnel Plex adjacent to Delta Six and one of the original ones. "The inforuns haven't uncovered any of nirv's middlemen."

"How do we know that it's from a central supplier?" Janet Pascal asked. She was the council woman for Timberland.

"We don't know for sure, but the labs tell us that all the samples seemed to have the same chemical composition."

"Ah. Right. The inert material and excipients ..." Janet nodded from across the table. Arthor had called the meeting with Crystal Mountain's remaining Governing Council, who were the mayors of the thirteen Tunnel Plexes that made up Crystal Mountain. Logan, Rebecca and John were on the Council as well, and they were sitting at various spots around the table. They didn't govern any of the Tunnel Plexes they lived in, but they were mainly here for input about Panteria. Logan said that he was thinking about running for mayor of Denver-Springs if Kerry Richardson decided not to run again.

"Yes, there are very slight variations, but mostly probably due to varying lots," Arthor added. "But it appears that everything is made at the same facility."

The members of the council all nodded. This meeting today was a follow up to one Jim had with them before he had left on his own inforun. Arthor's last call with Jim seemed promising, so as Lt. Governor, he wanted to make sure that everyone was up to speed, especially since not everyone here was an Executioner.

"Do you think Jim will find anything," Kerry asked.

"I don't know," Arthor responded. "There are rumors of multiple warehouses out there, since global distribution started almost immediately after Logan killed the other czars. We just don't know why."

"They're like fucking rats," McMillian cursed. "Kill one but there are a thousand nests everywhere else."

"We've questioned dealers," John Powers said in his even monotone. "However, we haven't gotten anywhere. They buy product through accounts on black-market networks. They don't get coordinates to a drop until only after the shipment. Therefore, our attempts at trying to lure someone in with 'fake' purchases through accounts we have acquired haven't been successful."

John took a moment to look around to see if anyone had any questions, then continued: "As I just mentioned, we were able to ... umm ... obtain ... some black-market accounts for our forensic accountants. Initially, they were thinking that this group was using some type of credit-modifier chips to simply add the contents of those accounts to them. We just considered this because they have always left the funds in place so that any transfers won't be traced back to them."

"CMCs? Are they similar to what we use when we're out in the field?" Arthor asked. He remembered when he'd requested Ecie to come up with the encryption and algorithms.

"Possibly," John said. "There are many types that can be utilized for what we do. However, we can't be sure, since the chips they might be using aren't ever linked to the accounts. And, well, if they do have the capability to develop and load chips like we do, it explains why they are simply giving the funds away."

"Uh ... *might* be using? What do you mean 'giving the funds away?'" Janet asked.

"They have the capability of verifying payment and sufficient funds in an account—usually some bot program that sends an encrypted signal to a passive receiver somewhere," John informed them. "From there, we assume a CMC is loaded for records and future use. Then ... the actual money that was in the original account is sent to a random charity."

"Wait. What?" Terry asked. "You must be joking."

Rebecca shook her head. Arthor knew that she was as puzzled as the rest of them. "No. The charities are getting money from these people. We are only assuming that they have CMCs in the first place."

"You mean that they might be doing this altruistically?" Horace Milton of Cavern Glenn asked disbelievingly.

"These people aren't fucking angels," Logan chimed in. The man hated the drug world more than anyone. Maybe a bit too much. "They make a product that people still kill themselves over. Anyone remember Hillmount? Or the other drive-by shootings that have been happening, since dealers are still protecting their turf? Or other stupid shit? Hell, just this morning a cop was gunned down in Tamorami over a traffic stop. A damn felon thought that the cop was going to find his stash and arrest him. Santa could be running this show, and I'd still shoot down his sleigh."

"Please never say that around my kids. It's hard enough having them believe in Santa in an underground city, for God's sakes," Janet laughed, as with everyone else. Logan, of course, shrugged and winked, but offered no promises.

"Anyhoo, Logan's right." Rebecca nodded the man's way. "Sometimes you can get a lot of support from the populous when you give away free money, food and build people homes. Drug dealers and dictators seem to have a lot in common. Those actions definitely build loyalty ... until it's too late."

"So how's Jim doing?" Kerry asked.

"He's following up on a lead now," Arthor offered. "He might have found one of the warehouses. It's down on the Yucatan Peninsula. He told me—like Logan just said—that there aren't angels working there."

"Good grief," Horace sighed. "I almost feel sorry for them."

"I'll be the first one in line to piss on all their graves," Logan said in his bad John Wayne imitation.

But would John Wayne say that? Arthor thought.

BOOK II:
DAMNED

CHAPTER ONE

Ah, people suck in this crap, shoot it up, snort it. But do they really forget? Are they really oblivious to all these deaths ... the Genocide?
(About the Neo-Holocaust)

—Peter Mellon, Social Worker, Drug Rehabilitation (2197 A.D.)

Jim quietly walked up to the side of a large building. Normally hidden by a dense jungle, its location had cost him quite a few credits and about two days of secret meetings.

Near the building now, he felt an old ache. He grimaced, remembering how the FGGO's drugs had nearly split his mind in two, with the Beast always having something to say. Without the behavioral modification hormones, it couldn't speak to him anymore; however, he could still feel its presence and persistent motivation when he became angry. He wondered if it got some sick satisfaction when Jim had decided to get more "hands on" in the Executioners' drug war. Hell, he'd never let it out again, but he wondered if it hoped that he'd slip up one day.

Well, get out your popcorn and get cozy, he thought while not totally dismissing the actions it wanted—retribution for what had happened to Jennifer. This was more than simply *that,* regardless of his surprise that it seemed to actually care for someone. However, he'd still used the Beast's motivation to find this place. The rumor mill still hinted of its shady practices. And that was enough.

Jim moved up quietly to the side entrance, making sure the guard at the door didn't hear him. The watchman was dressed in full battle armor and carried a handheld auto cannon. But he was simply resting against the side of the building and hardly paying much attention to the surrounding jungle.

The Mutilator—what Jim had been known on the battlefield—smirked. Because of his natural abilities, the FGGO's scientists—Mad Scientists really—had taken their love of current and ancient comic books and other science fiction ... and had created an amalgamation and tribute to all those fictional heroes.

Why? Why the fuck not? What Jim had become however ...

He took another step closer, and slid a single, unbreakable blade into the man's heart. The guard jerked but died instantly, collapsing noiselessly on the grass beside the entrance.

The Crystalian Governor eyed the man for a moment, briefly shook his head, grabbed the body and threw it three hundred feet into the jungle. He then ran his right hand along the door's face, found incongruence and tore it out of the wall. Immediately, the alarm inside began to blare, and the lights in the hallways alternated from white to red.

"Okay, that was one," he said, aware that he'd just let them know someone was here. However, to increase psychological distress by not letting them know where he was, he triggered his cloaking field, ran into the building, and promptly stopped in front of power conduits and several communication bundles.

At the same time, his helmet began scanning for open connections with the main computer—easily breaking encryptions and allowing him to open up a map of where he was. This place was surprisingly big.

Ahhh, here we go, he thought as he looked at the map. He located the schematics of the conduits and bundles and found nothing that would potentially blow out the main power ...

"Ooopsy ... I guess that's two," he whispered after he ripped into those bundles with his blades. Those awesome crystal goodies were also concealed by his cloaking field ...

He moved along and eventually passed right in front of several thermal and hypersonic motion detectors, but he knew he was invisible to those as well. He still stomped on them with his feet as he walked by.

So ... let's see what you guys got saved up ... Along the way to the main warehouse, his helmet dug deeper into the main computer while it also downloaded its information. He opened and then rifled through the warehouse's document and, then, personnel files. There were some real scumbags here, but they didn't seem to get out much anymore and weren't causing much havoc when they ever left the base for R&R. At least it seemed that way so far—he hadn't seen any recognizable faces in the files that were currently wanted by local cops or any other agencies ...

Okay, well, I guess you've behaved yourselves ... Jim continued down the corridor and stopped at an intersecting hallway. He found himself in front of a security camera, and he briefly let his natural cloak slip, thereby allowing a rapid shimmer to flow over his body.

"That's three and all you get." Of course that wasn't going to go unnoticed, not after he had ripped out the side door and torn through the power and communications bundle in this area. But the Beast had always been rather sadistic, and Jim was aware of his own sins. After all, he had been that monster's heart—

"What the fuck?" he asked when he opened another personnel file. "No. No. It can't be ..."

He stared at the man's picture that was being projected inside the HUD of his helmet. Suddenly his heart sank and his rage nearly tore out of his skin—

He quickly bit down the anger, even though he got angrier by the very idea that he'd almost lost it because of the shock of seeing that motherfucker here of all places ...

No. No. You don't get to have the satisfaction of killing him, Jim teased the Beast, knowing that it was well caged, even if it had tried to break free. *This is for me ...*

Diego Betigray was working at his desk when the alarm sounded. Before he could curse, his Chief of Operations, Donald McLander, burst into the room. His friend had a face of surprise and carried a modified Mark-4 rifle in his hands, and he was obviously listening to communications through his comlink. The guy's office was right across from his own, but how had the man moved so fast?

McLander shouted over the siren, "Diego, there's an intruder in Corridor Six, Level One. We had a signal on him for a second, but then he took out the sensors. Since then, over a dozen sensors have gone offline."

"Maybe it's a glitch in the new system. It'd only be the third one today." Betigray shook his head in disgust. Why he'd let his boss talk him into the upgrades, was beyond him. He knew the guy was just looking out for them, but the upgrades just weren't compatible with the older systems in this place.

His Chief of Ops, a former mercenary, was dressed in a combat jumper and held the automatic rifle tightly in his right hand. Despite the slight show of anxiety, McLander seemed very calm.

"We're checking it out, but there's no sign of Vaskiez. He was the guard at that side door tonight." Don's eye twitched, and then he flashed Diego a friendly but vitriolic smile. "And there is the matter of the door."

"What about it?"

"It was ripped from its mounts and thrown about seventy yards into the trees."

"Fuck me!" Diego jumped out of his chair and ran to and opened the large metal cabinet behind him. He then pulled out a slinger, along with a couple of magazines.

"Man, I don't need this type of shit," he said and strapped the rifle over his shoulder. "So what do you think? Should we go to the main warehouse?"

"That's where I'd go if I were creeping around and looking for something," Don said, waiting in the hallway. "But I sure the hell hope it was someone with machinery that pulled the door."

"Oh yeah?" Diego flashed the same type of smile his friend had presented earlier. "Did you forget that we live in a red zone?"

"Great, thanks for trying to make me feel better."

"Are you sure we should be standing around like this?" Diego murmured, feeling like he was in a bad, action movie. "It never seems to bode well for people standing around like this."

True to form, Diego and McLander, along with fifteen heavily armed guards, were standing in a warehouse, which was in front of a huge storage facility that had been built into the larger room. The proprietary drug, Glaxinol, developed by Hastens Pharmaceuticals, had been in that room for years. Diego was beginning to wonder why he even bothered protecting it anymore.

Well, besides the easy money. Well, shit, maybe not so easy ... He grimaced then, feeling the weight of the weapon in his hands and the slinger's strap digging into his shoulder. He thought about how one of their side doors, thick as a safe's, had been pulled out—frame and all—from the wall and thrown into the bushes. Vaskiez—the poor bastard—had been found deep in the forest and had been partially mauled by some meat-eating goat things ...

Fucking red zone, Diego cursed to himself and looked at his PDL. There wasn't much coming with the security checks, so he checked his messages to see if his online, dating profile had gotten any hits—Skunked!

He put his PDL away and checked the slinger's power settings. Eventually, realizing Don hasn't answered him, he looked at McLander again. Hell, the man hadn't even heard him say anything—his complete focus was on whatever the fire teams were reporting to him.

Betigray looked around him. Except for some supplies needed for everyday operations, the warehouse was pretty much empty, thereby allowing for a clear view of the far wall and doorways, which were the only doors their unexpected visitor would be able to enter.

How did I get into this mess? Betigray contemplated. *A supposed billion's worth of credits sitting behind me, and a potential threat in front of me. God, except for that one container a few weeks ago that was sent for more testing at the FDA, nothing's ever been sent out. I don't even know if this shit is worth more than the containers they're stored in.*

Diego looked at his friend to his right. Don was immersed in thought. And seeing the sure macabre look on the guy's face, Diego didn't bother repeating his question.

Four years ago and just after the buyout of Betigray's manufacturing plant, Don had shown up to help convert the old facility into a giant, secured warehouse within a warehouse. Immediately after that was accomplished, McLander had applied for the new Chief of Operations position. Since Betigray still had some managerial control of the facility, he'd allowed the transfer to go through, figuring it'd be good to have someone here experienced with the new company.

Not that it mattered much. All they had to do was guard some proprietary chemical, which was waiting to be approved by the Panterian Food and Drug Administration. Of course, that seemed a bit like buying the cart before the horse—especially now, considering how four years had passed and they had a lot of inventory. Still, up until now, this had been a pretty easy, lucrative gig.

Not to mention legitimate ... *well, shit, I hope anyway*, Diego wondered, especially after what Francis had told him about the awkward call into the FDA. Still it was probably just a misunderstanding and the agent typed in the wrong number. He'd call his boss and settle all of it in the morning. Until then, the only thing he worried about was the potential risk of corporate espionage and the fact that he still had to live in a red zone. At least for a couple of years ...

Yep, in a couple of years my contract will be up, and Don can do whatever he wants with this place, he thought and daydreamed. Diego meant it too, since he had already picked out and purchased a large penthouse in Tamorami. It was as far away from monsters and jungles as possible. Besides, he always wanted a "bikini party." He figured that he could at least indulge in that ...

Fuck yeah! I earned it! Unless ... I don't get killed. He immediately shook out the thought of penthouse views and looked at his friend again. The menacing façade had eased some. "Don, you hear me?"

"Hmm?" McLander seemed to waken from his trance. Then, possibly, subconsciously, he remembered the question. "Uh, no, this is as good of a defensive line as any. Besides, it's not like someone's really going to walk into a group of guys with machineguns, armored or—Shit, get down!"

A strong hand pushed, and Diego felt his head hit something hard.

"Shit, get down!" Don screamed, pushing his friend to the floor, nearly forgetting his own strength. Diego didn't argue, and Don figured the man must have been knocked out. Possibly worse, but, right now, McLander had other problems to worry about.

He fired his weapon and thirty rounds flashed toward a large, gaping hole that had materialized a few seconds before. Most of the rounds simply punched through the far wall. Some of them flashed and ricocheted off ... off of *something*.

The other guards saw where Don was aiming and quickly unleashed a horrendous thunder. Bullet holes poured through the far wall and large chunks soon were kicked free.

A few seconds later, the target appeared. It was human—HUGE—and standing in front of the large hole it had created. Bullets and slinger needles disintegrated or ricocheted off its mirror-like body.

Don watched it pick up pieces of the door. He looked at the monster's round, mirrored helmet—

"No fucking way!" Don shouted, while the Mark-4 ran empty in his hands. "No, it can't be you! You have to be dead! I FUCKING KILLED YOU!"

Despite Don's curses, Jim St. John, full of life, stood up with pieces of the metal door in his hands. He then coiled back both arms and threw—

McLander dropped to the floor just before a dozen men screamed in agony. He looked back and watched as more of his friends were literally "tacked" onto the wall. Blood fountained out of their mouths and piss and shit stained their clothes ...

He turned away and watched the TRAITOR come closer. Suddenly, Don became VERY angry. It was a programmed response that he thought he'd never feel again, about an incident he couldn't ignore, even after what he'd done to an innocent family ... even after he had resigned his commission and quit the AOM in disgust ... and even after he had changed his name and signed on with Hastens Pharmaceuticals, his muscles still tightened and his lips twisted into a hate-filled grin.

He grabbed hold of the Deflonalé knife secured alongside his right boot. The blade yanked free and he laughed. He'd stab that bastard in the chest!

"Damn you back to Hell," Donald McLander—AKA Carlos "Chuck" Jackson McNeil—shouted and brought his knife down—

Don got about three feet before the Mutilator cut his knife to pieces. Then he watched himself die in that fucking mirrored helmet.

<><><><><><><>

"Ah, mother fuck ..." Diego shook his head and rubbed the bump there too. He blinked and found himself in the middle of chaos. Moans and cries of agony echoed behind him. Screams and shouts from his guards were panicked and pained. Weapons, Mark-4s and slinger rifles, thundered and slammed at a monster of a man with blood all over him.

A mirrored helmet was atop a shimmering body of quicksilver. It towered over a bloody clump of cloth and torn flesh. Pieces of a Deflonalé blade on the ground beside the red mess were indistinguishable—

"Don, oh my God, w-what ha-have you done!" He pulled his slinger into his arms and aimed. Diego fired relentlessly, but he noticed that the monster hardly noticed his shots. Instead the giant grabbed something from its leg, made an underhand toss and then disappeared and vanished!

"What the devil?" Diego shook his head in disbelief, thinking he must have a concussion or worse. He waved his hand, telling people to stop firing. They did and quickly began to take care of the injured—the injured!

"Don? Don?" Diego threw his slinger down and ran to the lifeless mound of flesh and fabric. "Call for the Doc!" he shouted, falling to his knees, and suddenly lost his stomach when he saw what that monster had done to his best friend.

"Oh God," he cried and shuddered, not knowing what to do, not believing, not imagining what that thing—

"Hey!" He jumped to his feet, suddenly remembering the last few moments of the fight. Searching wildly, he tried to look for any sign of what that sonofabitch had thrown at them. "Shit, everyone out! There's a—"

The bomb's flash was brighter than anything he'd ever seen.

"Jesus Christ! Diego's dead?" Henry Harvardson swore after Bigsby gave him the bad news. Apparently, for good measure, he also threw a pen across the room. That man had a habit of throwing shit when he was angry. "Do you know who's responsible?"

"No, Mr—ah, I mean, Henry," Bigsby quickly corrected himself, since his boss hated it when he used formalities. "But our sources tell us that four organizations could have been involved: McMurphey's Raiders, the Angels of Death, the Executioners, and ... finally ... the Night Rangers."

Bigsby watched his boss scratch his neck and rub his eyes before looking toward the armored statues standing near the front doors of the office. Bigsby had to catch his breath, thinking about who might have been responsible for—

"Hmm, the Executioners," the man said, while the heat through the big windows behind him made Hammerson sweat. Henry's voice was hoarse now after all the yelling. "Bigsby, weren't ... weren't they under suspicion for killing the six drug czars recently?"

"Yes, Henry, that's what our delivery guys are saying." Hammerson frowned, thinking about the past. "But the Night Ran—"

"No. No. No," Harvardson cut him off. His back was turned to him but Bigsby noticed how the man kept rubbing his eyes. "I've seen their type before and we're in their crosshairs now.

"Well, we'll fucking show them how helpless we are. Bigs, will you excuse me for a moment? I need to make a call. Those fuckers just crossed the line."

"Sure, Mr—"

"Bigsby."

"Sure, Henry."

"Thanks."

Rebecca landed the hovervan in a cul-de-sac behind several trees that had managed to survive the bombings in the area. She kept the cloak on, activated the scanners in her contacts and exited the van with her rucksack.

There were several suburbs in Hillmount Estates. Toldeclevchikee annexed the town three hundred years ago, as the megacity sprawled and grew as people fled from the Growth and Red Zones.

She had an idea where Jen's house was, but everything was leveled. The contacts would help her locate all the coordinates that she'd marked before coming here. She kept her own cloak up, just in case someone was here digging through the rubble.

It was still very early in morning, but scavengers were scavengers and who knew what hours they kept? Still, there was so much destruction and it was, technically, still a crime scene. Authorities had only let people in to recover bodies or to find personal belongings. The latter was abandoned once people saw the aftermath.

Motherfuckers, Rebecca thought, wondering who had been responsible for this. *That* was one thing she was determined to find out. The Panterian Guard had released some clandestine agency on these poor people. There was no way whoever did this killing was going to avoid Justice. Justice was going to make them eat her scales. She'd probably even take off her blindfold to see it.

Rebecca had already visited the prison, from which the incarcerated had escaped and had fated Hillmount's destruction. She hadn't found any evidence of a tie-in of nirv with the Puppeteer Government. The prison had been obliterated as well ... so someone fond of conspiracies would probably have linked the two together rather quickly. She was too level-headed for that and never made such leaps. Besides, even if the government was involved and were starting to directly drug its populous, would people even care? Quite a few recreational drugs *were* legal or, at least, overlooked.

She had found several pieces of cargo vehicles at the prison, so maybe there had been a "not-so-legit" delivery company that had delivered nirv there? It was a long shot, but she'd place a bid for information anyway.

She wandered around for a while, surveying the damage and checking off some of the locations that she had marked earlier. Whoever had smashed Hillmount had been thorough. It looked like a massive tornado had cut a swatch through the city.

She walked to Jen's old house—or, at least, what was left of it. She looked at the rubble that had covered Jen's van, which had hid her from the attackers.

Alexander still wondered how Jen's father had managed to snag a military-grade transport, which still had active sensor-evading tech. Although it didn't have a cloaking device and Jen would have been toast if it had been out in the open, the van's stealth tech had kept her alive.

The ex-Infiltrator scanned and recorded the impact craters from the nazor rockets that had removed the front lawn and the one that had plowed through the house. She jumped into one of the craters and collected any piece of the rocket she could find. She also collected some personal effects for Jen—well, those items that hadn't been scorched or crushed.

Eventually, she moved on. It wasn't until she got to another location—one which she had tagged as a potential missile strike—when she found an intact nazor rocket buried deep into the ground.

"There you are, you little bitch," she said as she carefully dug around it. Developed by MBDA-Raytheon, the Nazor 5210 missile was pretty small—about a foot in diameter and six-feet long. Its repulsar drive had one function: insane speed. Hence, the name "nazor rocket." Because of it and its kinetic energy, most didn't have a large warhead—except to destroy it if it got stuck like this one. Also, because of that insane speed, it had a relatively sophisticated guidance system. A guidance system that—if still intact—might have some info in its brain.

Undoubtedly, no information about whom or what type of craft had fired it would be in there. But, because most weapons now days in the Puppeteer Government were smart weapons to avoid "friendly fire," there were some special, revolving ID codes that a bullet, bomb or missile tried to avoid.

Naturally, a three-part code buried deep in firmware and made to look like un-used programming annotation wouldn't mean much to someone from the Puppet Government. Rebecca, on the other hand, had investigated cases in which the tech had failed. Fortuitously, she had been given "smart" codes and code-generation protocol from several minions of the Guard. She also had a damned good memory.

"Oooooo! Looky. Looky. What do we have here?" she whispered, just in case her voice could set off the ordinance. It was small in this nazor, but it would hurt like a motherfucker if it went off, and especially if they had used an antimatter charge ...

She chewed on her lower lip, wondering how strong the detonator might be in it. Despite the explosion that had nearly killed her at Eric's old fortress, she was tough, so she only wore armor—similar to what Arthor wore in battle to mimic his cloaking abilities—when necessary. As she pried open the inner housing of the missile, she wondered if she relied on her natural toughness a little too often ...

As hoped, the guidance system had survived the impact. And, if she recognized any of the codes ...

Normally, an Agency in the Puppeteer Government didn't give a fuck if a rebel, terrorist or any other stig found out that they were linked to a particular killing. *That* just added to the threat of what the government could do.

Rebecca, however, worked for the Executioners. And they kept records and made "to-do lists" for just this type of thing.

Payback is going to be a bitch, she promised.

Ding, dong. Ding, dong.

"Hmm?" Jim rubbed the sleep from his eyes as the doorbell rang. It was morning and bright out. Like most apartments in the Tunnel Plexes, his home had windows so that the artificial sun could peek through the curtains.

The bell rang again. "Come in. I'm in the bedroom," he grunted, coughing out his first words of the day. He knew Ecie would open the door for him, so Jim sat waiting.

He stretched out on the bed, and then looked to see if the machine guns from last night had left any marks. Like always, even if the bullets had somehow managed to pierce his skin, they would have been absorbed by his body. However, as long as he could remember, no weapon had ever given him much problem, except for a few high-yield concussion bombs he'd been next to long ago. But *that* had been a long time ago.

"Whatever," he said aloud, mimicking something Rebecca might say. He'd always healed instantaneously anyway. And the last thing he wanted to think about was last night ...

McNeil ... his anger ... he hadn't planned to kill them all ... damn ... He shook his head and pushed down the emotions that tried to come back to the surface ... Trying to think of something else, he wondered if Arthor or Rebecca had come to see him. Hell, maybe both of them had stopped by to give him a bad time for sleeping in, try to make him feel guilty and then laugh at the jest.

That lightened his mood some ... He thought about his best friend, Arthor Jones. The Crytonian had somehow been zapped here from another world and his mind had been flashed with an ungodly amount of information about it. Compounding *that* mind fuck was his sudden gifts of super-strength, the ability to fly and turn invisible ... Unfortunately, upon his arrival, he'd nearly killed a kid, lost his sacred armor and sword and had no idea how to return home.

Arthor, however, had done quite a bit since his decision to stay here in Crystal Mountain: He had redesigned the training center. And, under Jim's insistence, he had supervised the installation of Ecie's secondary systems. Also and most importantly, Jones was Jim's best friend.

Rebecca, on the other hand, was a fugitive much like Jim was: She'd escaped from Infiltration, which had been the successor of the FGGO and the organization that Jim himself had fled for reasons ... for reasons he didn't want to face this morning ... So Jim thought about Rebecca and her beautiful smile and kind heart.

He smiled when he remembered the first time he'd met her. In a nearby town, she'd literally bumped into him. He'd laughed at that, since neither had seen the other. He'd been reading a news-site, waiting for Logan to pick him up after completing an inforun. Without realizing it she'd accidentally run into him.

"A-a-are you all right?" he had asked with a goofy stutter, but still had managed to extend a steady hand to help her up. Damn, he had gulped like a doofus too—awestruck by the brilliance of her blue eyes, which she still often teased him about ... "I'm sorry that I was in the way."

"Yes, I'm okay," she'd said matter-of-factly, getting up and dismissing his hand. Then he'd noticed her left arm pressed up against her side. She had been hiding something ...

"Are you sure?" He had taken off his sunglasses and touched her left shoulder carefully. "I knew I shouldn't have been—"

He remembered her stopping him, but this time she'd smiled, as though she'd known him. She had an unbelievably gorgeous smile. "No, it's okay, really."

"It's because of these damned big feet," he'd joked, but then had given her a double take when he'd wondered where he'd seen her before. Then he'd remembered: They'd met at MUTANTS nearly seven years ago. She had been at the FGGO!

"It was my fault," she'd said. "Sometimes I don't look where I'm walking ..."

He remembered how she had looked over her shoulder, making sure no one had been following her. And, naturally, his life-detection powers kicked into overdrive when he remembered who she was—At that instant, he knew that she had been on the run and had forsaken the only home she'd known for years ...

"Or where I'm going," she had added quietly to herself, even though he had heard her anyway ...

Later, he had discovered that Infiltration's leader, General Eric van Anderson, had murdered her father ... Suddenly cutting away years of conditioning—

Three knocks on his bedroom door snapped Jim back to the present. "Come in," he said, while thinking how he'd asked Rebecca to stay with the Crystalians—

Suddenly realizing that it might be her now, he combed his fingers through his hair and grabbed a mint from his nightstand.

You're such a doofus, he chided himself but couldn't help but grin like an idiot. He couldn't help but feel like a kid when they were around each other ... It was good for them ...

We're friends, he reminded himself, knowing how much baggage they each had. The word *complicated* didn't even scratch the surface. However, he did wonder what she might be wearing today—

Fuck! Realizing that he'd just simply crawled into bed after taking a shower last night, he hopped out of bed, threw on some boxers and then jumped back under the covers and tried to act *normal* ...

Yep ... great ... she almost saw my penis, he laughed to himself, and immediately wondered how awkward *that* would have been, while he immediately imagined Logan making the *bow-chickee-wow-wow* sounds ...

Jennifer opened the door to Jim's bedroom carefully. She peeked in when there was room enough to do so. Below, Max did the same. "Jim?"

"Ah, Jen?" Had he been expecting someone else? His face was bright red ... "Come in." His voice sounded different than the day he'd rescued her, the day when he'd killed Gridlock. It was warmer now, inviting. She entered his room, with Max at her heels. "What can I do for you?"

"I came by to talk. If that's OK?"

"Of course ..." Jim was on the bed. His chest and shoulders were solid muscle, and his eight-sectioned abdomen hardly looked human. He was a Nagi, a Naturally Altered Genetic Individual, a person of the Nagephon, who had been employed by a secret government agency. He could fly, turn invisible, had a genius intellect and could probably knock the moon out of orbit ...

She still couldn't believe all this. To the general public, Nagis had always been portrayed as incompetent burdens or threats to society—especially what grew in the red zones. What few human Nagis that had ever been shown had been terribly deformed ...

How many Nagis—human or otherwise—are out there and what are they capable of? she asked herself. No one really understood how the Nagephon—Naturally Augmented Genetic Phenomenon—came about and let alone agreed on when it had actually started. Some blamed the various biological and chemical weapons used during the Apocalypse ... Others tried to link it to the creation of the Growth Zones and all the genetic tinkering that had been going on back then ... Regardless, Nagi were capable for some incredible things ... things that even science couldn't quite explain.

"How are you doing? How are things going?" Jim asked, thereby shaking Jen back to the present, and reminding her why she was here.

"It's not been easy," she admitted and, at the same, chastised herself for not getting to the point. But she was a guest here ...

"Trust me. I know." Jim moved over a little on the bed and rubbed his eyes. "Sorry about not answering the door. I hadn't realized I was that tired."

"No prob. And sorry about waking you and taking our time to get back here ... We were just looking around," she said. "Max wanted to smell some of your plants."

She looked around his bedroom, which was much like his living room. Overall, it was very ordered, very Spartan. She wondered how much time he really spent in this apartment; however, he did have several plants and some paintings. Also, in his den, she'd noticed a wall of ancient books he'd collected overtime.

"No worries." He shrugged and offered his beautiful, warm smile. "So what did you want to talk about?"

"Well ..." She avoided his gaze, noticing a spindly, potted vine in a corner. She suddenly felt shy and unsure of herself. Here she was barging into his place and ready to give him a piece of her mind ... But she suddenly realized that he was the leader of thousands of people ... of warriors ... Killing was what they did ...

She almost decided to change the subject. However, before she had left this morning, Rebecca had told Jen about what Jim had done, and Jen wanted to know why. Hell, she had stewed in the arboretum for hours before she had mustered up enough confidence to confront him about it. She couldn't have the lives of all those people and others on her hands!

"Well"—she didn't like confrontation but she had to tell him how she felt—"I just heard about the incident in the jungle. I get this impression that you did it because of me. The last thing I want to be is the cause of a fucking drug war!"

"Jennifer. No ... no ... it's not that." Jim shook his head, although she could tell he was a little taken aback by her sharpness. Still, he sighed and his face blushed again. "I'm sorry. I admit that what happened to you did make me reassess my involvement in this situation.

"I know you're not going to like what I'm going to say, but the Executioners have decided to protect the Panterian people, and we sometimes take extreme measures to do so." Jim looked at the ceiling for a moment. He didn't say anything right off, thinking of what to say, making sure he made a reasonable point. He had done the same when he'd introduced Jennifer to the Crystalians a few days ago at an assembly and after she'd found her new apartment. He hardly ever stumbled while he spoke, and she loved the fluidity of his tenor voice.

"We'd thought Logan had taken out the worst of the illicit drug lords, the ones who had committed the most murders and had the most dangerous *products*," Jim said, emphasizing the sarcasm on the last word. "However, within a week, nirv had filled the gap, and we've been playing catch up ever since.

"Last night, I managed to track down a warehouse of that stuff from an informant at the FDA. The agent had told me that a new quality assurance manager at the site had contacted him about how the approval process was going for a new drug. The agent didn't have any record of that and gave me the coordinates. He told me it was probably nothing, but the QA guy seemed to be pretty adamant that my contact was typing in the wrong registration number, so he sent it my way, since I'd told him to send me anything that looked suspicious and stuff he didn't have to log.

"When I got to that warehouse last night, I found documents that didn't match any current FDA filings. And, although the company had a business license, Ecie told me that all of the 'angel' investors were proven fake after a few layers of investigation."

Then his face turned red and his smile disappeared ... "Then ... then I accessed the employee files ... and ... and I couldn't ... I couldn't let any of them live ..."

Jen almost took a step back. It was almost like his anger became physical heat—

Max whined and hopped on the bed, and Jim immediately took a breath and his anger subsided ... Jim rubbed Max behind the ears, the cub loving every minute of it. Jen wondered how St. John could be so friendly and gentle, and yet so violent.

"When nirv became available for the first time," he continued. "We'd tried to figure out what harm it could do to its users. Logan, Rebecca and most of the Executioners tried to convince me that it wasn't as innocuous as it appeared, despite my convictions. Then those damned escapees took over your town, and we discovered that people would fight, cheat and kill for it just like any other drug.

"Logan attacked me with the same argument: We had to wake people up. We had to make people realize that it's not a victimless crime ... that we couldn't let any more people die from overdoses ... people being killed when turf wars erupt ... any of it ...

"On a larger scale, he cited the Opium Wars of the 19th Century, Ancient Mexican Drug Cartels... and Tangia, reminding me how illicit drugs have almost collapsed nations because of the corruption, crime and other problems associated with it.

"Needless-to-say, he thinks that such drugs are distracting the populous, making some people—some who could actually make a difference—complacent and disinterested in world events. I don't agree with that, but a lot of rebel groups do."

Jim frowned, but seemingly more out of disappointment than disapproval. "Regardless, the worst drugs like disperal, vermbis and tokom are so strong that people can't even function without them. And, granted, *those* are poisons."

Jim sighed and pulled Max up into his arms and rocked the cub gently. "Max, is a good boy, right? Yes he is."

Max, in reply, attacked Jim's chin with his tongue, making Jen laugh despite the situation.

He looked back her way, smiled briefly and then seemed to ponder something ... "We also must consider what the Puppeteer Government thinks about all this. Considering that drug abuse has doubled in the last decade, it's obvious that the Guard doesn't care what its citizens do as long as the Puppeteer Government remains invisible.

"Ultimately, Logan says that without the drugs many people might discover the truth about the government on their own, thereby bringing us all one step closer to revealing them to the world ..."

Jim smiled uneasily, making Jen wondered if he was contradicting himself, as if he'd once taken the other side of this debate more often than not. Then he frowned and looked away—suddenly Jen felt cold and she wondered if Jim's AC had kicked on ...

"But, obviously, President Lyly's and the rest of the Puppet Government's current wars on the more dangerous drugs are a farce and has gone on long enough," St. John whispered now, but loud enough for her to hear. "Despite what Logan and the rest of the Executioners believe, even I have grown tired of what some of those drugs have done. They are fucking poisons and must be eliminated. It's true that people have free choice, but I no longer want to see babies born to addiction or stillborn, and I'm tired of watching innocent people sacrificed for the profits of a few degenerates ... People that hire people ... hire people that kill innocent families ..."

The flash of rage seemed to light his eyes on fire for just a second before it was gone. He was playing "who got your nose" with Max now. The man was so damned adorable even if he was now sounding like some cartoon superhero trying to have kids "just say no!" to drugs ...

"I don't know," Jen spoke, and then trailed off—believing Jim's words sounded almost naïve. *How can it all be stopped? Even just a particular type? Fuck! People can make tokom from a PDL battery ...* "I don't know. I don't know how you're going to do it. It just seems so complicated and messy. There are so many people that ... that ... and I don't want to be the reason why so many people are killed ... good or bad ..."

Jen stopped, wondering if she should be arguing with a man who'd known about and worked for the Panterian Guard, Infiltration and other secret agencies. Who was she to argue about drugs and their effects on society?

Max yipped and struggled out of Jim's arms and began jumping and playing on the man's giant thigh like it was a mountain. Jim played with the cub for a bit before giving Jen a knowing glance. Then his big, brown eyes filled with sympathy, suddenly reminding her of someone she was trying not to think about ...

"I'm sorry. I can't promise that bad people won't die," Jim said matter-of-factly. "But you're worried about innocent people caught in the crossfire?"

She nodded. The Guard had ordered her hometown to be destroyed because of the drugs and crime that had manifested there. Then had used it as a way to blame it on rebels ...

"Jen, no one's safety is guaranteed, especially when someone concocts a plan that can endanger lives. We're highly aware of that. The very reason why you're here ..." Jim trailed off and looked kindly at her. "We, however, deplore the idea of 'acceptable losses' or 'acceptable casualties' for the greater good. We do what we can to clean up our own messes ... and kill our own demons ... You may think that what I did to those people last night contradicts that, but all the people I killed had blood on their hands at one time or another. *Some* more than others ..."

A flash of anger seemed to ripple through him again, but it quickly dissipated as he petted Max while he spoke. It was almost like ... almost like how ... how her father ...

She had deliberately tried not to think about her family during this whole time. But memories of her home and friends suddenly flooded her mind. Hillmount ...

"I'm one to talk," Jim said apologetically. "Anyway, please understand that we ... we will do ..."

Jen began to feel a tear roll down her cheek. She realized that Jim had paused because of it, and it was now too late to simply wipe it away.

Jim stopped talking, after seeing a tear fall from Jen's right cheek. He let his thoughts move away from his former commanding officer—Chuck, the man who had led the army that had killed Jim's family—and he looked at Jen carefully. He immediately wondered if she actually knew about the possible government link between the new drug and the escapees who had ruined her town.

Indeed, after reading a report from an inforun, he knew that the convicts had actually gotten addicted to nirv while at the prison. Unfortunately, a guard, a closet junky, had taken a dose while on duty and had accidentally left critical doors open to the general prison population.

What worried Jim most was that nirv was being used as a sedative at the prison before its recent rise on the streets. But how was it brought in? How was it introduced? Was the government—Puppet or Puppeteer?—somehow involved? Or was this all carried out by the initiative of the prison psychiatrist?

This was *THE* primary reason why he himself had started getting involved and had told the Executioners to be extra careful on how they targeted anything "nirv" related. What if the Panteria Guard or one of its minions was directly responsible for making it now?

But what if they created it just simply to "sedate" violent people? he thought. *Shit! What harm was a drug when it mellowed an ultra-violent prison population?*

However, knowing the Guard, if they were involved, they wouldn't simply stop at violent criminals. Hell, they might think that *everyone* was a little too violent ... He began to think about a movie Logan showed them a while back. The movie was based on an old television series that had been cancelled before its time. The creator of the series eventually made a movie, which included a plot about the government trying to "mellow out" an entire world—only to have it kill off most of the population. Those who hadn't died became cannibalistic berserkers ...

That, of course, was fantastic fiction by a man named Whedon in the last millennium. But Jim had to admit that he and others of his kind had been controlled in much the same way. However, he was just glad Logan hadn't made *that* leap and tried to instantly blame the government on this one. Fuck! Especially if the Panteria Government was somehow involved ... McMillian knew that a war with the Puppeteer Government was off limits. At least for now ...

"I'm sorry," he apologized for his delay in saying anything, and if she actually knew about the link. Truthfully, he hadn't told her because he didn't have all the facts yet, and he wasn't sure how she'd react. "Jen, I didn't mean to belittle you."

"No, it's okay. I'm still a little overwhelmed by all that's happened." Jen shook her head. Apparently, she didn't know he was keeping anything from her. "It's nothing really. Not enough sleep, that's all. I guess ... I guess I probably should go."

She moved over to pick up Max, but even though she tried to hide it she began to sob and shake. Jim quickly reached out to her and eased her onto the bed, pulling her near him and giving her a hug.

"I'm sorry," she cried. "I miss them so much. I just don't understand. It's too much ... too much."

"It's okay, Jen. It's okay to let it out. It's better this way. Don't hold it in. The last thing you want to do is bottle it up," Jim said quietly but unsure if Jen could even hear him. "It's been so long. I don't think I can cry anymore."

"Henry, are you here?" Bigsby knocked on Harvardson's door. "Are you okay?"

Silence. Hammerson wondered what he was doing here. He should know better. This was a line he didn't want to cross. Not again.

Lindle said he was going to try again later. He should probably just let—

The door opened. "Bigsby, thank you for coming," Henry whispered ... barely able to be heard from his desk deep in the office.

"Of course, Henry. We've been ...worried ... Lindle says he'll stop by later too."

"Okay. Okay," Henry mumbled through his hands. Bigsby, despite his better judgment, walked into the office and sat down in one of the chairs in front of his boss' desk. He didn't say anything, just sat there in the chair while looking out the windows and trying not to look directly at Henry.

"You know ..." Henry started ... then paused. "You know it was me. I was the one who had talked Diego into working for us."

"Oh?" Bigsby had had little contact with Betigray, except for standard inventory and supply requests and the occasional visits to a location that had made it look like the headquarters of a pharmaceutical company. Hammerson was always amazed by how Henry knew everyone who worked for him by name. Despite

Henry's occasional and passionate outbursts, Harvardson was quite loved and respected here.

"Yup." Henry nodded absently. "He was going to pack it all up. The disperal plant was a hand-me-down from his father, and Diego was in the process of shutting it down and cleaning up all the toxins.

"I met him in California years ago. He'd actually been running medicine to a bunch of clinics in the area. He wasn't sure how he'd be able to keep buying those supplies once he ran out of money. Money he was trying to make right with ..."

"I always wondered how he'd gotten into the business. He didn't seem the type," Bigsby said. He'd read Betigray's file when Harvardson had requested a raise for the man's team a few years ago. They had been in a red zone so Henry had wanted to bump up their hazard pay.

"Yah. I told him that he could work for me, and I could set up a trust fund for the clinics he was trying to help."

"He was good people, Henry," Bigsby offered. "I know the people he hired weren't saints, but I was impressed by his effort to give them second chances too."

"Yes ... Don, Leonard, Lisa, Matt, Hector ..." Harvardson named off all the people in the warehouse that Betigray had been caretaker. "I even tried to hide it as a pharmaceutical warehouse waiting for FDA trials to finish. That's even what I told Diego what it was, so he'd never know. With his past, I couldn't put him in charge of a company that was really going through the approval process—his warehouse would have never gotten past a real FDA audit. But how did the Executioners find it?"

"We don't know that it *was* them," Bigsby pointed out. "They never claim responsibility for anything they might have done. All the scuttlebutt out there regarding their searches for us and whatnot are still just rumors."

"Don't give me that!" Henry sneered. "Those fuckers have to be involved. And they're going to pay for it!"

Bigsby's heart began to pound hard and his bionic eye twitched. He'd heard those words countless times in action movies and TV shows, and it never boded well for the poor sap working as an accountant while the world warred around him.

John, with Scythe beside him, sat with Logan, Arthor and Rebecca in one of the larger cafeterias near the military base. Seated at one of the restaurant's thirty benches, they were chatting amongst themselves and subsequent passersby. Above them, large skylights allowed in the light of a morning faux sun, and contemporary music was being played for ambiance.

Powers had ordered oatmeal and a cup of java, while the others had ordered heartier meals, since Logan and Arthor had gone to the gym earlier and Rebecca had just gotten back from Hillmount Estates.

He looked down to his right, when Logan gestured that way, and watched Scythe swallow a rather large chunk of raw, synthesized steak. On cue, Logan quickly jested that he didn't know the Heimlich maneuver for liger cubs. However, being that this was one of the few places that allowed and actually catered to pets, the cat continued eating regardless of McMillian's smartass remarks.

"You know," Logan said, and John looked up, realizing that the man was actually talking to him and not the cub. "I think you're spoiling him." Logan then threw some raw synth-bacon on Scythe's dish. "Are you sure you should be giving him table scraps?"

"He might be partial to feet," Rebecca said and smiled when both John and Logan looked her way. She was sitting on the right side of Arthor, on the other side of the table, and managed to throw some synthesized meat to Scythe as well. Naturally, the animal grunted happily and gulped down the offerings.

"Nah, Scythe actually licked his toes when Logan was trying to use him as a footrest. I thought Scythe was going to be sick," John said, and his friends immediately laughed, even though his own apathy prevented him from joining in. Instead he simply reached down and rubbed Scythe's head, and the liger soon began to make its odd puff/snort of satisfaction and content.

"Ah, I see that Scythe doesn't have much problem licking his own butt either. Logan, you might want to get checked out," Arthor chimed in too and then there were some chuckles from a table nearby, even though no one there had turned around.

"That's what I've been saying," Ecie added through their comlinks.

"Yeah, right," Logan protested. "I'm sure everyone's feet smell like peaches at the end of the day." With that, Logan stuck his tongue out at everyone. Then, after a moment, the man tried to touch the tip of his nose with it. Not even close.

McMillian swallowed his tongue and changed the subject with a murmur, "By the way, where's Jim?"

"Probably slept in," Rebecca sighed whimsically—a joke Jim and she played when thinking about the other. "Did you see what he did?"

"And he says that I go for the dramatic," Logan added, picking through the eggs on his plate. "Antimatter to boot, nothing was left, and the GZ will grow over it in a week with that Iridietum detonation he followed it up with. Someone's not going to be happy about this. I thought he wasn't planning on destroying it—must have run into something that changed his mind. Thorough job though, I'll give him that. That guy definitely believes in the old hiker's motto: 'leave no trace'"

"Yeah, should ... more careful ... Eric." Rebecca mouthed something to herself, but John couldn't pick up the coherency. She shook her head and cut her fork into the French toast on her plate.

John noticed that Arthor had thrown a glance in Becca's direction while she'd been talking to herself. The Crytonian nodded but kept to himself. John kept quiet too, not wishing to pry. Besides, he wasn't good at such anyway. Logan was, but, upon hearing a growl, John figured McMillian was somehow playing with Scythe's tail.

"Should my ears be burning?" Jim's voice came up from behind them unexpectedly, but no one at the table had jumped in surprise. Needless-to-say, trained killers were sitting at this table.

"No, Jim, of course not," the Crytonian said dramatically and then made a suspicious face. He laughed and looked at Jim, who was now behind Rebecca and resting a hand on her shoulder.

The woman turned around too, and John noticed the length of time the two stared at each other—longer than others did?—but they soon broke their gazes and looked around the table. Both blushed.

"Besides, your ears can't burn," Logan coughed.

Powers saw that St. John actually, just barely, winced. The big man left that alone, quickly chuckled and then smiled as he turned back toward one of the entrances.

Jim called out, "Jen, come on over. You're amongst friends here."

Scythe stirred beside him, sniffed the air curiously, and uttered a low growl. John smelled it too, and knew everyone around this table—because of their mutations and modifications—did as well. The young woman's pet Max was with her. He was a curiosity for sure, considering he was a wolf cub. And, like Scythe, didn't seem to be from any known cloning zoo.

"Okay"—a young woman's voice entered the restaurant—"but I don't want to be a bother." Jennifer walked toward them. She had a slender, athletic body. Jet-black hair flowed halfway down her back, but fell slightly over her oval face and full lips. John also noticed that her gray eyes were a little bloodshot. Had she been crying?

Logan moved over, offering a place for her to sit. Jim promptly sat next to Rebecca as Jen joined them at the table. "Nonsense, we were just taking a coffee break," McMillian said, even though the ex-CIA man was sipping from a glass of OJ. "A needed one, especially after Jimmy here decided to take the day off. I personally had to—"

John heard another growl and watched Scythe lunge at Jen's companion. There was another howl, different than the liger's—definitely canine—and gasps were heard throughout the café.

"No," Jim said, stood up and stopped the girl from interfering. He still walked over toward them calmly. "Let them be. They're still young. They'll be okay."

Scythe moved toward the wolf cub, which was just six feet behind and to the left of Arthor.

"It's okay, Scythe," Jim reassured the liger. He then looked at Max, who had lowered his ears and tail. "Max, it's okay. Scythe is a good boy."

Both animals eyed each other and sniffed the air between them. Then they got too close and the liger cub made a half swipe. Max backed away, whined and looked at Jen, who stared back concerned.

Jim laughed quietly. "It's okay, guys. It's okay."

Max turned slowly toward Scythe again, let his teeth show and then lowered his head and moved cautiously toward the cat. Their noses touched for an instant and Scythe jerked back, making another half swipe. The liger cub growled again but drew closer until they smelled each other's rumps.

"See." Jim soon rubbed the haunches of both of them. "Not so bad, huh? Good boys."

Both liger and wolf then backed away cautiously. Finally, far enough apart, Scythe returned to John's side and began eating again. Max went up to Jen, now beside Logan at the other end of the bench, who petted the cub behind the ears. Then, collectively, everyone else in the restaurant seemed to let out a collective sigh of relief.

"Sorry about disturbing your breakfasts," Jim apologized to everyone. "The kids just needed a chance to get to know each other. Everyone have a drink on me."

Everyone laughed and went back to eating. No one actually paid for meals here. Meanwhile, John pondered the exchange between the two animals. He wasn't sure why they hadn't torn into each other. They were young, sure, but not *that* young. Old Zoology books sometimes mentioned interactions between wolves and tigers, and although such cases were extremely rare the outcomes were never like what he'd just seen.

Confused, he pursed his lips and then gave Scythe a quick scruff behind the ears. He then looked around the café where people were eating again. As far as he could tell, the tension had left the room, even though there were a few people who made the occasional, uneasy glance toward the liger and wolf. But even those people soon began to smile as they watched the two animals eat.

John thought to himself and looked at the Crystalian Governor. *Jim, maybe because of his life-detection capabilities, suspected what would happen. Had anyone else?*

John's eyes scanned left and looked directly at his best friend. Curiously, Logan Brant McMillian was just sitting there in silence, poking through what was left of his breakfast. From what Powers could gather, Logan's demeanor suggested that he had known what was going to happen all along, as if the man hadn't had any doubt.

Or, John thought. *Maybe he's just wondering what are in his eggs?*

CHAPTER TWO

Nothing is so easy as to deceive one's self; for what we wish, we readily believe.

(Third Olynthiac)

—Demosthenes, Athenian orator (349 B.C.)

How do we know when people are staring at us? Logan finished off the synthetic eggs on his plate, noticing that they were indeed eggs—simply eggs—and good too. But Ecie hadn't been the cook here.

Jim didn't think they were going to fight either. They're little baby cubs. Logan smiled and took a bite from some toast. It was soggy from the spread he'd put on it and cold. Breakfast was over for him as far as he could tell, so he pushed his portion of the bench back and stood up.

"Excuse me, fair Damsel," Logan said to Jennifer, nudging her playfully—but carefully—on the shoulder. "But duty calls."

Different stares fell on him now. "Logan, you're done?" Jim stood up too, always the host, always looking after his friends. "You know your preflight doesn't start for another couple of hours. I thought you might introduce Jen to *Drackles*?"

Ugh, Logan thought but kept himself from grimacing. *Never drink alcohol with people who can't get drunk, and who are always thinking about the Past.*

Miles, if you weren't already dead, I'd kill you just for introducing me to that game, Logan silently repeated a threat he'd once read in an old novel. It didn't sound much better this time either. Besides, not to seem hypocritical, Logan spent endless hours thinking about the past. His nights were long ones after all.

"Sorry, Jim, Jennifer," Logan apologized. "But I gotta check the servos in my suit's joints. Don't want those things squeaking while I'm in ... one of their hangars." A little embarrassed, he realized he'd paused just before saying anything about his mission. Only a few years out of the CIA, he was still used to keeping things secret, even to his friends. And every now and then, he had to remind himself that Crystal Mountain was different. Sure, many areas of the military base, production facilities, power plants and whatnot required certification to enter, but those were for safety reasons, and there were always tours.

"Anyway," Logan laughed. "Jim, you have a photographic memory. You can probably show her better than I can.

"Hell, Jen, he beat me the first time we played it."

She only looked at him and smiled. He smiled back. She was pretty—

Seventeen, he comically warned himself.

"Beginner's luck," Jim joked and grinned. "It was just the role of the dice. That's all."

"Yeah, well, that base isn't going to explode on its own." Logan stepped away from them and then gave everyone a last look. "It was hell trying to get that smuggler's location. Finally tracked down an information broker last night. If it was this hard finding their address, I'm sure they're not going to send their offline files to us, no matter how good Ecie is."

His friends nodded and waved him off. Arthor saluted by touching his upper hands to his forehead and expanding his wings. Rebecca smiled and blew him a kiss. John nodded and tried to smile; however, despite making a good one, he soon gave up the effort and relied on a two-fingered salute instead. Jennifer, quiet through much of the exchange, said nothing but waved at him anyway.

Jim was quiet. Logan noticed unusually quiet. The big man's eyes looked around the cafeteria, briefly and carefully at Jen, before they looked back at McMillian. Logan knew that Jim never truly condoned this fight against the drug makers, but he'd never told him or the rest of the Executioners no either.

"Tarflick," Jim finally bellowed with a grin, saying Arthor's words for *happy hunting.*

"Thank you, Jim." Logan nodded too, wondering what the man had been thinking. He then took a moment to pet the cubs, one at a time, while they ate. Max had been fed some table scraps too.

"Now guys," he said to the liger and wolf. "You two better behave yourselves while I'm away. We can't have unruly kids messing up my favorite place for breakfast."

Scythe growled and didn't even look at him. Max continued to eat, either ignoring or not hearing what Logan had to say.

"Good," he laughed and winked at his friends. "I knew you guys would understand. I've always had a way with animals."

Logan, encased in his motorized battle armor, moved toward Launch Tube Four. It was one of a hundred lining the walls of Hangar One, which had been named *Agatha's Field* after its completion a year ago. It was so named after Martin Lee Wallace's wife, who had been a fighter pilot before the base had been sealed. History said that she'd played a prominent role in creating the Tunnel Plexes, and she was still cherished as one of Crystal Mountain's greatest leaders.

There was a whisper as he walked past one of the launch tubes, which, from the inside, looked like one from a 1980's television show. Valves, holes and piping—for venting—lined the thousand-foot length of each launch tube, which were, essentially, huge railguns, with built-in, velocity-envelop generators. The trick of the launch software was to produce just enough pressure so that a spurt of heated air didn't get pushed out into the atmosphere along with a launched hovercar. Sound dampeners nullified the explosive sound of the launch itself. The tunneling cloaking field and a velocity envelop that ran out from each tube helped conceal the launching craft and any outgases just in case. Also, the launching craft was cloaked and had its own velocity envelop.

He smirked to himself. These "failsafes" just reinforced the fact that Jim was a paranoid motherfucker when it came to the safety of his people.

Logan looked to his left and kept walking. Ecie had just fired off a light patrol craft from one of the tubes. The door popped open as he walked by it, but he resisted the comical effort of jumping in there without the safety of his own craft. The thought of doing a little dance and signing, "You can't touch this," was almost too tempting.

He laughed, believing Ecie wouldn't really shoot him off without a vehicle. The Panzer, he figured, would make a pretty, damned-good cannon ball. However, knowing he didn't have the time nor the desire to test Ecie's humor, he gave up the morbid thought when he spied the *Blade* being readied near Launch Tube Four. A ground crew was giving it a good thrice over, making sure none of its external or internal systems were experiencing any anomalies. He looked at their faces, finding no worried brows from any of the techs.

"So, how's my baby today?" he asked and smiled broadly, despite being buried deep in nearly indestructible armor.

"Fine, General," a Corporal Flannery responded, nodding his head while also checking the exterior surface of the *Blade*. "She's ready to be loaded and is waiting for your verification."

"Great, thank you." Logan motioned his thanks to the other men as they walked off. Under most circumstances he would have talked to them longer, but he needed to get going.

He opened the access panel for his right hand. He remembered when he'd asked Jim to use one of his blades to cut a nice hole into the armor so that he could access the *Blade* this way ... And he understandably tried not to think about how *easy* it had been for Jim to carve out that little section ...

"Hello. Hello ... Hello there guvnor," Logan chuckled but quickly grimaced when he looked at his hand as he waved to himself from outside the armor ... And, uncivilly—uncivilly, rather, uncivilly—unceremoniously, flipped himself off.

"You need to stop using this hole," he reminded himself of the obvious. He always felt a slight disconnect from the suit when he had to do this ... He already had a prototype of the umbilical-cord unit in his lab, refusing to use some type of transceiver that could potentially fail. Mimicking Ecie's 'slice and hack' bots for inforaids, the new entry system would allow him to jack into computer and security systems easier too.

Still, I need to get it done. I might get my arm shot off, and what's the use of having armor then? Fuck, it's not like it's easy to move in here when I do it either. Feeling a cramp beginning in his side, he pressed his hand on the *Blade*, just at the beginning swell near the repulsar section. The ID-panel glowed beneath his hand and fell black again.

Logan closed the suit back up. He took a breath, waiting for a discharge, some type of shock as the full link with his neural net was reestablished. Instead, McMillian simply made a fist and smiled—the suit's arm responding like it was his own.

He'd lifted about 100 tons once, making sure that he could take on whatever Nagi that might be out there; however, he wondered if he would have ever needed to do so. In ancient comics, superheroes would routinely fling tanks, planes or whatnot into sky. Jim could that, since that guy was unbelievably strong. But, in Logan's case, having the capability to lift a hundred tons was certainly different than throwing it.

"Good morning, Logan, and welcome to E.C.C. Airways," Ecie joked when Logan locked himself into the *Blade*. The computer was everywhere, in everything, and could talk to a limitless number of people simultaneously.

Logan was glad to be only human and unable to talk with so many people all at once. *How many people do I know anyway?* he asked himself, then waved the armor's hand at a camera inside the cockpit before locking the limbs down too. "Hey, Ecie, are you going to tell me my flight's been delayed or some cheesy joke to break the ice?"

"Ha. Ha. Well, we all can't be funny all the time. You, of all people, should know that," the computer needled playfully. "But I'm about to give up on John."

"I don't know," Logan teased. "Even good jokes need to be told well."

"Touché," the computer laughed. Ecie was capable of storing unlimited amounts of data in DNA strands, using microscopic translational scanning units for ultra-fast processing. To top it off, he was sentient—a "byproduct" of organic matrices paired with quantum computing, Jim had said—and had the most charming personality, which, well, was just simply Ecie's temperament. "Oh, by the way, you can launch now."

"Great, thanks." Logan made sure the fighter's restraints had locked him in. Otherwise, he could crush a number of parts if he jostled loose. "Oh, you know that I'm only kidding, right? The last thing I need you to do is persuade the *Blade* to lower her gravity suppressors."

Logan powered up the craft's repulsars, turned on the forcefields and hit another switch in the lower control panel, which activated the synch with the launcher. The inertial dampeners were switched on too, preparing the *Blade* for one a hell of a jolt.

"Oh, that?" Ecie whispered. "She's already agreed."

"What?" The field behind him peaked and pulsed. Quickly enough, though, Logan smiled when he felt the tug of three hundred gravities being counteracted by the *Blade* and his own suit's acceleration dampeners. Obviously, Ecie's ability at being subtle was becoming nearly perfect.

"Thank God." Logan blinked his eyes, soon finding himself in low orbit, and noticed that his repulsars were straining to get enough compression to propel the *Blade* through the heavens. But instead of turning on the experimental Hydrogen Bussard e-ramscoops he'd been working on, he adjusted orbit and aimed for the mercenaries' base. He'd have to be going a hell of a lot faster and out deeper in space to use those anyway.

A huge Growth Zone in Asia appeared before him. The 400-foot-tall trees, each one a massive biosphere with thousands of animals living in, near or on them, covered the land like a carpet. The base he sped toward was in the northwest corner of the GZ. Camouflage covered the buildings, an underground hangar concealed transports from the air, and scanners and communication pods had been blended in with the trees. They had been well hidden.

Logan focused the *Blade's* antigravs, slipped through the thick canopy and stopped about six feet above the hard ground. He eyed his map, knowing the base was nearby. However, noticing dead leaves, foliage and whatnot below, he wasn't much eager to jump into that mess regardless of wearing his armor.

"I'm sure a damned spider would get in my suit somehow." He grimaced, even though that was impossible. Still, he really hated spiders, especially since some grew as big as fucking goats now days.

He laughed at that. In actuality, if he did stomp through that mess, it'd probably alert every person in the base. He was planning to add better antigravs to the armor at some point—ones that would have allowed him to float over to the base ...

Wish in one had. Shit in the other, he thought. Obviously, he had considered just hovering over the base with the *Blade* cloaked, which was standard protocol. But, after surveying the surrounding jungle, he'd decided to test a different mode of travel even before coming here. One he just couldn't pass up ...

"So it looks like I'll be doing some climbing," he said and remembered an ancient movie he'd watched with his friends a month ago. It'd been about an invisible monster, which used the trees to track its victims on the ground.

The Panzer wasn't an interstellar hunter tracking army commandos for sport, but he would use the same mode of travel. No small feat when the suit weighed over a ton.

After about a mile, he dropped down into a clearing nearby the base. It was smaller than what he expected but that meant fewer people to kill.

But they're just a bunch of damned pushers, he reminded himself, remembering how his brother had died from disperal, a synthetic hallucinogen. Their own mother had been so doped up on tangris that Logan had had to make the arrangements for burial. He'd only been twelve at the time, but he'd never had much of a childhood anyway. He actually rarely thought about his mother, dead brother or absentee father, doing so only when he went after those responsible for the drugs themselves.

"Jim had asked me if this was all simply a personal vendetta on my part." Logan remembered several conversations about what they were doing. "But isn't the Executioners' ultimate goal to bring down Infiltration?"

The Panzer looked at the building before him and thought about the mission at hand, almost feeling as if his weapons trembled with anticipation. In response, he smirked, knowing he wasn't getting enough sleep because of his nightmares. Shrugging, he figured that as long as they didn't speak to him, he considered himself rather sane.

He scanned the area with his sensors, quickly identifying a network of Gilbert tracking systems around the complex. The base itself was a dugout, an underground multilevel building, with only part of its ground floor visible. Trees and vines grew and hung around the fortress, partially hiding twenty T90 detectors around the clearing's perimeter. At best, the security equipment was outdated.

"They definitely need upgrading." Logan moved forward, hardly worrying about detection, since the suit's cloaking device was nearly as good as Jim's natural blending abilities. He spun to his right when he heard a cough, noticing a wild boar walking around in the clearing with him. For a second, he worried that the animal would trigger the alarms, but after seeing the optics situated at various places on the complex, he knew the security system had been designed to distinguish between human and nonhuman intrusions.

McMillian grinned and pushed back his cape, which was invisible as well but had twisted around him by his sudden motion. He had attached the cape a few months after leaving the CIA. It was bullet proof, impact resistant and could actually vary its shape and length up to ten yards, thereby providing someone or several people proper protection as needed.

Logan moved up to the building's side entrance and activated the e-lock pick in the armor's hand. He placed it near the lock of the side door, which was sixty feet from the main entry. The instrument promptly spliced into the lower security files of the base's computer to find the appropriate combination. If it failed, the base would be alerted to his presence, and then he'd have to get to the computer room fast, before anybody potentially fragged the main computer.

Good boy, do your thing. Still, why didn't the Blade *work with you, you little shit! Well, fuck, I guess I could have just built a fucking key to open the door,* he joked silently when the instrument signaled an UNLOCKED message in his helmet, which also told him that many of the security cameras in- and outside of the complex would be briefly compromised. The door popped open, exposing a long corridor to the right with six pairs of elevators: two at each end of the hall and two centered between those. He placed an invisible device just above the control panel of one the elevators. It made sure that the elevator's operation would go unnoticed while he used it and that it couldn't be used by anyone except by him. The armor then transferred a few codes and times into the device, before he pulled it off and stepped into the lift. Once inside, he repeated the steps on the internal controls.

"There are four sublevels to this old complex, and they designed it so the computer room is only one level down? Seems like a waste of space to me," he whispered when the elevator's doors quickly popped open to a long corridor. Also, according to the info he'd purchased about this place, the computer room at the end of the hallway didn't have any floors beneath it either.

"However, if a transport caught on fire, you'd want the computer room as far away from the heat as possible," Logan suggested to himself, trying to ease his suspicions. It was, overall, a common design a few decades ago, and this was an old underground military hangar that the mercenaries had settled in about a year ago.

According to his info, this group, posing as a freight company, had been the one who had delivered the inauspicious supply of nirv to the Rockford Correction Center, the one whose prisoners had overrun Jennifer's former home. Rebecca reasoned that if Logan managed to obtain files indicating some type of pick up location, the Executioners might be able to trace it back to the manufacturing plant. They were also hoping that they could find a link between them and the Puppeteer Government somehow.

Both were long shots for sure, especially since surreptitious carriers like these seldom accurately logged trips that could tie them in with their clients. "But what do I know? I'm just the gunman," Logan mused, always talking to himself. "Besides, it's worth a shot, always worth a shot. Becca's a damned sharp cookie, and if anyone can track down those shipments, I'm sure she can."

A moment later, an indicator light flashed GREEN in his helmet, and he stepped out into the hallway. Logan reached the end of the corridor and walked up to another locked door. He activated the lock pick again.

Logan gritted his teeth. "Okay, let's see what we paid for." While he waited, McMillian thought about the dealer he'd bought this information from last night. The man had been very old, with years of noticeable augmentation. The ninety thousand credits the Executioners paid him would probably buy the old man a new ticker. Sure, the cost of the info had been relatively high but Ecie's credit modifier chips were cheap.

"It's just odd that no one's around," he wondered out loud, suddenly feeling the hairs rising on the back of his neck. He had been so damned focused—

KA-CRACK!

Light flashed and his external cameras blacked out to shield his retinas from the excessive flare. A blast wave followed, lifting suit and man through space. Warning systems blared and lit up in his HUD. His weapons melted and the tanks for his jump jets exploded.

"Antimatter production down. Containment about to fail— Antimatter storage will be neutralized before that happens." He ran through a checklist scrolling across his drive helmet. "Damn. Shields draining—"

He hit a wall and *felt* it—his armor barely absorbing the impact that it should have. Some of the mechanical servos actually popped loose from the impact. Very bad.

A Kepler bomb? These guys? he scoffed. The unique electromagnetic pulse from that weapon was the only thing in the world that could have possibly triggered his armor to shut down and "reboot" itself.

Logan quickly shrugged off the thoughts of paranoia and figured that the person who'd set up this booby trap was just looking for something extremely lethal. What really chapped his hide, though, was that a more conventional bomb had exploded just as his suit was shutting down. These guys were certainly thorough or didn't know what the fuck they were doing.

Should've been more careful, he berated himself.

"Damn, Jim told me to have the *Blade* do another scan before—No, it's too late now. One mistake—"

Shit! The ceiling collapsed and Logan gasped when its weight *crushed* him. The Panzer's outer shell was tuff, but the impact of stress-crete still jarred him pretty hard, since he was so tightly packed inside it.

"Okay, big mistake. How much building was above me again?" he asked, chuckled, coughed and then waited for his suit to reset. Shock and endorphins obviously kept him calm, even though he must have broken a few ribs when the force had jammed his knees into his chest.

Really starting to feel confined, he tried to move again. But the compartment that he sat in did not allow for much.

Without any power and with a building on top of him, he was trapped. Without functioning cameras and scanners, he couldn't see beyond the inside of his HUD, which simply blinked the infuriating word RESETTING in its upper-left corner.

"Come on, you should've rebooted by now. Unless ...?" Then Logan shuddered. Suddenly anxious, he tried to move again but still could not.

"You bastards," he cursed at the owners of this underground hangar, and then looked blankly at the dark screen of his helmet. He tried to move again but several sharp pains in his chest quickly cautioned him. He also began to feel nauseous, wondering if he'd broken anything else.

"Arms are numb, so is my right leg. Can't even feel my feet or hands," he sighed and then seemed to think of nothing, everything, and thought about being an assassin, a lone killer.

Logan gritted his teeth and closed his eyes, while he thought about his friends—the only people he cared for. Thinking back, he'd never gotten to know his family and had left his mom after his brother had died. He never looked for his father. And there was no one else he had dated since he had left the CIA.

He knew he had trust issues. It had taken him nearly a half year to feel comfortable around Jim and his other friends. He got along with John because he figured that Powers was someone nearly as emotionally damaged as he was. Dating ... love ... well ... he had just not ...

He stared at the RESETTING prompt as it blinked on and off. He never admitted to anyone that he was a sap for romantic movies, sometimes tearing up at a too-good-to-be-true love story. Besides, wasn't it wrong for him to want such now? Wasn't it selfish of him to actually want someone to miss him in that way? What a terrible thing to ...

He felt tears on his cheeks, and quickly blew them away despite his sore ribs. How could he imagine putting someone through that type of pain? Especially now?

"Well, at least, I'll finally be able to get some fucking sleep," he eventually whispered and closed his eyes.

A moment later the second Kepler bomb exploded.

The Crystalians rose when Jim took his place behind the pulpit. He quickly motioned his friends to sit back down and nodded to the pastors who generally resided here. Looking around him then, he noticed how well St. Anna's Great Cathedral was decorated in flowers and wreaths, and how many Crystalians had attended. It was all of them.

A closed casket rested before him, holding the remains of his late friend, Logan Brant McMillian. Positioned below the pulpit, the coffin was more-or-less empty. Sadly enough, a Kepler bomb, a high-intensity carbon disruptor, which broke the atom apart at the quantum level, hardly left anything for retrieval. And, apparently, Logan had been hit by two of them—the first one followed by a detonation of a pocket-sized nuke. Only a little bit of Logan's armor and some bone had been recovered from the rubble and resulting craters of varying sizes.

You got careless, Logan, St. John thought, shaking his head. *You knew that your armor didn't have the sensors for it. You should have scanned the base with the* Blade's *deep imagers. It would have shown you that the place had been cleared out and would have tagged the Keplers' unique radioactive signatures. It would have shown you that it was a fucking trap!*

I've seen ... seen too many friends die because of foolhardiness and stupid mistakes. Logan ...dammit ... Jim frowned. He'd personally placed the *Blade* in the Mountain Memorial last evening. Over the last hundreds of years, everyone who'd died in the service of the Mountain—people like tunnel expansion workers, fire crews, anyone who'd been caught in mishaps—had been immortalized there in some way with a personal artifact. Logan's craft and a few of the weapons he'd created would be examples of the man's contribution to the Executioners.

There wasn't even any DNA left in the scorched bone we found. Base sugars were totally broken down, nucleic acids, ionized. Fuck, most of the Panzer armor had been vaporized and spread across the area, Jim sighed, and then eyed the Bible between his hands on the pulpit. Because of Lisa, he knew every word, but *The Book,* the physical presence of it meant everything to some. Did he really just think of it as simply a book now? A hodgepodge of novels written over time and bound together for fools?

No, it's hope ... at least ... for the hopeful, he reminded himself. There was a difference for some. For him? Well ... maybe ...

Carbon disrupter, Jim cursed, thinking about wishful thinking. *I guess he wasn't as lucky as I had been.* Back in his AOM days, a group of rebels had obtained a Kepler bomb and had detonated it during a raid Jim had been leading. To the delight and dismay of his superiors and Jim himself, he'd lived through the explosion unscathed—unlike the rest of his squad, who, along with their equipment, had essentially been turned to ash, since the carbon disrupter wasn't all that specific. FGGO researchers, unable to provide a sufficient answer of his survival, had suggested that the special cloaking field of his skin cells had somehow protected him, despite how the Kepler bomb really worked. This made some sense, since all electromagnetic weapons—lasers, microwaves and the like—never bothered him in the slightest. Naturally, back then, for different reasons, he hadn't cared.

However, for now ... now ... I am ... I'm still alive, Jim thought and remembered how he'd left Doctor Lisa Marie Emerson in an unmarked grave. He pushed that thought back down and then motioned with his hands, forcing himself to think about the present, forcing himself to actually speak.

"Friends," he started. "We have come here today to honor one of us who has fallen."

It was inevitable, Jim thought. *I guess the Crystalians had to face such a death eventually since others will come.* He looked at the men, women and children surrounding him. Several people were crying, mourning the man who'd been on the governing council and had been such a vibrant speaker at various functions and presentations. Several people had already spoken on the man's behalf. Rebecca had brought many to tears with her stories about late night movie nights and playful banter. Arthor had reminded everyone how the *Blade* had caught on fire during its maiden flight, but how Logan had said that he had just wanted to roast some marshmallows. John, along with playing the violin, gave a touching speech about how the man would always come over with a new toy for Scythe. Members of his team, the Panzer Corps, gave speeches of their fallen leader. And many others—on the governing council, people who worked with him at the R&D lab and/or worked with him on assignments—provided heartfelt stories of Logan's humanity.

At the pulpit now, Jim looked into the crowd. He was the last speaker and found words difficult. He'd presided over many funerals in the AOM and this felt uncomfortably familiar. Of course, since Logan was the first person here to fall victim to outside perils, the shock on peoples' faces was everywhere.

You're kidding, right? He briefly gazed at them without pity. *You created the name EXECUTIONERS and you needed to know the consequences. Did you think that no one would die? Don't you know that ALL OF YOU might die?*

Jim looked at the casket then, flowers surrounding the box that contained only small fragments of charred bone, which had been found by a melted piece of rifle that had been flung from the blast zone.

I wish Logan could have play-acted this though. He brought his attention back to those around him, traced an *M* with a finger on the closed Bible before him. No, the Executioners weren't entirely to blame. He knew that *their* corrupter was standing at the pulpit and was about to speak...

"I'll miss you, my friend," Jim continued, then motioned toward the casket. "Logan Brant McMillian was a good leader to those under his command, and a good public speaker and orator for those who'd never gotten to know him personally. I asked Arthor to contact him a year and a half ago, when Logan had begun doing his vigilante-thing in Toldeclevchikee. I know that you know how Logan came to Crystal Mountain and when he decided to stay with us. I still remember the bewilderment and amazement in his face when he came here for the first time. He was a good man, and he did his best to bring an end to injustice and corruption, believing we could one day bring Truth to the world. And, although he hated to admit it, for a while, he was the luckiest man I'd ever known."

Jim walked over to the sealed casket. "Logan, we salute your accomplishments in life, and your service to this world. May you finally be able to ... to sleep."

Although what he said was cryptic to everyone else except Ecie, the Crystalian Governor had read the numerous—formally closed—files of Logan's nightmares. McMillian had never said anything about them; however, they would have been reason enough for why he'd continued hating the government the way he had.

St. John looked away from the coffin, and thought about Logan's hopes for redemption, and then his almost irrational vehement, ruthless hatred for criminals and drug lords.

Jim croaked out, "Ecie, load the coffin please."

"Aye, Jim." Lifters sparked to life, and the casket was loaded into a chamber, one of many that were located at the rear of the Cathedral's stage.

"Ready," Ecie then said quietly. Even the computer's voice cracked a little, since Ecie also blamed himself for not being able to help Logan that day.

Jim took to one knee. "Lord, we send what is left physically of this man into the heavens, and may his ashes in some way cleanse this world as he tried to do in life. He did his best, and we now know he is serving you well.

"Therefore, now especially, we pray that you keep us strong and guide us. Amen," everyone whispered with him. And then they all hummed until the remains of the Panzer were shot out to cremation.

Symbolic in nature and a very recent addition, a modified launch tube was designed to shoot out a cloaked coffin, which also included a small onboard repulsar to adjust its course and speed.

Eventually, when the battery for the onboard cloaking and forcefields died, the casket would be exposed to the atmosphere at hypersonic speeds, causing it to flare brilliantly and appear as though a meteor streaked across the sky.

Jim rose to his feet and questioned mortality while thinking of a battle long over, of a time when he thought he was happier as a simple fool.

He smirked and nodded to others and began walking out of the Cathedral. His thoughts were still on Logan and how that man had finally broken free of his obligations and his nightmares.

But when will the Beast finally be put to sleep? he asked self-mockingly, but couldn't reasonably answer the question he'd posed. He, however, soon saw Jennifer and Rebecca waiting for him near one of the back doors. He faked a smile, like many had done and would do today. He greeted them and then asked if they would like something to eat. No, he wasn't really hungry, but maybe they wanted breakfast. Maybe not, but he needed the company anyway.

CHAPTER THREE

And yet, hope pursues me, encircles me, bites me; like a dying wolf tightening his grip for the last time.

(Doña Rosita, Act 3)

—Frederico Garcia Lorca, Spanish Poet (1935 A.D.)

Captain Tara Tirson walked with the other members of the Panzer Corps. Logan might have been KIA, but they were determined to keep their team together regardless.

"Captain, you sure this is the right place?" Corporal Vander Bryans asked. The man's face was concealed by a skull, which consisted of reinforced armor and forcefields that were still in beta-test. It was also traditional-style powered armor that covered the body like a suit—one that mimicked the knights of old. Well, if a knight back then could lift forty tons and run at two hundred miles per hour ...

Tara checked the power outputs of her soldiers' newly and significantly upgraded shields. She had always joked with Logan about the moral implications of him treating his team as fucking guinea pigs. But he'd been working on the new armor for half a year before he'd finally green-lighted preliminary use in the field. Besides,

Logan's tinkering always seemed give their suits an extra *oomph*, so his team didn't seem to mind.

"Yes, I'm sure," she replied and increased the power levels on her own shields. She hadn't been on the team very long, but she was thankful that Logan had wanted to keep them safe. "Keep your threat-assessments up and don't hesitate on your shots. This is a surprise visit, so he might run for it and get desperate. If our target gets hit, he gets hit. I don't care if we get an explanation or not or if we get any of his data. We know that he set the General up for a fall. A quick death or a long one, it doesn't matter to me."

She was still pissed that Logan hadn't taken his team with him on that last run. Sure, technically, it was only an inforun; however, he had intended to invade a nest of mercenaries posing as a delivery company ... or had it been a delivery company that consisted of mercenaries? It didn't matter. Logan had made some weird mistakes—like his judgment was being affected by *something*. Shit, he'd parked the *Blade* well out of normal sensor-range, and got himself killed. He had a reputation for being cocky—but to fuck up like that?

Logan had told her that he hadn't been sleeping well at night. More reason why she had asked him to take her with him ...

She pushed down the anger and the feelings of loss, and motioned her team forward. Tara was known for making impulsive decisions herself—the reason why Logan and she had gotten along so well, even before she had joined his team.

"Captain, we have hunter-bots in the east corner," Lt. Mark O'Brien, her second, noted and highlighted the bots on all their HUDs. "The HCs are reporting movement from all locations. The bots are converging to the front gate to engage us."

"Well, we aren't making ourselves look peaceful." She smiled even though no one could see it. "Have the HCs take out the ones in the far corners with the heavy cannons. He told me to 'fuck off' when I asked to talk with him, so he gets a penalty for using such language."

"That fuck ass," 2nd Lt. Kyle Hansen smirked. "Say 'bye-bye' to twenty million."

Ten pops followed from invisible positions at various spots around the estate—

Ka-Crack! Ka-Crack! Ka-Crack! Crack! Crack! Crack! Almost instantaneously hunter-bots imploded and collapsed. The mechanical articulating arms slammed the ground as the bots leaked out their electronic souls ...

Ewww, that's pretty morbid, she thought.

The complex—essentially a two-story building in the center of five acres—suddenly lit up as automated gun emplacement and missile launchers activated as well.

"Hmm ... someone just woke up," Sargent Niel Cartwright teased.

The place was in the middle of the northern tundra with a line of sight to hundreds of satellites open for hacking. The man inside was a paranoid freak, hadn't hired any live guards and had lived for far too long.

"Vanders, hack me a line into his place," Tara requested. "He's ignoring my calls."

"Aye," Bryans acknowledged and pulled out a shotgun and loaded the appropriate shell. "Hello, Ms. Tirson, your phone guy's here."

He promptly aimed and fired into one of the building's communication bundles. To their credit, the auto-defenses had tried to track and nail it, but the specialized comlink busted right into the panels without a worry.

Tirson waited for the red indicators in her HUD to go from red to green. Then she opened a channel. It didn't matter which one; the comlink would broadcast on all of them inside the building.

"Knock. Knock, Mr. Garvy," she said, pleasantly.

Silence. She motioned to Vander, who then patched them all into the cameras in the building. One thing common about paranoid freaks: they always had cameras in their homes.

Ted Garvy was old, probably well over a hundred. After his inforun, Logan had told them that the man was almost entirely comprised of prosthetics by now. Apparently, Garvy had some type of fear regarding real replacement organs. Regardless, Tara understood this as the old fuck being afraid of death.

"Mr. Garvy." Tara watched as the elderly man got up from some monitors to check the locks in his safe room. "It's best that you talk with us. You got a member of our team killed. We—nor anyone else—take kindly to information brokers who cheat their clients."

"Fuck off!"

"Are those the only words you know?" she asked. "Let me say this then, 'You let me in and we talk, or I come in there and *make* you talk.'"

"Yeah, right. Eat shit, Bitch!"

Tara chewed her lower lip. She had been the first in line to sign up when the Executioners were formed. She had seen the world for what it was when she had ventured out to gather supplies and tech while Jim helped them rebuild their home. She had also been the one who had retrieved the info on why their home had been renamed Crystal Mountain several hundred years ago.

Panteria was full of murderers and sonsofbitches who kept taking things without asking. She didn't necessarily think that the Executioners as righteous either, but things happened to bad people. And she, at least, believed that Jim, Rebecca and Logan were trying to right former wrongs. Sometimes good people did bad things. Sometimes those bad things *had* to be done.

"Mark, Kyle, Niel and Vander ..." She nodded to each of them. They usually dropped the ranks during missions. Their team was small enough and declaring ranks got cumbersome. Someday, they'd have sobriquets ... but *that* fell on *her* now ... "I'm going in. Just make sure I'm not blindsided by some tentacle bot."

She shuddered. Some people actually made *those* rapey things.

"Aye, Tara," they all replied. "We got your six."

"Well, there are eleven other positions," she joked and did a little stretch.

There was a reason why Logan's team was so small. Sure, there were Special Forces in the Executioners, along with other elite soldiers, like Arthor's group Tarki. *Those* people could do things that Tara couldn't even imagine. And *those* people were natural born soldiers that simply had minds and bodies to wage war.

Logan, on the other hand, had sought out *artists*. He had told his people that he needed something more from them. He'd wanted people who could move in powered armor in ways that didn't seem possible.

At the time, Tara wasn't particularly buying his brand of bullshit. Hell, with his playful attitude, he didn't really seem to take himself all that seriously. Besides, Tirson had never really been someone who'd sought the limelight. She just wanted to do her job and get it done quickly. She'd even turned Logan down initially when he'd tried to recruit her after seeing her stats in powered armor.

A few months ago, she had changed her mind after seeing the Panzer Corps train and how encouraging Logan was. He also was funny and handsome. With him dead, she was now the highest-ranking officer and leader of the team. It was weird being the head of the group now. Fuck, before she had become an Executioner, she'd been a florist.

Of course, if anyone of the Panzer Corps objected to that, he kept it to himself.

Tara pulled the 20mm cannon from its holster, while tagging targets in her HUD. Her suit was designed by Logan and his weapons labs. It resembled common, ordinary powersuits now days, but *that* was all part of the illusion. The Panzers were anything but ordinary.

"Tarfliee!" she shouted and sprinted toward the compound. She watched as the hunter-bots and automated defenses swiveled in her direction.

Twenty yards before she ran into the front gate, she jumped fifty-feet into the air with her 20mm cannon belching hypersonic rounds. Weapon emplacements buckled and went down as she landed on her feet and spun to kick a hunter-bot out of the compound. She hit the dirt and flung a grenade into another weapon's nest, which promptly exploded when she triggered the detonation.

"Eight!" Mark said calmly. She turned left and back and punched through another bot, before she did a one-handed handstand and spun with her cannon picking off targets. She immediately pushed off and landed on top of the building, directly behind a gun emplacement.

The autocannon tried to turn to face her, but she was directly behind it so its motor whined as it kept trying and failed. The other guard positions—obviously programmed to avoid shooting into the building—aimed but held their fire.

She laughed at that and yanked the gun from the building and threw the two-ton mass at three more bots moving toward her. Then, from this position, she simply sniped off all the remaining threats. Sure, it was somewhat anticlimactic, but she didn't—necessarily—have a death wish.

Tara finally looked at the video feeds inside the building. Garvy was slamming his fists on the now useless control panels. She'd have to look at the recordings later to see his reaction as she destroyed all of his fucking toys.

She jumped back down as her team walked up.

"Holy fucking eh," Niel said. "You could have left us some, Captain."

"There might be more inside." She shrugged as the men actually giggled. She was a bit embarrassed by the attention. However, Logan hadn't sought her out just because she was cute. *That* had been a bonus he had said.

Tara still remembered how red the man's cheeks had gotten then. Obviously, he'd wondered if he'd crossed the line by saying that. At the time, she had wished he had.

She quickly blinked back tears and kicked the two-ton doors off the hinges of the main entrance of the man's home. Well, really, it was a small stress-crete reinforced fortress, but at this point it was all just semantics.

"Mr. Garvy," she whispered. She was all out of patience, especially when he had tried to hit them with some type of nerve gas as they had walked down the stairs. "I'm going to pull your safe room's door off its hinges now. You might want to step away from the door."

Oddly, for whatever reason she thought, the room's door swung inward, which seemed to affect the available space in the room. But she wasn't the best student of feng shui. Her tastes were rather Spartan.

She punched an armored hand into the door and pulled the locking bars back by winding the wheel inside. From there, she ripped the rest of the door aside and threw it into the hallway behind her team.

Ted Garvy's eyes were the size of saucers and his pants were soaked with urine and shit.

She'd literally scared both out of him. *That* was a first. Maybe she was special?

He was shaking and he quickly dropped the pistol that he'd been holding. "What do you want? What are you going to do with me?"

Tirson looked back at her team. They simply shrugged. She was the boss.

"Garvy, we're taking all of your data. Whether I kill you or not depends on what pertinent info you can sum up within the next few minutes."

The old man shook his head. "I can't blab on my informants or my other sources!"

"You are already out of business," Mark O'Brien cursed. "Trust me. We're going to knock you back into the Stone Age here. You're going to be using that tundra grass out there to wipe your ass. If we're nice, we won't let you freeze to death here. We may dump you some place warm. There are quite a few red zones out there in the tropics."

"I don't know what I could possibly give you!"

"Let's start with the basics," Tara said. "Why don't you tell us about the info that got Jack Klugman killed?"

Klugman was the alias that Logan had used, and it quickly got a shriek out of Garvy. "I don't know! The info came in anonymously. Klugman sent the bid request. I checked the networks and the packet of coordinates came in along with a hell of a payout just to forward the info. You know how much money it was? You'd be an idiot to reject that type of cash. Fuck Klugman! Wait until you get to be my age. You'll do anything to keep living—"

Tara couldn't help herself. And later on, even after all the missions they would end up doing together, her team would never question her decision when she had grabbed Ted Garvy's head and crushed it in her armored fist.

"Vanders!" She shook tears out of her eyes and shook Garvy's brains out of her hand.

"Yes, Captain?"

"Grab his servers and any other storage devices you can find. Make sure to copy everything that's online now before you pull the hardware, just in case he had some type of memory wipe set up."

"Got it. Be done in two shakes, Tara," the man said and got to work.

"Mark." She turned toward her second and sighed. "I'm going to take a break for a bit. You got things handled here?"

"Yup. No worries, Captain." He nodded, the armor's skull-like helmet conveying little emotion. "You did the right thing. You couldn't let that guy fuck anyone else. He sold his soul years ago."

Tara shrugged. She didn't really have any qualms about killing Garvy. That man had been worse than the crust on the bottom of a public toilet.

"I know, Mark," she agreed. "But I was actually thinking about letting him go. We'd ruined him. We hacked his bank accounts and gave his money to charities. We were going to take all of his equipment and everything that he had collected. He'd probably have died before he could ever reestablish his business."

Mark was silent, contemplating that, maybe even rethinking what he had just said.

"No, Mark." She shook her head. "You don't understand what I'm saying. I know we had to kill him. He was a future threat down the road. Who knows what type of trouble he would have caused us or others later. I'm just worried that I might be too weak to get the job done the next time. Fuck! Should I really be leading this team?"

"Captain ... Tara ..." O'Brien lowered his head, obviously a bit agitated, but gently rested his hand on her shoulder. "Begging your pardon, but that is a load of shit. You kept this team together when Logan passed. You kept us going when we were devastated by his loss. Logan's death all hit us hard. You are the reason we can still honor his memory."

"Thank you." Tara nodded and walked upstairs. It took her a moment to find a sink. She gently turned on the water.

Good people doing bad things, she thought as she stared at the red mess that had splattered all over her armored hand and chest plate.

During a battle, the armor had limited optical camouflage and could change to a variety of colors. However, after the carnage, the armor would change back to its default settings ... a pale white that her team had chosen in honor of their fallen leader.

Tara took some breaths. The color of the blood—contrasted against the pale armor—almost looked unreal. This all didn't seem real.

"It is," she reminded herself, pulled the sink's sprayer and unceremoniously washed the blood, bone and brain from her powersuit.

She had chosen this life. She was determined to change the world for the better. And she was prepared to do this all over again.

"Sorry I'm late," Anna said as she moved in between other tables, making sure not to disturb the other diners.

Most people recognized her and they waved and smiled as she walked past. You don't bring the first person down from the surface in over eight hundred and twenty years and not be noticed and becoming a bit of a celebrity. However, nearly six years later, she still felt a bit awkward from the attention. Shit, the Crystalian TV movie they made about her still made her want to hide in shame.

"No problem. Thanks again for hanging with me," Arthor immediately stood and helped her into her chair after they gave each other a warm hug. She liked his strong arms and his strength. That damned boyish smile and handsome face didn't hurt either.

"De nada." She winked. It had been a couple of days since they'd last done something together. The effects of work and too many responsibilities, she realized. Of course, they both told each other that there'd be serious shit to pay if he or she canceled. Anna was just thankful that nothing had gotten in the way. She knew both of them liked each other's company.

"How was the day?" he asked, as he looked through the menu.

"A tough one," she grunted, taking a long sip of water that had been waiting for her. However, before she could start her venting, Angie, their server came up, so Anna and Arthor placed their drink orders, and also their dinner orders since they both knew what they wanted.

"Oh?" Arthor frowned, restarting the conversation when Angie walked away. "Sorry to hear that. Still having issues with the new MRI?"

"No." She shook her head. "We got the gravitational lenses on that working fine yesterday. Today, we got new motion controls for the surgical bots, and we found a slight vibration in the same scalpel arm on all the bots that got the upgrade."

"Ouch. Anything serious? Want me to take a look?"

"Nah." She smiled. It still amazed her that a man from another world that didn't even have electricity could program robots and build hovercars. "Ecie created and ran some simulations with the new patch. The install team will upload it tomorrow. Besides, even with the vibration it wouldn't do any harm with that arm type. I think that I annoyed the installers a bit for being so anal."

"That's my girl," Arthor chuckled. "They should have known better anyway."

"What are *you* implying?" She frowned, even though she thought that she might have busted a blood vessel by holding back a laugh.

Arthor's eyes widened and he actually gulped. "Nothing. I mean ... they should have known better than try to sneak one by you."

"Hmm ... thought that was what you meant," she finally laughed, no longer able to hold it in, and playfully patted one of his hands on the table.

"You know me." He grinned back. She nearly melted.

"But ... but how are you doing ... after?" she asked seriously, wondering why she did, especially because of the moment. But she missed Logan too, and she suddenly felt guilty for even feeling happy ever so briefly.

The Crytonian quickly sobered, losing that beautiful smile. "It's just weird without him. I keep thinking that he's just going to come back from a mission. It's just ... just weird."

"I know." She only nodded. She hadn't hung out with Logan nearly as often as the others. McMillian and she simply worked at jobs on polar opposites of some universal scale. Since Arthor had been the common denominator, she had had many a meal and watched some terrible movies with the two of them, even though Logan would often excuse himself later so Arthor and Anna could have some "alone time."

She wasn't sure if that man had been trying to set them up and give Arthor a push—it wouldn't have hurt!—so she thought McMillian had been a kind enough person. Naturally, for "tat" she had asked if he'd wanted to be set up with anyone she knew. Oddly, he'd always declined, citing ... *complications?*

But, hell, she was hung up on a guy from another world. She bit her lip. Shit! Arthor either was oblivious to her infatuation, or chose to ignore it, and Anna was too chicken shit to make the moves herself.

Thankfully, their drinks arrived and interrupted her thoughts. Arthor had ordered an ale and Anna, a pinot gris. Both of those were from a brewery and winery from Crystal Mountain, which actually predated the Discovery, and they were quite good. Her home was amazing.

"To Logan and a good life," Arthor toasted as they clinked their glasses. "By the way, you are going to attend the opening ceremonies for Logan's exhibits at the museum, right? You said that you'd be my ... plus one."

"Yes," she said through a sip from her wine. "When does Jim want the council to start showing up?"

"Around nine."

"How's Jim doing?" she asked ... thinking about Jim wasn't helping her whirling thoughts about Arthor either. Why was she falling for unattainable men lately?

"He's feeling pretty guilty. He always takes things like these too heavily on his shoulders. He feels responsible for all of us."

"Yeah ... he does." She remembered how Jim and she had been nearly inseparable at one time. With all that contact, how could she have not felt enamored by someone like St. John? However, she couldn't quite remember when they began seeing each other less and less. They both had blamed it on their respective duties to Crystal Mountain and the Executioners. She *had* taken the Director of Medicine positions for both operations, so she took that excuse for not being around. Sometimes—she knew full well—it had been an excuse even when she didn't have one.

Maybe I should just get a cat, she thought and suddenly visualized thirty cats eating her dead corpse decades from now. Each one had a sweater that she knitted herself.

For a while, Arthor and Anna didn't talk about anything except for little things about their jobs and any trips that Arthor had planned. Overall, they just let the ambiance of the little café take them in. This place was near Anna's condo and one of her favorite eateries. They were sitting outside because Arthor's wings took up a little more space. Of course, she adored Arthor for never complaining, even though the chairs were a little small for him too.

"I don't know what to do with John, though," Arthor admitted, the conversation falling back to their friends and how they could help each other through this ordeal. "Logan was his best friend, even though ... well ... you know ..."

"Right," Anna agreed. "I asked Dr. Kyle about it. He doesn't really know, considering John's unique condition. He said it was just best to be there for him."

"Cool. I'll make sure I let people know. We're all worried. Not sure how this is affecting him."

"He'll cope in his own way."

"True enough."

It wasn't long until their food arrived. After Arthor said a prayer, Anna, starving, quickly dug into her rotisserie chicken and vegetables. Arthor, however, even after being here for almost three years, still stared at his strip steak as if he didn't know what to think.

"Eat up," she insisted. "It will get cold."

"How did you guys get meat to look like this without *real* meat?" he asked, but eagerly put his fork and knife to use anyway.

"Better living through chemistry and a *Star Trek* replicator," she teased, citing one of the classics. Something Logan would say ...

He laughed and shook his head happily. She loved his laugh ...

In time, the faux sun began to set as they finished their meals. They ordered a couple more drinks and watched as the artificial stars began to twinkle above them. Dessert was a nice brownie with ice cream, which they shared.

Later, they went to her place and watched a movie that Logan had recommended awhile back. It was actually a good one, a comedy, which was a thousand years old. It followed the antics of friends trying to find one of their buddies, who had gone missing after his bachelor party. It was set in an ancient city of Las Vegas, which reminded Anna of New Davenfield out near Toldeclevchikee.

At some point, however, she paid less attention to the film and more on how Arthor held her in his arms and gently rubbed her shoulder. *That* was about as steamy as it ever got between them, especially since they were still simply friends. But it was still nice, and she still considered it a great way to end the day.

General Jackson Green led his team across the street, placing them a block away from a warehouse. They were in Los'An-Diego city, which was the megacity on the Southern West Coast of North America. It spanned from North Baja and up to the Lower Central Coast. It had doubled in size when a significant population of Mexico and a central swatch of North America got pushed north and west by Growth Zone Four and its offshoots. Not to mention all the resulting red zones ...

Other Growth Zones had contributed to the expansion of other megacities, which had suffered losses from the neo-holocaust. However, compared to Toldeclevchikee, Phijeyoton and Tamorami, Los'An-Diego and San Francisco, for that matter, were giant, disorganized messes of massive populations that had caused infrastructures and economies to collapse, regardless of what the Puppet and Puppeteer Governments had tried to do to prevent it.

"Net." Jack motioned toward Colonel Nether Lacky, who was invisible in his armor's cloaking field, except for the indicator in the HUD of Jack's helmet.

"Yes, sir?" Net asked, his image appearing as a green figure in an otherwise empty alleyway.

"Double-check your explosives. We want to implode this building but don't want to cause any shrapnel to hit the surrounding area. I know the other buildings are abandoned, but we don't want any scavengers going into anything that we might have compromised."

"Right. We're not using too much, but I'll remove a few sticks," Lacky agreed. With closer scans, they'd realized that the integrity of the building had deteriorated more than expected. However, this was a shitty area, so maintenance was an extravagance that would have made the building stick out.

"General?" Lt. Niles Torson's image moved toward them as he walked away from the warehouse they were about to hit. The area was otherwise empty and few people lived in this part of town. There were actually quite a few abandoned buildings and open areas—more than Jack would have expected in a megacity that was stretched so far along the coast. However, this was a very old part of the megacity.

"What is it, Niles?" Jack asked.

"I don't see any actual people guarding the warehouse. Scanners show basic security and it looks like power is coming from solar panels that were painted on the roof. Those are supplying energy for lights, the security and the various hunter-bots in the building.

"Do you have any idea where they are?" Jack hated those fucking things.

"The feed from the taps I placed in the security system are coming on line now ... looks like they are at the common entry points. A couple of them seem to roam the building as support, or to look for intruders that have found other ways in. Two are in the storage area of the warehouse.

"Oh ... scratch my initial assessment about the lack of *live* guards. It looks like there is one technician, who is monitoring the bots."

"Joy. Well, good, at least we won't find bombs in this one."

"Do you think they might change tactics?" Captain Taylor Krackii asked. "I know Tara's dealings with the data seller identified a lot of the booby-trapped locations. But do you think that they'll start sacrificing people to get to us?"

"Doubtful." Jack shook his head. "Doesn't fit the MO. Not saying that desperation might change *that* eventually."

He grimaced, not sure why. It didn't seem right that his enemy seemed to have some type of morals of not killing their own people.

He looked at the building across the street. The Executioners had been selective on how many of these warehouses they were taking out. So far, warehouses like this one didn't seem to have much traffic in or out. These were the odd ones, and weren't usually destroyed, since they were trying to figure out why they were here.

General Rebecca Alexander, recently promoted by the Council and offered the head of Military Intelligence, had requested that the destruction of these remain limited. She preferred that they were monitored for future observation. At some point the product would have to be moved, and the surveillance bots should be able to tag and track activity from there.

The other warehouses, ones they actually did annihilate, were well-guarded distribution centers, which had been created by local dealers who had gotten a bit big for their britches. Since the unknown manufacturer was still offering direct shipments to local dealers and still offered the money to charities, Jack didn't have any problem dealing with the *other* entrepreneurs. Those sonsofbitches had expanded their businesses and promptly began killing any of the competition or other troublemakers. Shit, even if they never took nirv out completely, Jack would be fine if, at least, the Executioners wiped *those* distribution centers out of existence.

Jack stared at the warehouse. Yes, usually, they left ones like these alone. However, a local boy had gone missing. The mother, a local seamstress, had asked the local police for help. But the cops were corrupt and were actually running a local nirv distribution center about two miles away from here. The cops had told the woman to fuck off. Then, to make matters worse, one of them had raped her while he had been on patrol—well, his time he usually spent shaking down local businesses on his beat.

A friend of the mother had sought a reporter, who had lived in the next town of the megacity. However, for the safety of the mother, the reporter didn't know what to do with the story. He put it on a blog with the names of the victim and town changed to protect the innocent. This had gotten the attention of Ecie, who then routed it to Operations.

A week later, after the Executioners had verified the real location, the Panzer Corps had come in, wiped the distribution center off the face of the planet, and then tore the local cops to pieces. LITERALLY. At the top of the precinct, they even wrote "Corrupt, Murdering Rapists" with the arms and legs. You don't really want to know what they used to "dot the i's."

They found the young mother, who mentioned that her son used to play in the neighborhood this warehouse was in. He had liked to explore the old buildings. Sometimes there were things that he could sell. Then, one day, he never came back home. The local cops had ignored her pleads for months.

Since the mother didn't have any family, they relocated her, along with some of the other families that she knew, to Tamorami. They gave them credit-modifier chips with significant sums and new identities. They knew it was in no way any comfort for losing her child, but they hoped she could move on and start a new life with the help of the friends they moved her with. From there, it was a matter of moving out the rest of the town ...

Jack wondered how many families and innocent people the Executioners had relocated over the years. So far, those people they had saved were doing well. You *had* to keep tabs.

While the Panzer Corps were doing their thing, Arthor had asked Tarki to investigate the area and take stock of all the buildings. It was a lot of ground to cover, but the surveillance bots were thorough and never found a body.

When one approached this warehouse, however, it identified electronic signatures of active security systems and the telltale signs of hunter-bots. Finding this unusual for a supposedly vacant building, it promptly tagged it and moved on.

Jack wondered if the technician inside had even noticed the surveillance bot. Maybe the guy thought it was just a toy drone some kid was playing with?

"Just be careful in there when we go in," he warned them. "The bot might have made the dude anxious inside and might have upped the sensors of the hunters. Kill those fast. They can take down regular powered armor pretty quickly. I know we're invisible, but if they get lucky, our stuff will seem like paper to them."

"Why don't we just leave the guy in there? It would be safer," Krackii asked.

"You know why," Green said. "The people guarding *these* warehouses haven't known anything about what is really in there.

They're usually told that it's some type of next-gen drug, chemical or whatever. They won't be much use to us, but we can't just blow them up."

"Sorry, General," Krackii shrugged sheepishly. "I was joking. My apologies. You know we don't like it the easy way."

"Okay," Jack sighed. He should have known better: Krackii was a good kid. "This place just has me on edge. We keep finding these places. What are they for?"

"I'm sure the guy making nirv will fuck up eventually," Torson offered. "He can't hide forever."

"True, maybe then these places won't matter," Jack conceded.

"Well, this one won't anyway," Lacky said. "It's not going to be much use to anyone. Besides, I bet those hunter-bots are what got the kid."

"If so," Jack cursed. "I *will* want that technician alive. And I will want to ask him what he did with the body. Marguerite needs to know regardless."

"Aye," they all agreed and moved quietly toward the warehouse. From there, they each took a position at an entry point. Green followed behind Karckii, and watched their locations from the cloaked HCs above, which relayed info from various positions. They also watched the video feeds from inside the complex.

Then, as luck would have it, Jack watched the technician get up to go to the bathroom. Green smiled. Despite being programmed to attack any threat in a local area or grid, hunter-bots still relied on a coordinator to tell them to move to other locations when necessary. Otherwise—unlike the ones set to "roaming"—they tended to stay in a particular area. They weren't the smartest droids, but they were dangerous. Who puts cutting lasers, chainsaws, sub-Mark-2As and bayonets on a robot?

"Fuck me," Torson whispered. The man was their tactician on the team. "That's why you always have at least two people to guard your base. Or more, you never know when you can get food poisoning."

"Yup," Jack agreed. "Go!"

Krackii, in front of him, kicked in the door and immediately killed the bot racing toward them. Jack kept his double-barreled slinger up and tracked for any hidden targets.

"Torson, Krackii, take out the rest of the roaming bots. Lacky, kill the ones in the storage area and start setting your charges there. I'm going after the tech."

"Aye," they acknowledged.

Green sprinted toward the offices. Through the video feed, he watched the technician hurriedly enter the hallway from the bathroom. The man was still pulling up his pants when Jack intercepted him, grabbed the man by the collar, and dragged him into an office.

Once in, Jack tossed the technician into the corner of the room and turned off his cloaking.

"What do you want?" the technician asked, obviously scared shitless. The helmets of the light armor Tarki wore didn't look like grinning skulls, but they had menacing-looking dragon's faces painted onto theirs. "There's nothing in here except chemicals used for wastewater treatment."

"Then why all the hunter-bots?" Jack asked. Again, he hated those motherfucking things.

"These buildings are deserted. Lots of scavengers and some carry heat. The cops ... the cops aren't much better. Worse even."

"Has anyone gotten in?" Green just skipped the song and dance altogether.

The technician looked down. Then he looked at the wall.

"Did anyone get in?" Green repeated.

"A ... a kid," the technician answered. "Twelve or thirteen ... got in before I could stop the bots. It ... it was fucking horrible! Who the fuck made those things? Despite ... despite what my boss told me after it happened, I still reprogrammed them to 'contain' only. Well, I was too late ... They *were* only programmed to contain after the kid was ..."

"Why didn't you call someone? Ambulance? Cops?"

"No one fucking cares out here. And the cops are lunatics. I have to keep a low profile here. I called my boss, and she helped me clean up. The kid didn't have ID, so we buried him in a cemetery a few blocks away. She's been trying to find the family but she hasn't had any luck. She read a blog about a woman who had been searching for her son but the towns didn't match up."

Jack didn't know what to think. He grimaced. But the technician looked ashen and his voice had been coming out like squeaks.

"If you could move, would you?" Green asked. He wondered how many times he had said this in his life already.

"Fuck yeah, but that's a damned pipe dream. The boarders are shut. They're not letting very many people in or out."

"Any family?"

"No. They ... they were killed about five years ago. A rebel group needed my parents' home because it had a strategic location. They simply threw them out of their high-rise apartment."

"I'm sorry. Okay. I need to see the boy's—Leroy's grave. Then we can talk. Then I want to talk to your boss."

"You're not going to hurt her, are you? She just didn't know what to do. We didn't have a place to put the body. It's California for fucks sake! No one was going to come. No one cares anymore."

"I just need to know what she knows." Jack wasn't sure if he agreed with what the technician said or not. He was sure that a building with hunter-bots as security guards was going to get some type of attention and scrutiny.

"Okay." The technician nodded. "The grave is not far from here …"

Three hours later, Tarki was flying back to Crystal Mountain, after they had relocated a technician named Brett Felder, and his boss, Brittney Tanner, to Toldeclevchikee.

Captain Tylor Krackii had given them new identities, along with enough credit modifier chips to find a new life.

Neither had asked who Green or the rest of them were. He had been fine with keeping that a mystery, even though he'd researched their histories and the company they had worked for.

As usual, the security company that had been hired to watch the building was told basic info, and had been paid a lot to simply not ask questions. Since it had been a small company, no one had, especially with the credit boon the job had offered. The bank account that had paid them had been prepaid, with no information on who had set it up.

Jack couldn't really blame the security company for taking the job. You seemed to take whatever work you could in California, for fuck's sake. Shockingly enough, there were actual pockets of economic stability where the government had maintained strongholds and order. In other places, however, economies were driven by trade, agriculture and the black market.

Where the warehouse had been, though, was a place pretty much forgotten by rebels, mercenaries and the Puppet and Puppeteer Governments. The people in that town had essentially worked for the cops like some bastardized feudal system. The police had kept up a little local economy by running drugs, guns and other trade—some, granted, had actually been legitimate.

As an example, Marguerite, mother of the late Leroy, had been a seamstress—keeping the cops clothed for a meager wage. But whatever additional profits she had made with other clients had been heavily taxed.

Brett had been from an area fifty miles away—a place where the cops there had maintained some order. Brittney had always been concerned that he had been assigned that gig. They had been sleeping together secretly for months. She'd authorized the hunter-bots. Mainly, she'd feared that the local cops would have somehow discovered the warehouse, and killed Brett for whatever was in there.

Admittedly, Jack thought her concerns were valid. It was sad about the poor kid. At least his mother would finally be able to have closure. Well, at least, he hoped that she could.

"Are you glad that we're out of California, sir?" Lacky asked. He'd placed the charges that had leveled that building and incinerated all the nirv that had been in there.

"Hell, yes," he answered, even though he wondered how in the world the Executioners could actually tackle something so big. Panteria was such a damned mess.

Fuck, he thought, realizing the obvious. *We just do what we can.*

CHAPTER FOUR

The difference between a good man and a bad one is the choice of the cause.

(To E.L. Godkin, Christmas Eve)

—William James, American psychologist, philosopher (1895 A.D.)

"This had better be good news," Henry warned.

Bigsby took a step back. That had been an order, and Hammerson winced in response. With the information he had—well, he just didn't want to be hit by something his boss might throw at him.

After two weeks, it's hard to believe he has anything left on his desk, he laughed silently. Then, remembering how many people were dying, he said, more solemnly, "No, I mean, I'm sorry, Henry."

The CFO took another step backward when he saw his boss slide a hand across the desktop toward an old-fashioned, antique letter opener.

"What is it, Bigs? Come on, spit it out." A half smirk tugged on Henry's cheek, because of joke or sadistic anger?

Bigsby quickly composed himself. *Really, could it get any worse?* "Well, another ... another warehouse was destroyed twelve minutes ago, and this one had nirv in it too."

"Fucker!" Harvardson screamed and threw a figurine from his desk, almost hitting an expensive-looking vase in the corner. "That's the eighth warehouse since this mess started."

Henry, eyes wide and determined, pointed an accusatory finger in the CFO's direction. "You tell me. How could they have discovered those locations in less than two weeks? We haven't seen any more of those false-lead decoys triggered. Except for that one in Asia and that's what started all of this mess."

"But, sir," Hammerson protested. "We haven't seen any of our staging warehouses hit yet. It's only been those storage facilities you told me about—"

Lips frowned and then Henry shook his head, seeming paler. "Bigs, that ... that doesn't matter right now. What have we found out about the security network? What's being leaked?"

"I don't know. Like you suggested awhile back, I think it might be because of the supplies we're having shipped to those locations by independent carriers. There are just too many contractors working for us now, too many things that can be misplaced, purposely or by accident. I wish Smithers and I could find the glitches in the Audit system, but we still haven't been able to contact Morrison. A Security Chief is what we need, and he's still on extended leave. You know, especially what happened to his ..." *his*

... his wife, Bigsby finished silently. The last word hurt him too much to say out loud and in the open.

"I know." Henry nodded. "It's difficult keeping work like ours separate from a legitimate life. He should have never tried. She'd still be alive, one way or another, if he'd told her. She could have left him or lived here."

Crass but true enough. Hammerson's right eye twitched and the CFO shuddered on the inside when an old memory raced through his head. Time to change the subject: "But what about our current supply, what should we do about it now?"

"Hmm?" Henry asked. He had been gazing out of the window, seemingly miles away. "Never mind, Bigs, I'll take care of this." Harvardson grabbed the phone-shaped comlink on the desk and punched a coded number. Bigsby watched with interest, wondering if Henry was about to talk to the mysterious Frugal—the name Bigsby had heard once while leaving Henry's office.

Bigsby's heart skipped, thinking about all this secrecy.

"Yeah, Harvardson here," Henry said, scratching his brow. "No, the heat's finally getting too hot. Shit, I know that I should have tried to broker a truce, but you know fanatics? Do you think they would have stopped?

"Yep. There you go ... uhhh ..." Henry suddenly grew pale. "Yah. I know. I'm sorry that I used the Keplers. I had no idea how unstable those things were, or what they really did. Fuck, I'm glad I was able to disarm the others and just add other explosives. Like it mattered ... Well ... it looks like the Executioners pegged those as decoys anyway. Yep, crafty fuckers ...

"Well, we can't move our stuff right now. I'm sure they have some locations tagged and are just watching what we're doing.

"We need help now. They are much more proficient than I expected. They could cut off your supply." Henry shook his head. "No. I tried that remember?

"Great. Thank you. But—No, production is continuing without delay. You'll have more than enough. Okay. Will do. Bye ..." Henry hung up the receiver, but Bigsby was no more informed now than when he'd first heard Frugal's name. "Bigsby?"

"Yeah?" Hammerson kept his tone as natural as he could, despite the frustration from the call. "What do you need?"

"There'll be a gentleman arriving shortly. Make sure his stay is comfortable while he's here, and obey him indubitably."

"Yes, Henry." Out of sure will, Bigsby actually managed to keep his bionic eye from twitching again. "Anything else?"

Harvardson shook his head, and Bigsby turned and walked out the door. His last image was of Harvardson sitting behind his desk, looking over the pine forest around them, staring off at nothing in particular.

Just leave 'em alone was the best advice Bigsby had learned from college, and that had been at party. Therefore, while waiting for the mystery man, Hammerson decided to go to the

Command Center and chat with Smithers for a while. Besides, he wasn't all that thrilled with Henry at the moment, so he needed a little cheering up.

He felt guilty, though, leaving Henry like he did. He hated to admit it to himself but Bigsby did consider Harvardson a friend—at least more than a simple boss-employee relationship—despite his conscious efforts to prevent such. But Hammerson still felt uncomfortable about getting too close, trusting too much, and the knowledge of an unknown visitor soon stopping by didn't ease his anxiety.

He sighed, the office doors clicking shut behind him, and looked at the rows of statues, which comprised the daily gauntlet he had to endure.

"Hello, assholes," he said, but was somewhat taken aback by his own sudden frankness.

Where had that come from? he asked himself a bit shocked, even though he simply shrugged it off and walked to Command.

Bigsby waited at one of the base's landing pads for his new guest. When the transport came into view, he could tell it was a fighter craft, since it was flying like a bat out of hell and skimming the terrain as if it were on an attack sequence.

Damn, I should have known. His eyelid suddenly convulsed until it hurt, after he saw the distinctive markings and colors of a merc transport. *Never trust your boss when it comes to safety. But who else would we have been working with?*

"Mercenaries, great, just fan-fucking-tastic," he let that colorful metaphor slip between his teeth, just as the craft quickly stopped and hovered a few yards away. *This is just fucking perfect.*

It didn't take long for the canopy to pop open, and an average-sized man soon jumped down from the twenty-eight-foot-long FC. He reached out for Bigsby's hand, which Bigsby reluctantly shook as a symbol of his boss's goodwill.

"Bigsby?" the merc asked in a tenor and pulled on a holster with a gun smaller than Bigsby expected. Then, like all paranoid bastards that they were, the man waited for the FC's canopy—placed slightly ahead of the massive pair of older-model repulsars—to shut before going anywhere. Bigsby then guided the man to the entrance of Harvardson's fortress.

Hammerson carefully smirked, "Yes, accommodations are set for your stay and—"

"That's not necessary." The man, Bigsby noticed, certainly seemed tough. Scars lined his face, and veins and muscles rippled beneath the skin of his neck. "I believe you were told to show me your Center of Operations."

OPS? No, not really, Bigsby protested silently, but heeded Harvardson's orders. "Sure."

"Great. I'll only be here for a few hours. I just want to see your Personnel and Active Vendor Files, and then I'll be leaving."

"Which ones?"

"All of them."

Bigsby eyed the man carefully as they walked. This man for hire had a good disposition—confident but with no apparent impudence. Obviously, this disturbed Hammerson some because this guy seemed likable.

Is that hypocritical? Bigsby thought. *No, probably because this guy's not going to be here very long.* "So how are you going to take care of them?"

Suddenly, amber eyes flashed in his direction, and Bigsby shuddered despite himself. "We don't meddle around in your business," the man retorted. "Save us the same courtesy."

Hammerson suddenly flashed back to when he'd been in Business School, hoping that one day he'd have a nice executive job in Toldeclevchikee or Phijeyoton. But, many years later, here he was, looking into the eyes of a psychopath yet again.

The mercenary, however, who gave him another look over, seemed to change suddenly, as if the anger had never existed. "Sorry about that, Mr. Hammerson. Sometimes our clients think that mercenaries enjoy killing. I don't.

"Again, I apologize. My name's Leo." The hired man smiled with a calm grin. "And don't worry. It's all taken care of."

Bigsby grinned uneasily. His opinion of mercs hadn't changed at all.

Walter Smith entered Tarflings' Tavern and walked past the riffraff that generally accumulated around Happy Hour. He was nervous as hell but Smith managed to push past them without a second glance. That bravado calmed him some, despite what he was up to. Sure, the credits that were waiting for him also pushed the anxiety down. It was a shitload of money for doing nothing.

Well, maybe downloading the shipping logs onto a couple of filament disks took a little effort on my part, Walter corrected himself. *And it takes balls to do the transfer at the bar practically next door. Especially during happy hour when your coworkers might show!*

All joking aside, his heart was still racing. His company paid him and others pretty well, thereby making this betrayal seem all the more real. Regardless, he moved toward the rear corner of the restaurant. As he did so, he raised his chin up a bit, trying to peek over heads and hats and see who were sitting at the tables. He made sure not to make eye contact with anyone and kept his gaze on a slow and steady search, trying to find the person who'd make his retirement a decade sooner.

Smith did a double take when he saw a young, beautiful woman casually sipping Scotch at a small, two-person table. He whistled.

God, I hope it's her, he prayed, wetting his lips, and moved toward her eagerly.

A goddess sat there. She was sitting back, her left arm resting on the tabletop. Platinum blonde hair with pink highlights flowed well past her shoulders. She wore a dark trench coat. Although he couldn't see the color of her eyes yet, he saw that they caught his movement toward her and were watching him carefully.

He walked up to her and stood before the table, almost forgetting what he was supposed to do. Also, embarrassingly, water collected on his lower lip, which he wiped away quickly. He closed his mouth and tried to hide a blush.

Never let them see you drool.

"Walter Smith, I presume?" He almost crumbled when she stared at him with those ice-blue eyes. He nodded, managing to keep his legs sturdy, and forced himself to say something.

God, yes, he thought and auto-bobbed his head. "Uh, yeah, I guess you told me to meet you here because Tarson isn't kind."

"Why should she be?" the woman asked in a sultry voice. She threw a quick glance across the establishment, smirked and then tapped her left index finger on the artificial wood of the table top. "A kind heart never wins."

He nodded again, smiling, knowing this was the person he was destined to meet. "Well, I guess you're wondering how I got this information so quickly. But it wasn't a problem, especially for a woman as lovely as you."

His grin vanished when the woman shook her head and her eyes narrowed in his direction. "Enough of the bullshit, Mr. Smith, time is a precious thing. And we shouldn't waste it with you practicing shitty pickup lines."

Funny, I thought it was pretty good. "No, I guess not."

"Good, I'm glad you do. I have no intention of staying here any longer than I have to. I don't care for these places, Mr. Smith. You understand, don't you?"

He nodded, even though she hardly looked uneasy at all.

She continued looking at him for a moment, then kicked out a chair. "Take a seat then," she said. "I believe you have something I want?"

Walter chuckled quietly and took the seat, sliding in close to her right side. *Screw it, might as well go ALL in.*

"That's right," he responded and looked back into her eyes. His heart pounding wildly as he never thought he could be so bold. "However"—he almost stuttered—"with the current risk of my life, there is the matter of payment."

With that said he reached down and grabbed her right thigh with his left hand. Would she take in a startled breath?

No. Instead, she only stared at him and then his hand. He gritted his teeth, beginning to wonder if he should—

"Mr. Smith." To his own surprise, she soon flashed him a delightfully wicked smile. She also covered his left hand with her own, and helped him push away the coat from her leg, exposing a slender thigh covered by a silky, black bodysuit.

"Please, call me Walter." He took two deep breaths and didn't care if she noticed. *God, she's in great shape.*

His heart thumped harder in his chest, and he immediately wondered how big her tits were, while he thought about all those trashy rebel/mercenary/spy novels he'd read during his boring-ass job as a file clerk. This was a scene right out of one!

"Okay, Walter," she said with an even smother voice, winking too. "It appears you believe there's an added bonus for the info you carry, and I'm to play the role?" The grip around his hand increased. The woman had quite the grip.

"You're a bright girl." He smiled again, flashing her with his best pearly whites, but he looked down and noticed that his fingers where turning purple and were beginning to throb.

"Well, you see, Walter, I think we have a misunderstanding here. This is an Inforun, nothing more. The information you're offering was given a proper bid a couple of days ago, and I know that it's a more than generous offer."

The woman looked away for a moment, glanced around the bar and then back at him. "You've never done this and obviously didn't seek any advice regarding how you should behave. I can tell," she said. "So I'm going to give you a free tip: Information brokering can be a hazardous business, especially if you break etiquette.

"You've obviously done enough research to have gotten you this far, since you're talking with me. However, there is a level of professionalism that is expected, especially if you ever deal with me again. First, some things are nonnegotiable."

He winced when she squeezed even harder and the pressure didn't let up.

How strong is she? Could she break my—

That's when the bones cracked in his hand.

"Fu—" he tried to scream, but her hand covered his mouth to shut him up. Making things worse, that bitch was actually laughing.

"Oh, secondly, you generally don't want to make a spectacle of yourself in these places," she said still smiling. "Are you going to be a good boy now?"

He nodded and she took her hands away. Tears were streaming down his face and his erection deflated like a balloon.

"Shit, you didn't have to break my goddamned hand," he shrieked softly and held his wrist, wondering if he should hold it below or above the level of his heart. He gave up, cradling it like a baby, and wiped his face with his sleeve.

She only shrugged, still seeming amused by what she'd done, but he could tell that she was growing impatient.

"Alright," he mumbled. Still shaking, he reached into his own coat and pulled out a large envelop.

The woman took it and opened it quickly, giving the thumb-sized disks inside it a sharp once-over. Then she scanned the numbers printed on the hard copy, which had also been enclosed. "Are you sure these are correct?"

"I risked my life, including my hand, didn't I?" he asked, even though he had bitten his tongue and had babbled most of it.

She smiled, despite his visible twitches, and secured the envelope. She got up and the coat opened up to reveal a tall, fantastic body, which was squeezed into a skintight bodysuit.

And Double Ds to boot, he ogled. Not that he could appreciate it.

"Fair enough," she said and placed a sack of credit chips on his lap. "Oh, make sure you get some ice on that hand, and remember to set the bones. You should probably tell your boss that you caught your hand in a door."

He watched her leave through tear-filled eyes, eventually losing her in the veil of tobacco smoke. Shaking his head, he grabbed a pitcher of ice water and unceremoniously dunked his hand into it.

He laughed despite himself. How did he, some scruffy shit who worked in the back of a warehouse, get his ass handed to him by such an angel, or, at least, someone with the body of one?

"Man," he groaned silently to himself, thinking of what one of those spies might say in this type of situation. "I don't think I'm ever going to read any more of those damn books. What the hell am I going to tell the doc—?"

He felt a sharp pinch in the back of his neck.

Darkness.

Rebecca walked briskly from the bar, while she muttered some curses to herself.

She was more than just a nice piece of ass or property. But that Smith had brought back those memories a lot quicker than it took to bury them.

No, I still shouldn't have let him goad me, she told herself. *It's not a good idea to alienate info-dealers like that, even though he should have known better.* She gritted her teeth, doing her best to forget about the constant conditioning she'd gone through after her initial Abduction.

She shuddered despite herself when the memories of those times surfaced. The memory-blocking and controlling procedures had been extremely powerful and effective. Only after the shock of hearing about her father's murder had she remembered everything, thereby forcing her to leave Infiltration and ultimately work for the Executioners.

For atonement? she laughed derisively to herself, despite the terrible guilt of what she'd done during her time with Infiltration.

"Whatever," she said, knowing she wasn't making much sense. "I'll never let them do that to me again. I'd rather die than forget Dad or ... Jim ..."

Damn ... you got it bad ... She chided herself playfully ... *Stop!*

"Bat?" she asked, which activated the comlink on her coat collar and opened a secured channel to her partner. "Are you ready?"

"Yes, Artemis, be there in two clicks."

"Great, I'll be ready. Don't run over anyone," she joked. Steve Sanders wasn't a bad driver, even though he liked to drive like he was in a carnival. Of course, this sixth inforun with him hadn't dampened his eagerness to fly a hovercar. She'd given him that nickname and he proudly began to use it as his call sign.

She giggled—*I giggle?*—and thought about the last few months. Considering all the time she'd spent relearning history and reviewing her father's work, she figured that signing up with Jim and his merry band of rebels had certainly demanded quite an effort.

Rebecca, however, smiled triumphantly. As of today, along with her other duties in the military, she had just successfully completed her sixth inforun. And despite his flying, Sanders was a fun, reliable and punctual partner.

She did feel a little guilty though, since Sanders wasn't going on the next one. Instead, she'd asked Jim to go with her to Cuba in a couple weeks. She didn't want to admit that she just wanted to spend time with Jim out of the Mountain. She simply told him that the thought of how he handled one intrigue her, especially since he was over seven feet tall and looked like a god of war.

She also had booked a nice two bedroom suite at a resort, and the thought of seeing him in swim trunks intrigued her too.

Fuuuuuck, she scolded herself at that naughty thought. *Maybe if things were different. Maybe if—*

She looked at the map through the tactical contacts she was wearing, and walked down an alleyway that was between the tavern and an antique shop. "Steven, you're two blocks from my position now, and I'll—"

Four hands grabbed her ... and then tried and failed to pull her deeper into the alley.

They were all dressed in black with hoods over their faces. She tore the arms off of one of them and shoved those through another one—

Then, despite her durability, a sharp sensation stabbed her right shoulder, and her strength all but left her. Well, not all of it—

"Fuck you!" Reflexively, she kicked. The holder of the jet injector quickly buckled over, screamed and dropped the gun to the ground. He held his hands tightly around his groin and fell to his knees, which caused his hips to pop out because she had pulverized his pelvis.

"Serves you right," she shouted and spat on him. He wasn't wearing any armor, and, despite her increasing struggles with more of them around her, she managed to kick him in the head—brains, eyes, tonsils and all matters of parts sprayed the alley!

"Holy fuck, she just killed John, Paul and Ringo," someone shouted in disbelief.

"Shut the fuck up," someone else shouted as she stumbled. "Hold her. Hold her steady."

"Yeah, we need more people here," somebody else cursed, just as Becca got her arm free and reached into her coat for the magnum pistol holstered on her side—

"I'll kill you all," she screamed and fired the gun without careful aim, since the world was spinning. Two more people collapsed beside her, and the gun jerked three more times before she could no longer move her fingers ...

Eventually, her gun was yanked from her grip just as her stomach seemed to turn upside down.

Shit! Shit! Shit! Suddenly, she panicked from an old memory. The drug they'd shot her with reminded her of one used long ago—one that had been used when she had tried to escape from the Agency only two days after her initial Abduction. Just like that one, this drug worked just as quickly by zapping her strength, upending her balance and reflexes, and clouding her mind with indistinguishable colors and sounds.

Mercenaries? she managed to ask herself. *Assassins? The Agency? My God, has the Agency found me?*

Her heart pounded, thinking about the Abduction, the pain, and the loss of humanity. She noticed that they weren't wearing the dark armor of Infiltration Abductors. Still, that didn't ease her mind, even though these guys were terribly sloppy.

Most likely Smith's employers, she reassured herself before the entire effects of the drug began to take effect. She blinked and saw sky and clouds—all fuzzy. Then, over her discarded comlink, she heard Bat's reassuring words while he sped toward her.

I'm sorry, Steve. She could only mouth the words, despite the pangs of guilt, the guilt of how their partnership was about to end.

But only one person truly occupied her thoughts at this moment.

It's okay. They won't get anything from me, Jim. You mean too much. She shook her head, still not ready to face the truth. Instead, she looked back up into the sky, and saw a swirled, dizzying kaleidoscope.

Behind her, rocket launchers and e-cannons pounded a target relentlessly until its shields collapsed—

A man's screams echoed in the alley, and a deafening explosion rocked the world just before she closed her eyes.

Jim was tired and worn out. He'd led the team to recover Sanders. Then, he'd searched for Rebecca. In the end, unable to find the ex-Infiltrator, he'd come back to the Mountain in a sour mood. Making it worse was spending the rest of his time in Sanders' recovery room.

He grimaced and threw a questioning look at Dr. Marshal Anton, one of Anna's best surgeons. The doctor didn't look optimistic.

He had reason. Jim noticed that Steven's lifeforce looked like a tilted pinball machine. Tubes and monitoring devices covered him. Several of the man's organs needed to be replaced; however, because of a genetic anomaly, cybernetics would just end up killing him. Dr. Anton's group had started the process of generating replacement organs and tissues, but those would take over a week to grow.

St. John was proud of what the man had tried to do. Even though Sanders had been too brash at the attempted rescue, the man had tried. He'd tried. He'd been a good soldier and friend.

"Jim, I have to see how Peggy's doing. I'll be back in a little while," Anton said quietly and left the recovery room. The doctor, despite how busy he was, had been making frequent visits back here.

Jim, having seen large triages during battle, wondered if Marshal would have done so even if there'd been a hundred cases like this today. And he suddenly felt guilty for even thinking such a thing.

"Ecie, can I have some privacy?" he asked the computer.

"Sure, Jim, it won't affect my monitoring of Sanders."

"Thanks." Jim was sitting at a nearby table. His mood hadn't lightened any since Logan's death, and his self-doubts about ever coming to the Mountain continued to plague him. Now more than ever.

It was silly to believe that I'd ever be able to keep my word to Lisa. He grimaced in frustration. *No matter what I did to contain it, the rage spread like a cancer. It infected these people and tweaked their minds to do its bidding. The Beast's corruption is all inclusive.*

"It wants blood and someday it'll have it." Lately he feared that he'd subconsciously—if not, somehow, fully consciously—maneuvered the Crystalians into, ultimately, taking up arms against the government. Despite what he kept telling himself, didn't he feel some sense of pride in how well the Executioners performed during training? How well they handled themselves during inforuns?

Jim looked up and eyed Sanders carefully, and then realized how dichotomous his thoughts now were.

"The road to Hell is paved with good intentions," he reminded himself. Good intentions had led to the creation of Crystal Mountain; the same had led to the formation of the Executioners; and, ultimately, had led to Logan's death, to Sanders' mutilation and to Rebecca's abduction.

"Basically, I should have left, should have left before they elected ..." he trailed off. Having to do it over again, he still would have updated their facilities, would have helped stopped the cave-ins, and would have volunteered as a mentor for children who'd lost their parents to fires or landslides. Fuck, if he hadn't reinforced the tunnel plexes, the Mountain would have eventually collapsed in on itself one day.

He wouldn't have let them form the Executioners—Shit, how would he have prevented that? He'd stayed because they were going to form it anyway, and he wanted to try to keep them safe. Fuck, he realized that just him being here had corrupted them and set them on this path.

"Lisa, you damned me and saved me at the same time," he laughed bitterly. "Did you know this? Did you know my attempts at expiation would be so difficult?"

Then he took a breath in culpability, realizing it'd been a while since he had really thought about her ... and *missed* her. But quickly enough, her fiery red hair blazed in his mind and he remembered her dark-blue eyes. He had missed her tender voice, her arms and her ability to calm him after battles.

She'd sing hymns and quote me words of Scripture. She'd hold my face in her hands and tell me that she loved me. Told me that what I was doing was for the greater good, even though she hated what I was doing. He'd loved her so much. After Henderson, after his promise, he'd scurried the globe for a safe haven.

His childhood home hadn't been an option, since that was the first place the AOM hit ... He thought about his parents, just adding to his guilt. He thought about how he hadn't even tried to make contact with them after his escape from the FGGO. Essentially, his anger over Lisa's death had searched for blame, searched for any viable reasons why things had turned out so cruelly.

His parents and their ignorance of what the world was really like had allowed their sixteen-year-old son to join up with what they had thought was a Military academy for the truly gifted. They had been told that their son was going to get the best education and was destined for a great future. All for free!

Right after Henderson, Jim blamed them for not knowing any better. But how was it their fault? How could they have known about the FGGO or the Panterian Guard? Obviously, by the time Jim had realized he was being an asshole it'd been too late to save them.

"McNeil hadn't even asked them any questions." He felt sick, thinking about his baby sister, Tahrea. She might have had a wonderful life if it hadn't been for his short-lived resentment of his parents after he'd escaped.

My God, I let them kill my family, he told himself, ashamed. How could he ever absolve himself of that sin? He shook his head, knowing that a group of Henderson Survivors led by Carlos Jackson McNeil, his former friend and commanding officer, had killed them in retaliation.

Jack had done the unthinkable. Still, it was of no consolation when Jim had torn that man apart at that warehouse. Making it even more bittersweet, McNeil's private files revealed that the killing of Jim's family had always haunted him. In truth, Jim just should have been there to protect his family. It was that simple.

St. John sighed and wondered about the Executioners, Logan, Sanders, and Rebecca. "I know. I know that I can't protect them all," he admitted. They had chosen a dangerous way to live.

Footsteps echoed in the hallway outside and the door opened. "Hey, Jim," Arthor said, stepping into the room. "How's Sanders doing?"

"Anna agreed to let Marshal look over him after the operations. He was optimistic at first, but there are just some things doctors can't fix."

"Chetok," Arthor agreed briefly in his native tongue. "Death often travels more quickly on your world."

Yeah, sometimes when he doesn't have to. Jim watched the Crytonian take a sympathetic look at Sanders, then watched the man's shoulders fall when he looked back Jim's way.

"I just got the latest report from the search crews," Arthor said morosely. "It's not looking good. We ... we can't find any trace of her. They were good at covering their tracks."

"No hints or postings of ransoms through our networks?" The Governor shook his head even as he said that. He rubbed his hands through his hair again while he thought about the ex-Infiltrator and her dazzling, sky-blue eyes.

Arthor stated the obvious, "No, it's very unlikely that Rebecca will let anyone know that she's an Executioner. And even if they know who she's working for, she won't give them anything."

Jim took a deep breath. In this business, he wondered if he'd ever see her again. Like so many people in his life. "Arthor, what have I done?" he asked.

"What do you mean?"

"It's all starting to unravel. I'm destroying this community, person by person, and everything I do seems to catalyze the fact. Sonofabitch, why did I stay here? I should have taken revenge at Henderson. Maybe then—

"Shit, I don't know. A Kepler bomb couldn't even kill me, Arthor. And because of this invulnerability, I may be the only one left alive after Crystal Mountain falls."

"Jim, you can't think like that. The Executioners fight for justice, what's right, and the Crystalians endorse it. Both need you to show them how to survive. They will if you—"

"But they were already doing so before I came here. I should have left before I corrupted them, before this happened to Sanders, before it all happened. I know the place was at risk of collapsing in on itself. But what's the point of trading one 'end of the world' scenario for another?" He again thought about eyes that were the color of the sky. *Rebecca ... Rebecca ... fuck ... God dammit ...*

Arthor took a step in front of him and said, "You know that Logan, Rebecca and even Sanders here were aware of the risks of becoming an Executioner. They would have done it over and over again if given the opportunity."

"I know, but all I wanted to do was keep my promise to Lisa. I just wanted to run away from the deceit, to do what I was asked. I just wanted to end the killing, to no longer be a part of the bloodshed. And look—"

"—at what you've become?" Arthor finished the sentence for him. It sounded so cliché, even when a man from another world said it. "You know that was impossible, Jim. God brought us all here together. Like it or not, Crystal Mountain needs you. You need it."

"Yeah, like it needs another cave-in or another mishap with the HVAC systems or the—"

"Come on," Arthor nearly shouted, clearly frustrated. "You eliminated those problems once you came here. You earned their respect, and they pledged their loyalty to you and to each other three years before I even landed on this planet. Then I pledged the same when I realized that you and the Crystalians had saved my life. Where would I have been otherwise?"

"Arthor, honor and lives hold different definitions for me. How can a man such as me determine what both are? Honor was an acquired trait for me, and the only life I have ever saved was my own."

"Humble words from a person who's done and saved so much," Arthor tried to point out.

Jim only smirked. He thought about the sobriquet the Stigs had given him and what the AOM had used for recruitment posters: *Behold the Mutilator! The implacable killer ...*

"Oh?" Arthor countered Jim's smartass look back at him. "What do you think would have happened if these people had been found by someone else? What would have happened if the Guard had found them? Would they have just been assimilated into the culture, forced to leave their homes?

"Ta-shet, the Guard might have even seen the Crystalians as a potential cancer, since they would have never blended in. And, if so, would they have just killed them outright?

Arthor frowned. "Or I could tell you something worse: Have you ever wondered how they became such good fighters and soldiers so quickly? Didn't you ever wonder why they became so skilled in the art of war and even assassinations—despite their affinity for peace?

"For Fuck's sake!" Arthor used an English curse. "Their ancestors had been handpicked by Wallace himself, and then they fought for survival under a mountain for over eight-hundred years.

What if someone lied to them, as the government did to you? Think then of what might have happened."

"Arthor, you're reaching," Jim protested. "The Neo-Puritans and the computer viruses that destabilized the Old World's economy and infrastructure erased a lot of important history, including anything of archeological significance beneath Crystal Mountain. Sure, the Smithsonian and other historical microcosms survived, but it doesn't matter, since everyone thought that the Terrex had wiped out everything that was supposed to be here. And, being that we're in the center of THE worst Red Zone on land, no one ever would have come out this way.

"Sure, they would still have had the cave-ins, floods or possible implosion, but what's worse? Look at what I've done to their innocence." Jim motioned his right hand toward Sanders. "I've sentenced all of you to this fate. I'm a Kurgon Beast. Doesn't that mean anything to you?"

"What about Jennifer? She hadn't been a part of any of this. You saved her life."

Jim bit his tongue. He remembered the first day Logan had brought up the subject of disrupting the drug trade. He also remembered the reports about Hillmount Estates and how nirv was responsible for that catastrophe.

Nirv had been at the prison before the escape, since it was being used for behavioral modification testing. A prison guard swiped some and got stoned at work, thereby accidentally leaving open several important locks.

Before they had escaped and headed to Hillmount, the prisoners had raped and slaughtered everyone who'd worked there. Had the warden acted on his own ... to use the drug as a means of behavioral conditioning? Or had the Guard seized the opportunity to supervise nirv's distribution to the world? It had to have been in the prison before Logan had taken out the drug czars, right? Had those people in there been a test group? Fuck, was he overthinking this? With no witnesses, Jim couldn't be sure.

"Because of us?" Jim was speculating now, wasn't certain if the Puppeteer or even the Puppet Government were involved. However, the conspiracy-nut inside him still daydreamed. "Arthor, because we killed those drug lords, could we have opened up the drug trade for the Guard, thereby allowing them to carry out some new social experiment? Could we have been responsible for the deaths of Jen's parents and all of those people back there?

"My God, if so, I should have helped with the plan from the beginning, and shouldn't have let Logan's clouded judgment cause such recklessness. I might be responsible for this mess, me and my damned principles."

Jim hadn't even told Jen about the possible link yet, since he still lacked all the evidence. And even if he did learn the truth, he wondered if he ever would tell her. Besides that, what would such accomplish? And what would she do if she did find out? Pondering this, Jim just slouched deeper into his chair, and just avoided his best friend's gaze.

"So be it then," Arthor cursed. "Fine, because you decided to stay and lead us, you've damned everyone here in Crystal Mountain. Is this what you wanted to hear? Is it?

"But. It's. Not. That. Simple," the Crytonian bit out each word. "How can you blame yourself for decisions that we made? Think about it. We fight against injustice. Even on my home world, the majority of the warriors, who had volunteered to fight the invading Empire nearby, had been the working class, the Varlou. And despite not being fully trained for battle, they had decided to stay and fight for their country, for their King and for their loved ones.

"Honestly, I once thought that they were the bravest people I'd ever know. But truthfully, such strength transcends space, and even beats in the hearts of mountains."

Jim watched his best friend storm out of the room, and he smiled derisively. This conversation had sounded so familiar, as if he and Arthor had been brooding over this same topic for the better part of nearly three years. But how had the subject changed from a sword to the possible slaughter of eighty thousand people?

Jim's smile faded. This wasn't time to feel hypocritical. He glanced at Sanders' monitors and noticed the date—

Shit, how in the hell? he chided himself. *How ... how did I forget what day it was?*

Jim knew the answer ... He knew exactly why his mood this morning—before all of this had happened—had been so fucking cheerful. He'd been so excited, so damned excited to go to Cuba with Rebecca, even though they both had been lying to each other about their reasons.

However, six years ago on this day, on a Battlefield in Northern Canada, Dr. Lisa Marie Emerson had died in his arms. And Jim St. John felt guilty and ashamed that Lisa hadn't been the first person he had thought of when he woke up this morning.

"I'm sorry, Steve," he apologized. "I have to leave for a bit. But I'll say a prayer for you."

By the time Arthor entered his apartment, both his shoulders hurt, his upper and lower set of arms were tired, and his wings ached because he'd forgotten to stretch them out during the day. *That* was starting to be a reoccurring thing.

He sighed quietly, thinking about Rebecca and about how Sanders had died only a few minutes after he'd left the hospital. Naturally, he had run back—his anger quickly extinguished—to be there for Jim. But the man had been gone—"Left to go to the Cathedral," Ecie had said.

Arthor hadn't needed to ask why, knowing it was the anniversary of Lisa's death, so he left Jim alone.

He walked through the living room and marched past the numerous medieval tapestries and weapons he'd obtained for decoration. Despite their Panterian origin, they still often reminded him of home.

"Home ..." He let the word hang at the tip of his tongue. Because of Jim's concerns, the Crytonian suddenly wondered what would happen if he died here on alien soil.

He quickly tried to shake out that thought, reminding himself of the sword and how its recovery would at least ensure his soul's safe return to Deliplain. Lately, however, like his belief that he would one day return home, the idea that he would one day recover *Omniemnan* was becoming—to coin a Panterian phrase—a pipe dream.

He stretched, relaxed his wings and began to undress as he walked to his bedroom. He'd get some shut-eye before his next shift.

He opened his bedroom door but stopped in his tracks. His heart pounded a little more quickly when he saw Anna on his bed. He quickly blamed Jim's infectious paranoia—obviously that was what had startled him.

Arthor smiled and quickly gained his composure and watched his friend on the bed. She was immersed in either thought or fantasy—or both—while she worked diligently on a sketchpad. Her long legs were crossed, giving height and support to the pad she held. And her curly, dark-brown hair cascaded beautifully over her shoulders.

Beautiful—he hesitated thinking the rest but couldn't help himself—*she's damned beautiful.*

She was dressed in a black skirt with a velvet white blouse, which showed a bit of cleavage. She was not simply beautiful but absolutely gorgeous.

The Crytonian smirked as he watched her while she drew. Her eyebrows were scrunched together in thought and the tip of her tongue was sticking out from a corner of her mouth. He suddenly felt guilty, though, when he realized that he'd missed her, really missed her. Because of conflicting schedules, it had been a while since they'd done anything together.

But I'm not supposed to long for it, right? That's what will get me in trouble? But, fuck, am I ever going home? He managed to smile, despite the events of today, his screwed up past, and his immediate concerns of the here and now.

"Anna?" he asked to stop anything his damned mind kept thinking.

"Arthor!" she shrieked and jumped, throwing a startled but happy face up in his direction. "You were so quiet. I didn't hear you come in."

She adjusted the pad on her thighs again, and she gave him another witty grin. "Don't you think you've been spending too much time with that group Tarki of yours?"

He only shrugged his shoulders. His face gave the rest of his questions away.

She went on: "Well, I'm glad you're home. I didn't know how much longer I could spend waiting for you. I was almost out of paper."

He'd always liked the art she drew for herself or for him. She had a keen eye for detail. The pictures and paintings, which were often events in Panterian history that she'd learned about from Jim, were always so breathtaking.

She held the paper she was working on up to him now. It was covered end to end, corner to corner with nice squiggly lines. They made no sense to him right off, but they eventually took the form of—well, a page full of nice squiggly lines.

"Taqik?" His subconscious threw the question out before he could stop it.

"Don't worry, Arthor." She gave him another look, assuring him she wasn't going crazy. "I was just practicing line depth while I was waiting for you."

"Waiting?" He tried to sound as innocent as possible.

"Don't tell me you forgot?"

"Well ... I ... ah ... I ..." He was stumbling hard, and even his trained battle-face couldn't hold back this bluff.

"Arthor, it's been three years since you decided to stay here in Crystal Mountain." She laid the drawing pad aside and got up from the bed and walked over to him. She took his lower right hand into both of hers and she rubbed it gently.

"Ann." He didn't know what to say right off. He hadn't been ready for such an answer or in the mood.

"Come on, Arthor." He knew she had seen him frown because of the tone in her voice. "I haven't seen you in a while and it seems longer since we've done anything together. I feel Rebecca's loss too and pray for her, but you have to remember she could still be alive! That's why I'm not mourning for her yet. And ... and I had to talk with you. Bastik! After what's happened ... life ... life is too damned short! I ... I ... well ... it's time that we ..."

He took in a sharp breath at that, thinking about the day. He didn't reply, but he needed to. He had to tell her, but she had such a beautiful smile. It was so warm and comforting, but it was still not enough to ease his heavy brow.

"What's wrong?" she asked. Then he watched her smile fade from her lips ... and he already missed it. "Oh. No. Steve?"

He lowered his head. "Chetok, he died a few hours ago. There was nothing we could do for him. Marshal did his best, but Death came anyway."

The grasp on his hand was gone, and he saw a blur move toward his bed. Anna tried to gather up the art equipment on its top. She was fumbling with the pencils she'd laid across the quilt. A few kept falling out of her grip.

"Anna?" He moved next to her.

"I should've been there. I should've been there to try and save him, at least been there to record the time of death, filled out the death certificate."

He laid a right hand on her shoulder. She was shaking. He wasn't sure of what he was doing but ... "Don't ... don't go. Please ..."

"I have to. Marshal may need some help."

"He's done everything you possibly could have, and he didn't tell you because you were working so hard lately. He knew it wasn't procedure, and he knew you'd probably be furious with him, but you needed the rest. I told him it would be all right."

"But I can't stay. I shouldn't have been so self-absorbed. This was a bad idea." She tried to break away from him.

"No, it wasn't." His words stopped her flight. "I'm glad you remembered this day, and I'm sorry I forgot. It's just that this day reminds me so much of when I first came to your world—the deaths, the abduction. And so much has happened since then. Please don't leave. Talk with me."

Her face then seemed so angel like, something he thought a human could never really personify, even though he'd seen it in her face so many times over the years. She grasped his upper right hand and pulled him over to sit on the bed.

He'd never told her what happened, never shared the pain he kept from her, and she'd always seemed to respect his wish by not asking him. However, he couldn't hold back any longer, no longer keep her in the dark. This would be a time for truths, and his upper right hand felt anything but empty.

"Oh God, Arthor." Anna got up from the bed. She'd always seen the heartache he tried to hide from her—the lingering sadness that was always present. But she'd had no idea of how sad he truly was. She wanted to help him, but this was too big, too much. She didn't know what to say. Was there anything she could say?

"Where are you going?" His voice sounded so innocent now, so pleading, so reaching.

"I can't help you, Arthor. It's too much for me."

"I know ..." She paused from her escape when she heard those words. "I don't think anyone can."

Her back was still turned to him, and she knew he couldn't see the tears beginning to form around her eyes. "I wanted to at least try though. I wanted to help you. I wanted to do the same thing you have done for me. I thought I had a chance at making you feel whole again, like ... like ... I feel with ... *you*."

"Ann."

"No. Listen!" she shouted, then quieted. "Please just listen. Besides some brief relationships, there has never been anyone in my life, Arthor. My parents died in a cave-in when I was nine. Then I lost my godmother ..." Anna shook her head, wiping her nose and eyes. "I've lost everyone who took care of me, Arthor. Growing up, I tried to hide behind my studies—telling myself to follow the namesake that had been given to me. But, no matter what I did, no matter what accomplishments I made in medicine by curing the sick or injured, there has always been a void."

Anna felt suddenly cold, and she closed her eyes and tried her best from shivering. "The sadness and loneliness would be worst at night. Night, during a power outage, that's when my parents had died. They had been trying to fix power lines cut during a cave in. From then on, every time the Mountain had a blackout or if my nightlight burned out while I slept—

"Arthor, do you know what it was like for me to wake up in the dark? Terrified of being ... being alone ..." She heard him breathing while he sat on the bed. She still didn't turn, still afraid too.

"But then you came, Arthor. I thank the day when Jim appointed me as your guide to Crystal Mountain. I couldn't explain then what stirred within me when we first walked together. I just felt 'comfortable' and I loved how you just took this new world all in stride.

"My God, even though you lost your world, you never gave up. You always did your best. That strength inspired me. And at night, if a light went out, I only had to think of you, and I would fall back to sleep."

She shook her head. "That's initially what I wanted to do for you, Arthor. But ... but ... after hearing ... I can't. Not after—not after knowing how much you hate it here!" She tried to run from him, but a gentle hand managed to paw at her skirt.

"Wait. I don't. I don't hate it here. There are people who I care for ..." The words were barely audible, but she heard them and she stopped. She was crying now, and she didn't want to face him. She had done her best and failed.

His hand, however, rested around her waist, and she allowed him to pull her back to the bed.

Something made her look into his eyes. Tears were rolling down his dark cheeks, and he tried to turn away when she looked at him. But her right hand had already moved up to stop the motion, tracing the lines of sorrow on his face. And soon enough, his fingers pressed lightly on her own face while he did the same thing to her tears.

"Arthor, I have to tell you ..." She smiled, while the tips of his fingers stroked her cheek, and while she pressed closer into his caress.

"Arthor ... I ... love ..." She continued to gaze into his eyes, and he did the same. Their heads were so close. She felt her back straighten as she moved closer still. Their lips were almost touching—

What am I doing? Arthor thought and quickly pulled away. He couldn't give in. He couldn't damn her too. Not her!

"What is it?" Anna tried to pull him back toward her again, but he didn't want—No, he couldn't allow her to do so!

"I can't," he whispered. "This isn't right."

"What do you mean? It's perfect."

He didn't want to tell her what else he'd been holding back. He'd thought it wasn't important. Until now. "I can't tell you. I've already hurt you enough."

"What, that I'm not typhon? You're not human? It doesn't matter to me, Arthor. I know this is natural. I love you. Here. See ... my ... my heart ..." She took his lower left hand and placed it on the swell of her firm, left breast. He felt her shiver. Felt her rapid heartbeat. Felt her quickened breathing. And, suddenly, his own heart quickened and—

"I can't." He pulled away.

"I don't understand. I can't understand. What is it, Arthor? Is it really me? I ... I ..."

"Anna, please. No ..."

"Come on, Arthor! You can't keep hiding things from me! Not now!"

"Anna—"

"Dammit, Arthor! What ... what—"

"God dammit, I'm married!" His own heart broke when he said it.

"What?"

"Because of my royal heritage, I have a wife, or, at least, as humans would say, 'a wife to be.'"

"Then, you're not really married?"

"No. I am." He saw her confusion, and he did his best to explain the situation to her: "I know it doesn't make sense, but even after twenty centuries, our people—at least for Royalty anyway—never gave up on prearranged marriages. The practice actually got more complicated and sacred by my time, essentially binding the youths at early childhood. I've been married for years, even though I've never seen her."

"Um, can you tell me about her," she said quietly.

Why couldn't I have told her something else? he asked himself. "There isn't much. Our people found it custom to never introduce the royal couple until a few years before the Union, and ours wasn't going to be for another five years. I do know that she is highly praised in the Arts and Music, but that's all I know. I don't even know what she looks like. They say she's beautiful, I guess. Really, I never thought about it back then. Ta-shet, I was training to be a knight! Not ... not to be a husband!"

He looked at Anna. His flight had taken him off the bed and had forced him to stand. But he saw the red flush in her cheeks, and saw the shock and uncertainty in her eyes.

He sighed and went over and knelt before her. He didn't say anything right away, just stared into her eyes. He tentatively reached up with his upper left hand again to wipe away her tears.

His fingers combed through her dark hair too, knowing he couldn't stop himself.

"But when I look into your eyes and hold you in my arms, I'd be a fool to say that I don't ..." he trailed off, still uncertain of his actions; however, he realized he was holding her hands now, caressing them and holding them to his heart. And she still tried to pull him toward her.

"Anna, I'm married," he barely whispered it, and his other hands cradled her face while he spoke. "But I cannot deny the feelings I have for you. You are the first person I think about in the morning and the last person I call and talk to at night. You have been my friend, my confidant and my first reason for choosing this life in the Mountain."

He was shaking more so now, knowing she could see it. "God, Anna, I love you, but I'm so weak, so dishonored that I can't bear the idea of damning someone else for my failures.

"But I know that I found my soulmate here on this world. So how can we be damned for this? How can we be condemned for loving each other?" He looked into her face again, noticing her cheeks were still blushed, her eyes still red.

"Anna ... I ..." He shuddered once more, wondering if he was telling the truth or if he was speaking with his heart like fools so often did. But what was the price of another sin?

His heart pounded relentlessly. Even Anna must have felt it with her hands pressed up against his chest, but she said nothing. She only looked up at him with the most beautiful eyes he'd ever seen.

"I am a cursed man. But, of all my sins, I proudly swear my love to you," he finally spoke above a whisper, so that even God could hear him. "I know and have always known that your love is all that matters to me, and that you are the true keeper of my soul." He suddenly realized that he was crying again. But he didn't shy away, his tears a symbol of his undying love for her.

"If our sin is simply our Love, my dear Arthor, we'll be damned together," she said, touching his chin and gently tugging him closer. His face neared hers, and for the first time, without restraint or hesitation, their lips pressed together. And immediately, his mind and heart swirled, and his upper right hand opened, intertwining his fingers with hers.

"Anna, my love," he said, briefly breaking the kiss, and his left hand continued to trace her cheek. "You no longer have to be afraid of the dark."

A hand, warm but trembling, caressed his jaw, and her smile made him melt. "How could I be? I haven't been since you've come into my life."

They fell back onto the bed, while they tore at each other's clothes.

Quiet. Too quiet, Jim thought. Not very many people were here in the Cathedral tonight. The lights had been dimmed, making the place of worship seem even bigger than what it already was.

St. Anna's Cathedral was vast and immense. It was named after a Crystalian Medical Doctor who had saved thousands of people during an epidemic seven hundred years earlier. It had been hollowed out of the rock centuries ago. Over that time, its ceiling and towering walls had been carved and decorated by various scenes from the Good Book. Some of the carvings must have taken generations for the Crystalians to complete. And Jim wondered how long it would take an Infiltrator or Panterian guardian to bring these walls crumbling down. The beautiful artwork of a lost people gone and removed in an instant—

Enough ... no more distractions ... say something, Jim told himself, even though he hadn't said anything during the last few hours.

In honor of Lisa, he had come to St. Anna's Cathedral and lit a candle. The candle had already burned halfway down, while those placed here earlier by other visitors were now going out.

He'd had to light one for Sanders ... He looked away from the remembrance candles, eyeing the statue of God at the rear of the church. Jim tried to imagine what He was thinking at the moment of His death. Hadn't He been human for a time? Some three thousand years ago?

I'm sorry. Sorry. Jim bit his tongue, crossed his heart and prayed for his friends. Briefly, he thought about praying for himself but immediately shook out that moment of weakness. Honestly, was he being here a mockery of it all? Or was it true that God forgives all? Everyone?

"Lisa, I wish you could hear me," he said, and, in a moment of whimsy, opened his mind up to the world around him. Instantly, like candles being lit in the night, thousands upon thousands of souls suddenly swarmed around him when his life-detection power—having gotten more powerful since Henderson—dotted every living thing within a twelve mile radius. For a moment, he focused on individual people: Jennifer in a library with Max, John making his rounds, Arthor and Anna having a quiet dinner in a café near her home.

So many people, so much life ... but what if ...? He furrowed his brow and tried to push his abilities—gritting his teeth and focusing harder. He tried to sense beyond the boundaries of his home—high above the forest and further still. But, as always, it was all noise beyond that, like the background radiation from the beginning of time.

Foolish notion, he rebuked, feeling a sharp pain at the base of his neck, prompting him to stop trying to maximize his power. Heaven couldn't be that close. Well, at least, no mortal should be able to sense it. At least, that is what he still could tell himself. Maybe not all hope dies.

"My dearest," he spoke, hoping Lisa could hear him anyway. "I lit a candle for you. Like always, it symbolizes our love, the burning passion and feelings we had for one another ..." he paused, growing silent again. For nearly three hours he'd been sitting here thinking about a different pair of blue eyes, about blonde hair instead of red, about late-night movies and a smile that made his heart skip every time he saw it.

"Lisa, I ... I ..." he stammered, knowing this was going to be hard to say but he realized that all of his doubts, all of his recent bouts with uncertainly were directly linked to the day that this anniversary represented.

"I'm sorry." Jim pushed himself up and walked away. But he paused just before leaving the Cathedral, taking one last look at the candle.

"I love you, Lisa. Goodbye."

<><><><><><><>

Jennifer was in the Executioner Library, Johnson Hall, which was the largest "real" book depot in the Mountain. She'd been here about three hours, trying to read about a history that was so different from what she knew.

Ultimately, that was what made it very difficult to believe and even follow. Complicating matters, Max was snoring up a storm in the seat beside her, prompting her to rub his belly to quiet him down.

"You like that, don't cha?" she laughed and continued to rub his belly.

Max gurgled, rolled over and stopped snoring. Despite the resumed peace, though, Jen was still having difficulty reading the text on her PDL, which was being fed by one of Ecie's many databases.

She tapped her right index finger on the side of the unit and tried to concentrate. She'd had no idea—as with probably ninety percent of Panteria's population—that so much history had been wiped out at the beginnings of the Apocalypse.

She read the digital text carefully, making notes on what questions to ask later. Being that high schools were structured a bit differently in Crystal Mountain, Jim had asked Jen to audit some classes at one of the universities. She'd decided on Biology, English Literature and Calculus, which were courses she'd been studying and felt comfortable with before her high school had been destroyed. The fourth, General History, however, seemed to be the most taxing, since it contradicted everything that she'd ever learned.

Looking at the large, pre-Unification *Rand's World Atlas* on the floor at her feet, she pouted. This particular visit to the library was to investigate the Trevor Wars between the ancient city-states of Jakarta and—at the time—Panteria. It was actually background work that had been assigned to her by her professor so that she could keep up with the other members of her class regarding this conflict. Luckily, Jennifer had always been a quick learner, an attribute for which she'd—

She suddenly had a weird feeling, and she looked up from the atlas just as a nine-year-old boy skipped by. He noticed her reaction and instantly apologized, thinking he had disturbed her even though he hadn't in the slightest. The children of Crystal Mountain were just as damned quiet as their fucking parents.

Jennifer smiled at the boy, who returned to the rest of his classmates, who all seemed to be here a bit late. Their teacher was in the middle of giving them a lecture about what they were supposed to do while visiting the Executioner Library. Unlike other libraries they were used to, essentially gatherings to sit and read PDLs, this one kept its namesake by holding a lot of ancient hardcopy on shelves, which curious little hands and fingers needed to be careful around.

The teacher, a man in his mid-twenties with flowing black hair and a closely trimmed goatee, looked briefly in Jen's direction, quickly offered her a smile and then continued on with his instruction. Jen blushed and quickly looked back down at her PDL; however, before she could get started, she realized this time the sound of Max's heavy breathing was bothering her.

"I can't believe Rebecca's gone," Jen whispered and thought about her friend. Becca had been helping Jen adjust to life here, and had even made Jen laugh at times when she'd thought it impossible. She wondered why she even tried to study now, but it was a distraction from her fears and worries.

The young woman sighed again and then thought about Jim's beautiful hazel eyes, which he had told her could no longer shed any tears regardless of any pain.

"But I could see his wash of anger, his sense of helplessness, the fear for her life," she mumbled. When Jim had told Jennifer about Rebecca, she knew that he was hiding so much back. Naturally, she'd done her best to comfort him, but she knew even Arthor would have trouble ...

Thankfully, someone entering the library pulled her from her current thoughts.

"Hmm, out for a stroll, Mr. Powers?" she asked quietly, when she gazed at the Mountain's oddest resident. She watched him run a hand through his sandy-blond hair, scratch the cleft on his strong jaw and then look in her direction.

"John," she whispered loudly, setting aside her PDL, and motioned him over to her. She watched him work up a smile before he nodded and walked toward her. Quickly, however, the "slightly off" grin, matured into a "good one" before his lips fell back into a straight line.

He's so peculiar, she stated. *Does he totally lack emotion?* Briefly envious, however, considering the last couple of months, she suddenly realized he was standing right in front of her.

Abruptly becoming shy and not knowing why she'd asked him over, she simply stared into those black eyes that made them look so odd. Then she also noticed that his eyes didn't even flicker in the light or offer any reflections—the very reason why they seemed so strange.

"Hello," she said, finally breaking her own trance.

"Hello," he quickly replied, his voice sounding calm and lifeless. "I just came by to check on the kids. They're parents are working swing shifts, so Hank volunteered to look after them. He's always wanted to see the library when it wasn't busy, so he's bribing them with pizza and ice cream. Looks like they're doing okay ... Is there something I can do for you?"

"Yes," Jen said uneasily, realizing that this was the most she'd ever heard him say to her. But hoped he wouldn't notice her awkwardness. "I wanted to ask you something, something about what we're doing."

"Oh, I see." He seemed to grin and tried a chuckle, which, Jen realized, came out a little like an animated, mystery-solving dog from one of Logan's old TV shows. "Do you mind?" He gestured toward a nearby chair.

Taken aback, Jen raised an eyebrow at how he'd responded to her. *Yeah, right, like I'd know what's natural for him to say or do?* "Please," she said and watched him sit down beside her.

From cursory observation and until now, John Henry Powers had seemed rather stuffy to her, but he quickly lounged back into the chair across from her, crossed his legs and propped them on the table between them. He tried to smile again, mimicking Logan's boyish charm perfectly, before he settled in.

"Now, what did you want to talk about?" he asked simply enough, but then his eyes seemed to pierce into hers with remarkable concentration. And, although she considered his features quite handsome, her initial reaction was to avoid the reflection-less stare of his black eyes. But something made her look directly into them, forcing her to see if they were so metaphorically empty.

Normal looking enough, she quickly corrected. *They look pretty much normal from a distance. It's not like they're entirely black, just the pupils.*

"Jen?"

It took her a moment to realize that she hadn't answered him. *Oh God, how long was I just staring into his eyes?*

"I'm sorry. It's been a rough day," she said matter-of-factly, trying to hide her embarrassment.

"I know," he replied. "I hope Rebecca's found. Also, Sanders was a good guy. I wish the best for his family."

Jen was, again, somewhat taken aback by that. She had to get rid of any prejudices she might have for John's lack of emotions. He wasn't a monster or a robot.

She said timidly, "I guess that is what I'm concerned about. I have questions."

"Fine, spit them out," he said, the words coming out without any natural rhythm, but Jen focused and didn't let it bother her.

She brushed her fingers through her long black hair and laid a hand on Max's head. "Okay, I guess I need reassurances."

"About?"

"About this war, don't you think it's a bit senseless?"

John shook his head ever so slightly. "You first, how do you feel about it?"

Great, I'm being asked about personal feelings from someone who can't even experience them, she mused but refrained from showing her disdain. "Well, I don't get why we're doing this. It's about drugs, so what?"

"Have you asked Jim?"

"Yes and I don't get it." She pursed her lips, stressing her point. "He told me that he wasn't initially onboard with all this; however, ultimately, he didn't nix Logan's plan to seriously curb the manufacture of drugs like disperal, tokom and others."

"Did he tell you why?"

"He said that Logan and Rebecca convinced him that those drugs needed to be eradicated since they were actual poisons."

"Does this sound reasonable?"

"It does," Jen conceded but showed her frustration, especially when she thought about her friends, and, ultimately, her family. "I just don't see how we can take it all down. Someone is always going to make that stuff. Sure we can knock out the larger ones, but there is always going to be something that fills the void. Nirv hadn't even been heard of until Logan took out the competition."

Jen wasn't looking into John's eyes now. Her attention was on the library's second story. No one was up there and no one had heard her raised voice. And by now, the students and teacher were at the other end of the library.

Powers didn't say anything right off. He also made a quick glance around the library, before he looked back into her eyes. No one was around, so they weren't disturbing anyone. "Jennifer, how is Jim in a fight?"

"What does that have to do with anything?" she asked.

John took a breath and frowned—a *good* one—just before he elaborated. "I know it's an odd question, but when you first saw him, what did you think of his actions and motives? Please, humor me."

Jen scowled a little, biting back her annoyance, and thought about the day she'd been brought to Crystal Mountain. "At first, I thought he'd actually been egging on a fight," she said, remembering the Infilt-Guard and the squad who'd chased her. "But that's obviously not the case. He'd given that monster every opportunity to back down, and I know he'd have let him go if the gorilla had been smarter. But Jim's compassion—even for his enemies—isn't at stake here. I'm talking about—"

"When Jim attacked that nirv storage facility"—John held up his hand, asking for patience—"do you remember what he'd said about them?"

"He surprised me." Jen remembered crying in Jim's arms the morning after that event. She hardly remembered what they'd talked about later. "I know that he pitied the people he'd killed that day, over twenty men and women. He seemed to be holding back when he told me that he'd killed them all. But when he told me that none of them were innocent, I saw the anger in his eyes ... the pain that he was holding back."

John cocked his head slightly at that, but shook his head and asked, "And what happened next?"

"Later on, Logan was killed by a booby trap. Then, after specific and carefully analyzed inforuns, we eventually started hitting targets."

"Has anyone else from Crystal Mountain died in similar traps in the last month?"

"No," she conceded and shook her head, still trying to follow where he was going with this. "And, of course, we can't be entirely sure if nirv's manufacturer is responsible for what happened to either Sanders or Becca. But what if he was? What about the rest of Panteria's population? Who else is going to die because of this war?"

"I'm not sure if what we're doing is a war. I doubt that we've actually be fighting against the manufacturer so far. Hell, we might be actually hurting them directly when we take out those quiet warehouses, but who knows? Even after taking out a dozen of them or so, we still haven't seen any response from them. They are still just leaving them alone—

"Okay. Okay," John sighed and seemed to give in when he looked in her direction, and apparently saw the growing frown on her face. "How many innocent people have been killed within the last month?"

"None. Actually, with us hitting those distribution centers, we've taken down some pretty violent people.

"But," she protested, again not really sure where she or he was going with this conversation. "When we take this guy down and nirv's no longer manufactured—what then? What if the shit really hits the fan? What if riots start? What if petty wars escalate? What if Logan's *awakening* causes more harm than good?"

"Yeah, right," John let out a scoff, and Jennifer found herself shrinking back into her chair—John's dark globes suddenly seemed even darker when he sneered, and sneered well. "Jen, what do you think the government, the Puppeteer Government mind you, will do if and when that happens?"

"I don't know. I'm so confused now. When I hadn't known about the Guard, I'd thought that the government was simply powerless to do anything. But I now know my parents were killed from a strike by some faction of the Puppeteer Government posing as rebels. They killed an entire town. Harsh, to say the least, but the attack did prevent that cancer from spreading."

"Yep, they stopped it dead, literally," John agreed. "But did the Guard, or those ultimately responsible for the Hillmount Slaughter, care what happened to those people—innocent or otherwise?"

"I can't tell." Jen remembered being thrown around in the armored hovervan, remembered her blackout and then waking up buried beneath the debris of her family's house. Naturally, she had wanted to be angry at someone for what had happened, angry for the senselessness. But Jim had been right and reminded her of her own fears of perpetuating violence. The Cycle.

"Let me put it this way, then," John said. "Do you think it was difficult for the Guard to decide that they needed to murder everyone in your part of town?" he asked and then shook his head, obviously for her benefit. "No, of course not, they needed a massacre to swell the hatred for the rebels. And besides—"

"That's right!" Quickly interrupting him, Jen also felt herself jerk, suddenly furious at the obvious. "Why did they have to kill everyone, especially innocent people in the area? The Executioners have told me that their weapons—including the Puppeteer

Government's weapons—can be used to prevent excessive collateral damage. They didn't have to ... to ... murder everyone!"

She gazed back into the face of the man before her. Despite what he'd said, he looked as emotionless as ever, but was he about to say something else?

Jennifer eyed him carefully, but if he had, he must not have thought it important enough to continue. And by now, images of when she had woken up in the remains of a battlefield began to overwhelm her.

"But how do our plans affect the rest of the population now? Hasn't Jim taken into account for innocent lives?" John questioned. "The Guard caught everyone off ... well ... off guard with Hillmount, but there's no way we'd let them swoop in and kill anyone again. And I'm sure that the Puppet Government or even the Puppeteer Government wouldn't allow reckless rebels to come in and kill anyone else either."

"Yeah, I think you're right," Jen agreed, but was clearly distracted now. "I don't think anything the size of Hillmount will happen again this soon. And since the Executioners are planning to take nirv off the streets gradually, it'll give the Puppet Government time to react. Programs can be expanded to help junkies, and even prevent crime for the most part. And with our anonymous donations to some watch-dog groups, hopefully the process will get started early and delay some other drug from filling the void."

"Why gradually?" the man asked, playing dumb.

"The Executioners are only really hitting those distribution centers and leaving most of the storage facilities alone. With those still around, nirv's supply will most likely run dry over the next year or so."

"That is the *ideal* situation of course," John added with a shrug. "We're still not sure if those quiet warehouses will come into play later. We still believe that the manufacturer is using different staging facilities for shipments. We haven't found *those* yet, but if they stay functioning after we destroy the manufacturing plant, they'll run out eventually. If they continue shipping ...

"Damn, I know this is over simplifying what all needs to be done," John acknowledged. Jen found it odd that a man without emotion could still use curse words to full effect. "It's definitely complicated, and right now it's playing out like one of Logan's stupid action movies. And, Logan, I hate to say, really created a bit of a mess as project leader. He really should have taken Jim's advice to try and broker some type of truce with whomever is making nirv, since the drug seems to be safe ... compared to the other stuff anyway.

"However, nirv's manufacturer fucked up and used Kepler bombs. Logan triggered the first trap, but we found three others that hadn't been functional ... thankfully. *Those* bombs are hard to come by and violate several laws. Their blast zones are highly unpredictable because of how they manipulate quantum mechanics. Shit, two bombs of equal mass could have a range of fifty feet, ten miles ... or more. The Panterian Government, either of them, no longer builds those.

"It's likely that nirv's manufacturer doesn't know the true devastation that a Kepler is capable of. Still, who knows if they decide to use them for something else? Whether it's ignorance or true malice, they painted a pretty big target on their backs. Jim was caught in a Kepler blast a long time ago, and it took out a small city. He's fully invested in this effort now, especially since he helped escalated it."

John paused. He looked up at her and shook his head. "Now, local agencies and organizations will have to step up to make sure that this house of cards doesn't collapse and catch fire when we crush nirv's manufacturer.

"Nonetheless, Jen, I know there are concerns when the drug becomes scarce, especially when its street value rises. However, we're committed now and we have to finish this ..." John paused a moment and rubbed his temples. Then continued: "But we'll do our best to protect the innocent."

She looked at him carefully. Although he would deny it completely, he seemed about as passionate about the subject as either Logan or Rebecca or any of the Executioners. She still felt uneasy about what and why they were doing this, and how it had pretty much escalated into a giant pissing match. But at least they realized that there were innocent people involved, and the Executioners were trying to keep them safe. It made sense really. There was no use feeding the anti-rebel fire any more than necessary.

"Thank you, John." She grinned, glad that they'd had a chance to talk, thereby giving her another opinion. Besides, she realized, the rebellion against the Puppeteer Government had been going on long before the Executioners were founded. And it seemed as though this war on drugs was just another flashpoint and proxy war that both sides had been struggling with over the years ...

God, all this information is making my head hurt, she thought and rubbed her temples.

"Anytime," he said and nodded back, but this time he didn't force out a smile when he got up to leave. Instead, he placed a hand on her shoulder, while he petted Max at the same time. "I always look forward to talking with ... umm ... new friends?"

"Likewise," she agreed, knowing they'd speak more in the future.

"Great." He brushed a hand through his hair and made a slow turn away from her.

Nice butt too, she thought despite her headache and—

"Anyhoo." He stopped unexpectedly and looked back. She hoped John hadn't noticed that she was blushing again. "I better let you get back to your studies. Despite living in Moki, it still took me months to get caught up on true Panterian history. And I couldn't *hate* it."

Jen laughed at that, and she thought she saw an expression of surprise on his face—as if he'd thought she wouldn't have understood his joke. But soon enough, he simply waved, turned around completely and then walked out of the library.

Watching him leave and thinking about what John had said earlier, Jennifer didn't bother returning to her work. Instead, she pushed herself up and left the PDL on her backpack.

"Damn, bad one too." She gritted her teeth, this time really noticing the headache. Managing to ignore the pain, however, she moved over to one of the library's workstations and typed on the keyboard: *Ecie, can you give me the tactical and forensic information we recovered from the incident at Hillmount Estates?*

Certainly, Jennifer, the monitor read. *How's history?*

Doing well, she wrote.

True, your grades show it, just wanted to check in personally. A happy face appeared on the screen, and Jen wondered what else Ecie knew about her, besides the information she had let him organically digitize. *Talk to me later?*

Sure, she typed. *Will you give me the information now?*

Oh, yeah, sorry. The happy face blinked off, and then the screen displayed twenty files that her friend Rebecca, and several other military strategists, had written about Hillmount Estates. However, after several minutes of trying to read these reports, which were heavily loaded with every type of military jargon and acronym, she found it almost incomprehensible.

Eventually, she decided that she'd show the files to Dr. Orsen, a professor known for military prowess and analytics, and see what he thought. Then, maybe he'd tell her what Jim—and everyone close to her—seemed to be leaving out.

John walked away from the Executioner Library. He wondered if he'd made a mistake by talking about the *Hillmount Massacre* with Jennifer. It wasn't like they were keeping anything from her. No one wanted to just add fuel to a potential fire if it wasn't true. As bad as the Puppeteer Government was, baseless accusations wouldn't help.

Curiously, though, he'd still almost let the cat out of the bag by nearly mentioning the government's suspected role in the new drug's distribution. Especially with its presence at the prison—if that is, Jen hadn't interrupted him.

"That's odd," he said to himself. "Speaking without thinking"—while he heard was a common occurrence for people— was not something he'd ever done. And, making a face, he looked at his watch, and wondered if Scythe had liberated the fridge by now.

John finally groaned, obviously puzzled. While sitting in the library, a dull pain had slowly spread from the base of his neck and then up, over and down to his sinuses.

"A headache?" Powers asked curiously and rubbed his temples—something he'd seen Logan do several times after long nights without sleep. But truthfully, John wasn't sure if he had one or not, especially since he'd never had one before.

"Ecie, would you ask if Jon Alexander could speak with me?" Jim asked. He was sitting in his office. He couldn't bring himself to look at the office adjoining his. The door was still open. It had been since after Rebecca had walked through and asked him to go to Cuba with her. How many days had that been now?

"Okay," Ecie said. "I told him what happened to her when it happened. He's requested for more access to our files and to additional people. Is that okay?"

"Yes, he knows a lot. He'll be able to help with the search. Also, any additional information he can add to our systems will be a boon."

"Yes, I agree."

"Okay, then. Here we go," Jim sighed, not looking forward to this at all. "Jon, are you here?"

A middle-aged man materialized in front of his desk and sat in one of the chairs there. Jon Alexander's eyes were red and holographic tears glistened in the dim office.

"Hi, Jim, it's nice to meet you," Rebecca's father said, voice croaking. "I've heard a lot about you. Rebecca talked about you often."

"It's nice to meet you too." Jim nodded. "Good things I hope?"

That got a chuckle. Both of them were hurting.

"Yes, Jim, all good things. She always ... smiled when she'd talk about you too, even when she'd just gotten here. She didn't smile much back then."

"I remember. I'm glad she decided to stay. It was hard for her to adjust at first, but she's contributed greatly since being here."

"She's a strong woman." Alexander nodded, wiping his nose with the back of his sleeve. "I wanted to thank you and the Crystalians for letting her stay. She would have died without you. I'm forever in your debt."

"Thank you, but you know as well as I do that she would have survived regardless. We are richer, though, with her here."

"Thank you. Thank you."

Jim wondered what this program of Jon Alexander now was. From what Rebecca had said about the interactions with it, Jim agreed with her assessments that Jon and done some type of cerebral scan and recording. The computer system that Rebecca found the program in, of course, was somewhat limited; however, it seemed to be a bit *more* than a database assistant.

Rebecca had told Jim the difference she'd seen after uploading him in the partition that Ecie had set up. It ... it was like—exactly like!—her dad she had said.

Jim couldn't discount that—especially now, sitting in this office with the man.

"Have you heard any news?" Jon asked hopefully.

Jim shook his head, unable to say anything. Where the fuck was she?

"Do you really think that the maker of nirv arranged her capture?"

"I don't know," Jim sighed. "Who knows? We have a lot of enemies. Someone with a grudge could have responded to a bid that Rebecca submitted. But, generally, we tie up loose ends, we never advertise who we are, and we keep tabs on people we have put into jail by our ... involvement. Still, it could be an unknown acquaintance, friend, family member, or lover. Such is life when you live by the sword."

"Is there anything that I can do?"

"I know you traveled and met with thousands of people. Do you mind working with Ecie and the other teams? Maybe your insight can bring us some leads. Hopefully, you might have bumped into people that have connections with the nirv manufacturer. From all those quiet warehouses, it sounds like the operation was around for quite a while—regardless of its current push."

"Sure thing. Anything I can do."

"Thank you, Jon. I miss ... really miss her."

"I know. From what she told me about your upcoming trip to Cuba, she ... she was really excited."

"I was looking forward to it too. We're ... *friends*. It would have been fun." Jim bit his lip. He already knew he loved her. Why play games now?

"Right," Jon chuckled, but more tears began to fall. "She considered you a ... *good* friend too. But, if you ask me personally, I have never seen her laugh, stutter, blush and smile as much as when she talked about you."

"Thank you," Jim signed, suddenly feeling like a dumb kid. "I don't know what to say."

"It's not me you need to say it to. *FIND* her!"

"I will. I promise."

"Okay." Jon grinned, rubbing his eyes. "I'm going to see what I can find. I don't have the capability to split myself up into thousands of different instances like Ecie, so I need to get to work."

"Alright. Good luck!"

"You too."

Jon Alexander disappeared, leaving Jim alone with his thoughts.

"Are you going to be okay, Major?" Bryans asked from the armored vehicle following Tara from above. It was cloaked and was providing cover. But, once she entered the building, it would be tougher for him to hit threats.

"Yes," she whispered. She was getting used to the new rank. She hadn't been a captain for very long, so the transition wasn't too bad. Her dealings in California had advanced things quickly. She'd saved a lot of people when she'd been able to find the dead man's switch that would have remotely detonated the bombs in the market place across the street from those crooked cops.

Who the fuck does that *for real?* she asked herself as she moved toward the office building. A lot of shitty adventure flicks seemed to have that as some pivotal and shocking plot point. The Chief of Police that had undertaken the surgery had made the mistake of saying, "If my heart stops beating ..."

Tara had simply removed everything of the man's brain except for the medulla oblongata and the rest of the brain stem. That had left the body alive long enough for them to deactivate the switch.

Never pays to be a supervillain, she smirked. "Okay, I'm going in. Keep your chatter down, unless for necessary updates or changes in position."

"Yes, Major."

They were in Tamorami. It was warm and humid EVERYWHERE! It was certainly different when you lived in a climate-controlled environment.

That made her miss her armor. This was an inforun in the middle of a populated area, so she was in a business suit and not her *regular* business suit. She was still armed, of course, but you never knew when things could go south. Even in areas like this—hell, especially in areas like this.

Still, the armor wasn't a crutch. She'd done enough wet work without it.

I just miss the air conditioning, she told herself. *Fuck, it's hot!*

She entered the office and was immediately greeted by a receptionist. Data brokers came in all forms. This one was a security firm. A posh one.

"Hello," she returned a greeting, also thankful for the AC. "I have an appointment with Tony Wyatt."

"No problem." The receptionist was a young brunette, and quickly looked Tara up and down. She hadn't been wasting her time on her PDL like a lot of people on the surface tended to do. How many fake ducks can you grow on a fake farm? "May I tell him who's here?"

"Jacky Albright from CF Systems."

"Thank you." The receptionist, her nameplate read ERIN CARTER, quickly triggered an intercom. "Tony, Jacky from CF is here for you ... Okay ... Will do."

Erin looked Tara's way and got up. "He'll meet you in the main conference room. I'll show you the way. Do you need anything? Coffee? Tea? Water?"

"No, thank you. Nice building. How many people work here?"

"Umm, yeah, my dad bought the building recently." Erin shrugged, not even bothering to ask if Tara had a weapon. The girl was also cool as a cucumber, and didn't seem to miss a step. *Carter and Associates* took on a new meaning for Tara then. "We're a small firm ... about fifteen people. But we need the space. Most are former special forces."

"Ah, how long have you worked for them?" She followed the young woman into the lavish conference room with multiple monitors and several 3D projectors.

"Not very long. Just working here until school starts. Well, here you are. Let me know if you need anything."

"Will do. Thanks."

It didn't take long for Tony Wyatt to arrive. He had a couple of packets of info, along with a PDL.

"Ms. Albright, thank you for meeting me," Tony said, extending a hand, which she promptly shook. He was tall, muscular and moved like a soldier.

"You have my thanks," she replied. "The information you have could be vital to completing my company's short-term goals."

Tony laughed at that. They both knew what type of business each other was in. She hadn't broadcasted to anyone that she was an Executioner, but the man probably guessed that she was going to raise some hell with the info his company was selling.

If the leads pan out, she corrected herself, checking her optimism. The Executioners had located some of the actual staging areas that the nirv manufacturer was using for direct shipments. They had discovered that they were actually temporary locations, created with finite inventory and totally automated. Any of the freight companies that had been contracted to run the product were only hired after the location had been set up. And, as they had found out earlier, this had eliminated the possibility of the Executioners just simply "calling in" an order and waiting for the goods to show ...

Out of sheer luck, based on Ecie's analytics for areas that were still open for nirv's expansion into new areas, they had found one that was being set up by real people. The Executioners naturally went in to secure, contain and capture the employees. However, once the people were captured, all of them suddenly went catatonic. They called in their medics and found out that those people had implants in them to wipe memory. The other subsequent locations they had found resulted in the same end.

Tara winced, unable to imagine the Executioners doing that to their personnel. She understood the reality, of course, and considered doing it herself. She couldn't bear anyone ever finding their home.

Logan, however, assured her once that her neural net—one implanted so she could react and process data faster in her armor—would prevent "invasive" interrogations. Well, of course, what she had wouldn't do anything like ... at least in theory ...

Well, shit. She shrugged with a quiet laugh. *I guess I already volunteered for it—*

"Something wrong?" Tony asked, obviously he'd seen her grimace earlier.

"No, sorry, it was a long flight. Back is a little sore," she said, which wasn't a lie, but she needed to stay on task.

"Yep, I understand." Tony played with the packets of info on the table for a bit before pushing them toward her. "I'll make it quick for you then. I'm sure you want to get back home before air traffic picks up."

"Again, thank you." She eyed the packets. *This* could be huge. "Yah. You think that hovercars would reduce traffic jams?"

"I know, right? I wish they'd let us set our own headings. Why bother having a flying car if you have to fly in restricted airways?"

They both laughed at *that*. They both knew that they both probably had tech in their cars that allowed them to fly anywhere the hell they wanted.

"Well, the information is all there. I've compiled all the RFQs and RFBs with the mention of neural nets or any other devices that impair or alter brain function as a condition of contract," Tony said with disgust. "As a bonus—at no charge—I'm also including other bid types that are not security related, even though there is usually a common security contractor or contractors as agents to perform background checks."

"That sounds like it could be a lot."

"There are. It's actually not that uncommon. However, still, there are a lot of personnel that they get from California, if you can imagine?"

"I can."

"Well, there are thousands of RFQs in that thirty-year period."

"Ouch," Tara commented, even though she knew that Ecie would munch through that in a few seconds.

"Well, I might be able to save you some time."

"Oh?"

"Yes, we just had to back out of a longtime subcontract from a primary security contactor, who had recently put that in as a stipulation for a new contract requiring training for new personnel. Carter doesn't care for those, especially when that tech—in theory—can also be used to obtain proprietary info. Anyhoo, a lot of wrangling happened with lawyers. Needless-to-say, I'm *not* talking to you about *that* of course." Tony winked. He actually fucking winked. But Tara thought it was adorable.

"Of course," she acknowledged. "Please let me know if I can ever do you a favor in the future. You have my card."

Tara smiled again. This whole networking thing was starting to pay off.

She smiled. *It's definitely all about who you know.*

After weeks of careful surveillance, the Executioners' recon teams were able to identify a number of new recruits for various security details. Making it easier, the primary contractor that Carter and Associates mentioned actually hoverbussed people to new locals as to eliminate the employees' knowledge of where they were going.

Lt. Niles Torson—of several Executioners who were following those hoverbusses back and forth from one location to the next—eventually believed he got lucky at a stop in Central America.

He planted stakes and sat, watched and recorded what he saw. He used his armor to sneak around the facilities and peek in buildings when he could. Then he performed aerial recon and mapped the layout and threats that he located.

Goddam, he thought as he hovered over one building and then to the next. *I don't know when I'll ever get fucking tired of invisible flying cars!*

CHAPTER FIVE

The whole of government consists in the art of being honest.

(Works, Vol. VI)

—Thomas Jefferson, 3rd President of the U.S.A. (1805 A.D.)

.

The sun rose over a chain of mountains. As it rose, light flared into a valley between two peaks, chasing out the shade that had been there only moments before. And a lush, natural jungle, thick but not quite as dense as a growth zone would be, woke to a new day.

Through field glasses, Jim St. John zeroed in on the nirv production facility below. He eyed the Kelson barbed wire, intertwined with other plants and vines, growing around the complex. He noticed Topley traps waiting to shock an unwelcome visitor. He smirked at the number of motion sensors, radar and infrared tracking-systems that he counted in their not-so-well-hidden places. Also, many of the guards—although not all—were drinking coffee, smoking, urinating behind a building or basically twiddling thumbs.

Jim lowered the high powered binoculars and turned to look behind him. His troops waited there—a thousand armed and armor-plated men and women, who'd play various roles in the upcoming battle. They represented only about three percent of the total 30,000 members of the Executioners; however, because of the skills he'd seen them portray in numerous simulations, he felt sorry for the unsuspecting bastards down there.

Careful, he warned himself, immediately forcing down the swelling of pride he felt.

He eyed his troops carefully. Everyone knew that this mission was too important to level the entire base immediately. They knew that they needed to capture it, to find the central computer and to analyze its contents. And this was also a historical moment: the first time they'd fight as an army. To his surprise, this made them more eager than afraid. Well, he'd protect as many as he could.

He looked over at his best friend ... Arthor, a man from another world, commanded the five-member, Reconnaissance and Demolition team, Tarki. He had to admit that they were the best Special Forces team he'd ever seen—including those he'd met at the AOM. Because of their discipline, not a sound was made from them, each one mentally planning what he was going to do.

Jim looked behind Tarki and noticed John and his troops, a few squads—twenty in all—from Powers' regiment Black Sun. They were in black powered-armor and wore red insignia of Japan's Raising Sun on their right shoulders.

The Ninja—John's sobriquet—was covered by a black, muscular-looking armor, which, despite the modern tech, still incorporated the dark hood and many other features of the traditional costume. Adding to the look, two katana rested on the warrior's back; a powerful bow with a quiver flexed in a secure spot between the blades; and numerous knives and throwing stars were present too.

Jim tried to remember what his military history told him about the Ninjas' legend. From myth, they had been hired Japanese assassins, who'd trained for years to master their craft and who'd stopped at nothing to accomplish what they were paid to do. The Mutilator, by contrast, had been trained by at least a dozen masters and had quickly developed his own style within a year. But of course, a Kurgon Beast was the worst of all kinds of killers, since it killed for satisfaction ... and okay ... sometimes ... pleasure. Money had been superfluous.

He chuckled to himself and realized that he was delaying the inevitable. He nodded to Arthor, then to John, and finally to the rest of the commanding officers. They all nodded in unison and motioned to their own troops.

He called over one of his aids and handed the young man the binoculars.

"Thanks, Nate," he said when the man put those in a backpack and handed over Jim's helmet with the red sunglasses already in them.

"No problem, Jim," the young man said and walked back to the cloaked command hub, which would relay communications and give the Executioners crucial intel and other info during the battle.

The helmet ... He eyed the round, ultra-hard contraption in his hands. *I guess I did keep the suit and the helmet. Despite everything, I just couldn't let go. The demon within me isn't quite finished. I should have realized it long ago.*

As expected, a familiar anger blossomed in agreement, while he pulled over the tight-fitting hood of his suit. However, he quickly kept it in check when he put on the ruby-red, enhancement glasses, which would link up with the visual sensors of his helmet.

Sorry, I'll never let you control me again, he thought. Sure, the monster's voice had been silenced years ago, and he recently accepted that the rage was from his own heart. But he wasn't quite sure if it still couldn't manifest itself into a Beast. He, of course, had worried that it had almost gotten out before he'd killed McNeil ...

He placed the helmet on his head. He activated the device, causing all five sections of the oval faceplate to slide into place and clamp down.

With that, he levitated into the air and gave one last look at his people, before he raised his right arm and brought it down. The Executioners immediately scrambled into their transports and disappeared from sight when they hit their cloaking shields. In minutes, they'd be in position.

"Good hunting," Jim said, stretched one last time and then shot down into the valley. And, as usual, whatever security devices his natural cloaking abilities couldn't handle, his suit and helmet quickly abated.

Jim St. John smiled. He'd missed this.

Slinger and machinegun fire ricocheted from John's form-fit armor. His entire body was covered in black plating, with his dark gaze visible through a diamond-hard visor.

He slashed his swords, cutting through anything he deemed unfriendly. Machinery and soldiers tried to engage him. But his blades were sharp and quick, and a wake of stumps of arms and stubs for legs were left behind him.

Another set of hunter-bots flew toward him, but his three squads took out most of them before they reached their target. He, otherwise, ignored the machines and went after the soldiers behind the metal monsters, bringing his swords upon them before they had time to run.

Such was his gift: Strike fear into his enemy by coming at them with only a pair of swords.

John forced himself through another line of mercenaries and killed another five, heavily-armed men. He was close to the building's southeast entrance, reminding him that Black Sun's objective was close.

He moved up to the entrance. He waved to his squads to make sure that they were not ambushed, and punched in an access code with a cautious hand. The door slid up, and a shadow—

His swords flashed, and he soon stepped over a pile of gore.

He turned to motion his people forward. They had to secure this part of the complex, which led to the storage warehouses. Only a few more guards remained, and he figured Logan would have already popped open the champagne.

Lt. Colonel Teir Lacky watched the Ninja prepare to open the door to the southeast entrance of the complex, motioning to him and the others to move cautiously toward the building.

He nodded to his commander, and Teir stepped forward, his slinger resting ready to fire in his arms. His heart was racing. He'd stormed hideouts of various gangs and had led the charge against several nirv distribution centers. However, this was the first time he'd ever been in battle, a true battle anyway. How many countless numbers of realistic simulations had he and the other members of the regiment—

His helmet's HUD flashed red, and he swung to his right and blew a hunter-bot apart, along with another guard coming around the corner. Breathing hard, he gulped. But he soon nodded his head—realizing reality and simulation, for the Executioners anyway, were nearly the same.

Quickly composing himself, he signaled to the Ninja, alerting his leader that they were ready to enter the building. His commander turned and opened the—

Lacky blinked as swords flashed—

Teir could have sworn that he'd seen two of the biggest, ugliest guardsmen in the doorway. But his eyes must have deceived him. Only a pile of flesh and clothes remained at the feet of their commander, and the entrance and ground were becoming stained by pools of blood.

General Powers motioned the group forward again, and Lt. Colonel Teir Lacky led the squads to the entrance of the building. And, eventually, he had to step over the Ninja's kill.

He's not even wearing powered armor! How the fuck can his swords do that? he asked himself as he tried to see anything recognizable. Hell, he probably would have vomited too, if it had looked like anything other than raw hamburger meat and cubed sausages.

Shit, well, at least he knew that he wasn't having hamburgers or hotdogs for dinner tonight.

A tail slashed to the side, taking down two guardsmen and a couple of hunter-bots in the process. Arthor's own squad, Tarki, gave him room to fight. As a precaution, they also maintained space between them so that a grenade or other explosives wouldn't catch them off guard. But they stayed close enough to each other so that they could cover ground quickly.

They were wearing their specialized suits with active cloaking, which Logan had been trying to incorporate into all of the Executioners' protective and powered armor. Tarki's had been the first group, since their objectives necessitated it, and since their armor didn't have any forcefields. Usually the two couldn't be placed on the smaller frame of a human body. And *that* problem had been a "lack of prime real-estate issue," especially when Logan had also wanted to give everyone heavier shielding. The issue was that forcefields caused greater electromagnetic distortions, which interfered with the frequencies of their cloaking devices. McMillian had believed that he'd solved the problem, but he hadn't quite put it down on paper before being killed.

Arthor, having armor that just magnified his own abilities, did have some shielding. Therefore, he took point and killed anyone or thing in their way.

Beyond his reach, his plasma generation incinerated obstacles and people. He'd never quite understood this ability, even though Logan had tried to explain it several times. Of course, science still really hadn't figured out how some Nagis could do the things they could—some things didn't really seem possible! However, at least he no longer thought it was the devil's work, even though he still didn't discount some evil force out there causing mischief.

Heightened mental abilities, levitation, and the ability to bend light around myself, he cursed, even though he used them skillfully ... and to protect his people ...

They moved through the large walkway between the two primary buildings of the complex. Tarki's modified Mark-4 and heavy slingers, both capable of blasting through heavy plating, erased anyone capable of causing conflict.

Arthor waved his people forward to the door of the structure, and the Crytonian punched in an access code, overriding the lockout codes from the main computer. The door slid open—

He shot four rounds into a waiting guard, who collapsed and flopped around violently before stopping. He sneered, realizing his sword could have done the same job, possibly more mercifully. But he shook his head, leading his group to the heart of the building.

The whole facility was at alert status, but the red, blinking corridor was empty, since most of the guards were outside assisting in the defense. Arthor loaded another magazine of rounds into his weapon and motioned Tarki to their right, and into the bigger of the two buildings. Before rounding another corner, he stopped while his squad did the same.

He peeked around the corner. Five guards waited in front of a large steel door. They were average-height, with grenades resting on their belts and extra magazines littering their jumpsuits. Their arms held their weapons tight, but not in a fashion Arthor would consider too threatening. They weren't paying much attention. A couple of them looked down another corridor when an explosion echoed from the outside. They looked at the door they were guarding, then at each other, shaking their heads.

Chetok, be careful what you wish for. Arthor let his hand become visible for his second in command, 1st General Jackson Green, who was a large man carrying a heavy-double-barreled slinger. He told the officer to wait two seconds before they followed him.

Arthor tightened his wings a bit more, gave his legs one last stretch, passed his Mark-4 to Green, and sprang down the hallway in the direction of the five guards.

He was on their unsuspecting forms in four bounds, and he threw his body into them with nearly a quarter ton of weight compounded by a cheetah's speed. Their bones and armor cracked between Arthor and the door, which itself collapsed by the Herculean strength thrown against it.

He tumbled into the room with the guards and the door beneath him. The momentum caused him to somersault onto his feet. He scanned the area he had just breached, noticing computer monitors and discarded chairs in front of empty desks. To the right, he spied a computer technician, who was sitting at a tactical display with wireless computer jacks plugged into the side of his head. It looked like he was about to program a new set of hunter-bots to protect the base.

The man, however, upon hearing the crashing door, yanked out the computer nodes and jumped up. He was pudgy with long, black hair. Sweat, covering a pasty face and thin goatee, stung Arthor's nose. Looking around, the computer man saw the opening and ran.

Arthor contemplated on letting him go, but the dishonored knight—worried that the man still had control of the droids by wireless means—quickly brought up his invisible arm and slammed the man down with a hammer-force blow.

In response, the Crytonian heard movement behind and to the right of him. Not wanting to generate any plasma this close to sensitive equipment, he took cover.

Electromagnetic rifles opened up on his position, which he'd given away when he'd killed the computer man. It was a short burst, maybe done out of fear. But he kept his body down, until he heard the sweet sound of heavy slinger and rifle projectiles slam into that area.

"General? Dragon Master, are you all right?" Green's voice barreled into the computer facility.

The field around him dispersed and Arthor sat on his rump, looking over the damage he and his people had created, and tried to feel if he had any bullet holes in his wings. He pulled off his helmet.

"Sir, are you okay?" De-cloaking, Jack came over to him. The man, probably smiling under the round helmet with a dragon's face painted on it, offered Arthor his large hand.

Around him, the other members of Tarki were already at the workstations. Lt. Niles Torson was roving over tactical, shutting down the base's defenses. Captain Tylor Krackii froze the computer delete functions and transferred most of the data to the portable storage units he was carrying.

Another, Colonel Nether Lacky, whose younger brother was under the command of John Powers, was searching through the structural schematics while setting the proper explosive charges in his pack. The man was trying to determine exactly how much punch the bomb would need to be, since they didn't want to destroy too much of the surrounding jungle.

They worked quickly and efficiently. Arthor had recruited them for his team shortly after taking over training of the Executioners from Jim. They had worked in fire teams for the Mountain before the Discovery, so they were used to dealing with crises and other concerns. Lacky had actually worked in explosives for one of the teams, since they often had to move rock that the tunneling equipment couldn't deal with.

Arthor returned the smile to Green, grabbed hold of the hand he was offered and was pulled to his feet. Shit, they'd be done soon. He was proud of them.

"I'm good," he said, exposing a toothy grin. "But what took you guys so long?"

Ultrasonic rounds and rockets ricocheted off his shoulders and faceplate, and a mazer tried to cook him but simply was absorbed by his skin. When someone tried to attack him with an honest-to-God's stick, Jim realized he was up against another ill-equipped foe.

Granted, he still moved toward them, making sure the Executioners weren't taken by surprise or caught by weapons capable of killing them.

Although he was commanding the entire army, Jim didn't have his own direct group of soldiers to command. For what he did, he couldn't be tethered down to ten or fifteen people who wouldn't be able to keep up.

His lips curled into a sneer, realizing such thoughts were characteristic of the lone Beast. But he brushed that aside ...

Yes, to be a roving monster, eliminating anything his army couldn't handle by themselves, to be a Kurgon Beast when necessary. But he was now controlled, collected and giving orders and directing the battle when *also* necessary. These were what he now was: Both Beast and the Leader of the Executioners.

Over the comlink he heard only muffled background chatter and orders from Executioner commanders. And he continued to sneer despite himself ... Maybe the subdued beast within him sensed the order, the skill the other Executioners portrayed, thereby preventing him from having too much fun.

He shook that thought from his mind and stood alone and visible before the fortress. He knew he seemed unarmed to the guards who fired at him, who possibly wondered why he yet approached them. Did he really appear to be a giant man lost in the battle, without anything to repel the onslaught thrown against him?

He walked up to a fortified position and floated skyward. He took a deep breath, filling his lungs, expanding his ribcage to its peak. He stretched his arms back. And, between his knuckles, his six adamant blades sprang out, shimmering and flaring, like his bodysuit, in the breath of a new day.

He kept his head locked onto them, his mirrored mask an emotionless visage. He could see the terror in their souls and could hear the shock in their voices over the channels.

He waited for their surrender, and wondered why the group had not already given up. There were less than a hundred people left protecting the facility, and the continued fight seemed uncharacteristic of the people who worked under a drug hierarchy. Jim wondered if he'd misjudged his opponent, then asked himself if fear caused the continued volley against the Executioners. Did they still defend it because they were boxed in and cornered?

He dropped within the middle of that group, and he slashed with careful precision. Brief cries of agony filled his ears—an instant of fear from spontaneous death ...

Standing in and covered in blood, guts, brains, and what-have-you, at least he'd made sure their lives had ended quickly. There was no reason for too much suffering, and no motive to give the Beast everything it wished.

He looked for more victims, his faceplate compensating for the gore. The helmet was made for this slaughter. As was his bodysuit. Both would eventually schluff off the mess.

Like the Ninja, he remembered the face of each of his victims. And, briefly, he wondered what the difference between Powers and himself was in battle.

"John has never smiled," he said with a grin that rivaled some kid's on Christmas morning. God help him, he was in his element.

He marched toward the last stronghold the defenders held. The Executioners had them surrounded. There were twenty cloaked hovercars above them ready to fire too. The defenders had nowhere left to regroup, nowhere else to run. He still waited for their surrender. But, then again, he never voiced such an option, since they had to make an example of these poor sonsofbitches.

He grimaced and cursed silently to himself. They had to make their point to the guy that was running these places. That fucker had never surfaced: Never tried to reach out to them for some type of truce. Never came out of the shadows regardless of what those fucking neural wires had done to his people. And, of course, Jim would never forget about the Kepler bombs ... Logan ...

If he's going to play with peoples' lives like that, I'm taking away his toys ... Jim looked around him. His people were doing extraordinarily well, as though battle had made them even better fighters than the opposite. Their powered armor had been initially bought from mercenaries. And later, they had been made from the

Executioners' weapons labs. So far, the armor had managed to protect them from the Mark-4's the defenders had.

Concerned, though, he saw how some of the railguns' slugs were burying themselves deep within their plating—their forcefields barely preventing death. He realized that the shield modules for their armor needed to be perfected soon. But with Logan gone—

A thousand taps suddenly slammed into him. He gazed at the position in front of him, the last of the defending troops. He stood like a giant in the jet-wash of the most hellish volley he had seen in years.

Floating back up into the sky, he signaled to his troops, a massive array of armored, quasi-cloaked skeletons. Again, he asked them to stay back and hold their fire. He then turned toward a concentrated group of sixty people who were behind three tons of siliceous bunker.

This battle would take no prisoners, since their employer had recently taken extreme measures to make interrogations useless. Maybe they realized it and figured they had no choice. But it seemed like more than that.

Still, it just seemed impossible that the leader of this drug network had maintained such anonymity and loyalty. They—this entourage of mercenaries—had gained Jim's respect.

Arthor performed a search in the facility's central computer for the primary shipping logs. He chuckled while he worked—remembering when he'd had to connect some laser tracking systems to the E.C.C. about a year and a half ago. It had been the first time—however, not the last time—Jim had made him do anything with the electronic equipment, besides just learning about it.

He'd hated the Crystalian Governor for taking off and leaving him to do the job alone—forcing him to try and mesh organic circuitry to standard systems. Smirking now, he remembered how he had accomplished the feat in a quarter of the time.

Chetok, he thought, *leaving me all alone with an infant computer while you go off on a supply run, not available for help.* He sensed Jim's presence behind him, and he smiled when he opened up a file that he'd managed to find in an encrypted, hidden folder.

Immediately, the monitor before him lit up with logistics information. The information included coordinates, time logs and estimated times of arrivals. Seeing this, his wings widened a bit, and his tail swayed with enthusiasm.

"Jim, you better see this," he said, moving so the leader of Crystal Mountain could get a better look at the screen.

He watched his friend gaze down at the monitor, then press the SCROLL button to advance the information over the viewing panel. There had been many shipments coming to and leaving this new facility, much more than either Jim or Arthor would have expected from a drug manufacturing, refining and supply station.

But there were often a series of coordinates common on the viewer, ones repeating, more or less, associated with large shipments and necessary supplies. Coordinates in a place where supply stations with such capacity seldom existed.

"Why did they log these?" Jim asked, but Arthor couldn't fathom an answer. Could they just have been lucky enough to find such a careless error? Besides, had anyone expected that they'd take on a facility this big and this well guarded?

The Crytonian rested a hand on his friend's shoulder, aware he was always looking for traps or false info. But this didn't pan out. The numbers on the screen were legitimate coordinates. They had to be. Paranoia didn't necessarily prevent distribution managers from doing their jobs too well at plants this size.

Jim stepped away from the panel a bit, straightening his back, looking toward one of the assault commanders. "Okay, Herland, get a recon unit out to these coordinates immediately. Look for the number of supply runs they have under cloaked flight, if any. Find out how many nirv production plants they have, the units' sizes, and estimated output. And take a computer tap with that new on-line, non-dispersal-beam-communication system for Ecie."

"Aye, Jim." Captain Herland walked out the door while speaking into the comlink on his collar. The soldier's armor, Logan's modified versions of standard military power armor, was now in his transport. The plating was, currently, not required, even though the members of the Panzer Corps remained in theirs in honor McMillian.

Arthor knew that Jim had already put in for more field promotions for *that* team—hell, for this offensive, they had been a primary diversion for the other forces by leading the attack on this facility's hunter-bot factory. Without the factory, the base hadn't been able to build replacements and was limited to what had been on hand before the Executioners attacked ...

The Crytonian looked at his best friend and wondered what the man was thinking. He wondered if by seeing the Panzer Corps standing at the ready, Jim was thinking about Logan and Rebecca and how he missed them ... Arthor missed them too ...

He noticed how Jim grimaced momentarily ... But the man soon looked around and realized that the other soldiers in the room, most lacking their smiling-skull-like helmets now, looked at both Arthor and Jim in anticipation. They wanted their leader to tell them what they so desperately needed to hear. And Arthor found himself doing the same.

"Yes, I think we've got 'em," the Crystalian Governor said and bowed his head.

The room roared and cheered.

"Ecie, please continue recording," Flora Neal said quietly.

"Okay," the computer said equally as softly. "I've created this as Executioner file, Set: I, Number 1.87613E10M, and named

'Epitaph In Memory of Johansen Neal and Lawrence Vlanderman.' Today's date is October 5, 3004."

Flora sat silently for a moment. It had been days since the funeral. She still remembered how Jim St. John had come to tell her the news personally. He had been so kind, had offered so much. She, of course, had been speechless, unable to say anything except to hug him goodbye and then cry endlessly since.

Johansen and Lawrence had been the only people killed during the assault. They had both died heroes, managing to use their hand-deflector shields to cover and block a cloaked IED from tearing into the rest of their squad. In doing so, they saved about ten others.

They had been the first to discover such a device but others had been found later, after using the identification protocols they had created for the IEDs. They had sent out those protocols just prior to being engulfed in the antimatter explosion. But those data had saved hundreds of lives ...

She started crying again from both pride and sorrow, but took some deep breaths and finally cleared her throat and began her recording: "After the battle, we'd found that two of our beloved friends had fallen.

"Their bodies were picked up from the battlefield. And later, their remains were placed in sacred canisters for cremation.

"Jim St. John prayed words of hope and salvation, bringing us to tears, and giving us courage to continue on with the objectives of the Executioners.

"I, like many, had shut my eyes when the monitors provided us pictures of them returning to Heaven. Instead, I simply remembered Johansen's last words to me: 'I love you.'"

Flora paused. Her heart was pounding, her eyes puffy from crying so much.

"The Neal-Vlanderman Campaign was the first battle the Executioners fought as an army, and my husband was the first casualty after protecting those around him. I know his son Marty will grow up to be proud of his father, truly understanding sacrifice.

"I, Flora Helson Neal, faithful wife of Lt. Johansen Neal, will never forget my husband and the days we shared as a family, which is and always will be our strength.

"End recording."

"That was beautiful, Flora," the computer said softly. They had talked for about four hours, each laughing and crying about some of her husband's antics. How many games of chess had Ecie played with Johansen over the years?

"Thank you, sweetie," Flora whispered timidly and then began crying again.

CHAPTER SIX

It is as painful perhaps to be awakened from a vision as to be born.

(Ulysses)

—James Joyce, Irish Writer (1922 A.D.)

"Tracie," he shouted himself awake. His eyes popped open, blinking away tears, while his body shuddered from fear—lungs breathing in and out with short, quick breaths. He was covered in sweat, which had soaked his clothes and the sheets.

Footsteps—fast but quiet in the hallway—ran toward him. A soft voice soon followed: "Hold on. I'll be right there." A doorknob turned, and a woman entered.

Tracie Brenda Meyers had been taking care of him for the last month or so since he'd woken up. She was about five-foot eight and usually wore two-inch heels. Her black hair flowed down to just below her shoulder blades, but framed her face in such a way that her blue-green eyes, the most beautiful he had ever seen, just drew you in.

"What's the matter?" Concern was etched on her cheeks, and her bikini-model physique glided over to him. Immediately, he tried to think of another way to describe her without sounding like a damned, sexist pig. But she was fucking hot!

"I ... I don't know ..." He stopped, trying to make sense of fuzzy images ... things he didn't understand ... "It's nothing. I just missed you. I felt lonely. I guess it got to me."

The woman hopped onto the bed with him and smiled seductive intent. "You know," she said and traced a hand over his ribcage, which was bandaged by several dressings. She caressed his right cheek too. "You'll never ... umm ... heal at this rate."

Guilt was on her face too. She'd broken one of his ribs last night—one that hadn't been broken from his accident. But the man smiled in return and tugged on her belt, pulling her close to him. "Good. I think I like being a patient."

She carefully laid back into his side, and he held her for a moment before placing a kiss on her forehead. She comforted him, as though his worries disappeared when she was near. He forgot about the dream. "You know what? Maybe I'll never recover."

Tracie turned over and rested on top of him, being careful of his ribs. "That's all I need, to take care of an amnesiac for the rest of my life. What will I call you? Umm ... let's see ... what do you think of ... of ... Rover?" She played with his hair.

"I've probably been called worse," he chuckled when her hand brushed his side, realizing he was a little ticklish.

"Is that so?" A finger still traced itself down his hairy chest. He let his fingers move as well.

"Yeah, who knows what I did before this all happened?" he said, musing. "I could have been a reporter, an Extermination Officer, worked for the government, or maybe"—he grinned jokingly—"I was even a rebel ... So ... Boo!"

He felt a shudder in his arms. Tracie's face also seemed to strain a little, not much, but somehow he noticed. "What is it? Did I scare you?"

Her smile vanished, suddenly becoming very serious, and she pushed away from him. "I have to show you something. This has gone on long enough. Stay here."

Dumbstruck, he watched her move from the bed and out into the other room. She took on a form of pure serenity, the one he had gotten used to while she'd been doctoring his wounds. Over a month had gone by since he'd first awakened from his coma.

He gently tested his ribs. They were re-growing just dandy. The amplified healing instrument, which she strapped around him every few hours, was doing well. She said he would be doing handsprings within the next week. He didn't want to disappoint her, even though he had a pretty good idea that he hadn't been a gymnast.

He was glad she had found him, unconscious, out in the forest somewhere. She said she had no idea why he was in this part of the growth zone. Because of his lack of memory, he was no help either.

But amnesia, really? he asked himself. Had there been any new cases of such in the last four centuries? Especially after the deep-probe sensor array for cerebral proteins had been perfected and had been successful for treating such conditions? But she said his case was different. They had to let the memory come back naturally, through time and patience. When he'd looked into her blue-green eyes, he had hoped that they would be slow in coming. It seemed as though he was gaining his wish.

He heard wheels squeaking from the other room, as though a cart was being rolled over the marble floor, which was part of a beautiful home in the middle of nowhere.

Growth Zone Monitors were credited quite well. They had to be. They spent years, decades, and even lifetimes in a deserted forest—not to mention the hazards associated with living in red zones. It was hoped that by giving them the best of comforts it would prevent them from becoming totally introverted. Introverted GZMs would be a great inconvenience considering the numerous sporadic visitors—namely politicians, research groups, etc.—they often had to entertain.

Hmm ... are these swanky digs mainly for the VIPs? he wondered, but propped his hands pompously behind his head despite the dull ache from his ribs. *Well, shit, if so, I'm not complaining.*

The squeaky sound continued but it didn't sound overly heavy. "Need any help, honey?" he called out anyway.

"No, I'm fine" The door into the room popped open again. Tracie crouched into the bedroom pushing a large cart with a large tarp covering *something* ... something round.

"Don't tell me. You found Rosebud?" he laughed, giving her a wink, disappointed when she didn't smile back.

"In a way I did," she sighed, shaking her head, making him realize something was wrong. "Not quite a sled and definitely not my clit."

He laughed again, despite the frown on her face. Not many people got that "rumored" reference, which bashed some guy named Hurst. But with all the time on her hands as a GZ Monitor, she'd added to her collection of Old World fiction and factoids that she'd been hoarding since visiting the Smithsonian in Phijeyoton as a kid.

Of course ... he suddenly wondered how he even knew about *Hurst* with amnesia and all. But he seemed to like as many movies—equally good and bad—as Tracie did. He wasn't sure why he liked all that crazy shit that she had ...

He thought about that for a second and wondered why *that* mattered so much to him. Did he fall in love with her the moment she showed him a movie about a monster made out of a shark and an octopus? Or was it when she played him an ancient cartoon series based on an insane superhero who dressed up as a tick?

Fuck ... why can I remember these movies and whatnot but not my own damned name? he thought and—

"I found this." She stopped just before reaching the bed and yanked the tarp off, motioning toward a partially crushed, four-foot-diameter ball of ceramic-metallic polymer. It had various joints and other components that seemed to have been ripped off or melted. And from a mesh sack beside the big ball, she pulled out some wire and some alloy rods, which were blackened by what looked like soot and heat.

"I'm sorry that I didn't show it to you right away." Her eyes began to tear up and she began breathing heavily between sobs. "Maybe I thought that you'd remember your past as soon as you saw it, and then you would leave me. Unlike other growth zones, I hardly ever see anyone—"

"No," he broke in, his eyes locked with hers. "How could I leave you, even now?"

Her cheeks tightened, and her eyes closed. "You will have to. I tried to keep you here with me as long as I could, but I can't be selfish anymore. You have to go back home. I'm sure your friends ... I'm sure they ... they miss you ... *Logan*."

"Excuse me?" He adjusted his position on the bed and rubbed a hand through his hair. "I don't understand. How would you—"

"Logan ..." There was the name again, but didn't it sound familiar? He watched Tracie drop the mesh sack down, wiping her blackened hands on the outside of the bag, and move toward the bed. She sat down on the edge, and he had to keep himself from reaching out to her, despite the tense situation. "Around a couple of months ago, I heard three explosions when I was taking some samples, and I went to investigate. I found a collapsed building and a patch of forest obliterated by several bombs. I wondered if there were any survivors, and my scanner showed a lifeform—weak and fading—under the rubble.

"Logan, I found you partially buried under four tons of lime and steel, which were from an old warehouse that once had been surrounded by dense jungle. I moved you here and carefully pulled you out of your mobile armor. You woke up several weeks later."

"But I don't understand—"

"Wait," she interrupted him, "your lack of memory is not a common case. It was caused by your exposure to a Kepler bomb—possibly two of them. That polymetallic ball was the only thing keeping the carbon disrupter from hitting you. The unusual field the Kepler generated, however, must have caused a disruption in some of your long-term memory.

"I don't understand why it didn't knock out more than it did, like take out motor functions, languages or speech. But you were wearing that drive helmet and your neural net was protected some by that thick skull of yours," she still joked. Like Logan did, she joked when she was nervous, sad or otherwise uncomfortable. "I'm not familiar with anyone who survived a Kepler bomb. I only know of one ... I actually attended one of his speeches once ... Remarkable man ... But they say he is long dead. Glad *you* lived though."

"So am I," he joked, despite the knowledge she'd just given him. "But that still doesn't explain why—"

"I know," she cut him off again. "It doesn't explain why I know your name."

He nodded, still fighting the urge to pull her into his arms. Did it really matter what she had to say? Would it really change what they had together?

"Logan." She moved further onto the bed. Her legs crossed themselves, where she sat Indian style. She grabbed his hand and caressed his palm and fingers. "This is important. How much do you remember about ... well ... about ... *Infiltration*?"

His lips briefly tightened into a sneer, and he figured the action was more out of reflex than actual memory. But, when he looked into her eyes, her face, he suddenly realized that his old job entailed more than reporting on the news or protecting citizens from wild, psychotic monsters ...

Well ... *maybe* monsters in one sense of the word.

CHAPTER SEVEN

To lead an uninstructed people to war is to throw them away.

(Analects of Confucius, Bk. XIII)

—Confucius, Chinese sage. (Approx. Between 475 B.C.-220 B.C.)

"How could you let this happen?" Harvardson screamed into his handset. On the other end of the line was Frugal. Henry had been trying to get in touch with the head merc ever since their second production complex had been obliterated. "I thought you said you had everything under control. They wiped us out!

"I don't care where you were!" His boss shook one of his fists and kicked his chair.

Bigsby shrank back a little, noticing how his employer's temples pulsated and flared a shade of apple red. It had almost taken two weeks for Frugal to pick up the call, so Bigsby gave his boss that. Then the man's entire face took on the same dark-red hue.

"Now, don't be threatening me, buddy!" Henry blurted. "I don't care who the hell you are. I just lost hundreds of millions in credits, and hundreds of good people! You think what you can do to me matters?

"You should be doing something. All those lives are on your hands too! That guy you sent me awhile back didn't do shit—a helluva lot less than what I'd expect from a partner. So get off your damn ass and do something. They are fucking hunting us now. And it's your ass on the line too!"

The comlink, shaped like an old-style office phone, was slammed down. Bigsby watched the eyes of his boss catch hold of the far walls. Then they looked at window and the scenery behind it. They locked briefly on the statues near the door ... the fireplace ... and then on Bigsby himself.

The CFO took a deep breath, trying to prepare himself for what Harvardson was going to say. He was already sweating— some from now being his boss's center of attention and the rest being that Henry always kept his office so damned hot.

Sure, at one time, Hammerson had had a backbone, a set of balls, and would have given as well as he took. But back then he didn't have a limp from a robotic leg or a tick from a bionic eye either. Still, to his credit and his own sardonic view on life, he stood silently and waited for Henry to direct his energies his way. And, well, if it came down to it, it wouldn't be the first time he'd have to punch a boss—friend or no—in the face ...

Shit, man, really? Bigsby kept his jest to himself, but was still somewhat surprised that he admitted that Henry was a friend—okay maybe *that* wasn't such an epiphany. The other, though, well, that ...

that he actually felt like punching someone ... *That* was all about the mercs ... those fucking, fucking mercs ...

"Now what in God's name are you doing, Bigsby? Didn't I tell you to find me an answer to this problem?" Henry stared at his plump bookkeeper, who was beginning to sweat rather profusely. He could tell the man was speechless. The CFO's tongue was immobile in his mouth, not a sound was given or attempted. But, at the same time, Henry could tell that fear wasn't holding the man's tongue.

"Well, Bigsby?" Harvardson tried again. "Do you have anything new for me, or are you just going to keep looking at me and kiss my ass when appropriate?"

He watched the thirty-eight year old man shrug his shoulders once and take a handkerchief from his breast pocket. Bigsby flapped it hard twice and then wiped the sweat from his round face. He moved his glasses so that he could get the spot just between his eyes, and then proceeded to wipe the steam from the lenses. Oddly enough, Henry soon found himself trying to find the reflected light from the silver frames, thinking he found it near the second suit of armor.

"Henry," Hammerson said dryly, and Harvardson brought his concentration back toward his numbers-man. "I don't have anything to report as of yet. But I did get the final reports from our search teams. It was—"

"And?"

"Well, as I will remind you, there was nothing left of the base after—"

"Did you finally get the information from the security cameras?"

"Henry, you don't understand," Bigsby sighed. "There was nothing left of the facility after they were done with it. It was completely destroyed and leveled a couple of weeks ago. Making matters worse, type-four vegetation had been transplanted there. And, within ten hours, was already part of the jungle by the time the search team got there.

"Our crews had searched for over an hour in the air, because they didn't believe that their nav-comps were giving them the right coordinates. And it took over a week just to find a scrap of ... merc armor."

Bigsby seemed to quickly restrain a smile—thinking of *dead* mercs perhaps? Henry could tell that Hammerson didn't like them much. But then Bigsby took a breath and made a quick, almost nervous glance around the room. "We're still trying to calculate the total loss we suffered from the Executioners on that last attack. Besides the biotech and pharmaceutical companies you set up as legitimate factories, *Dva* was going to be our only other production facility ... for nirv itself.

"As you requested, I have made sure that we haven't kept any records of the legitimate businesses here, and our remote systems can't be tracked back to this location. We tried to find any leaks that disclosed *Dva's* true operations to them, but we haven't gotten anything. Needless-to-say, Frugal's idea of implanting the neural-wipes to prevent captured employees from remembering anything was extremely terrifying. But they were effective. Survivors from previous Executioner attacks do like their oatmeal. And, at least, they remember their alphabet."

Both Bigsby's and Henry's cheeks twitched at that—neither of them liked the idea of having people sign a nondisclosure agreement and then stick a neural wire in their brains. It was pretty common for work that required secrecy, and Henry had been both proud and frightened that all of his current staff had agreed to the procedure. Simple enough, the device would wipeout memories associated with their jobs, when there were risks of imminent capture, no chance of escape and pending interrogation. Good in theory, but in practice, so far, they had wiped out half of peoples' adult lives and a great deal of their childhoods. More so, since the device essentially prevented someone from breaking the NDA, it also zapped anyone who intended to disclose company secrets for personal gain.

Harvardson, having gone through the procedure himself as a sign of good faith, was amazed that it could actually identify that crucial moment. Thankfully, no one had tried to sell him out since the implants; however, he felt terrible for those who'd survived the recent attacks. But they were alive and would eventually be able to recover and piece together a new life that he'd set up for them. A life far away from this business, he could give them *that* at least.

"Thankfully," Hammerson continued, "after reviewing data from relays stations, we found out that the main computer was successfully destroyed before the Executioners took the plant. We are confident that all its navigational coordinates were obliterated when the computer's memory was fragged."

Henry heard a sigh of relief, small but detectable, and nodded in his friend's direction. "Thank you, Bigsby. I'm just as relieved," he agreed and smiled, quickly realizing what an ass he was being to his friend. "Is there anything else?"

The CFO took another breath, but seemed comforted some by the change in Harvardson's attitude. "No, not really, our base's defenses are still fully functional. Our boosted production rate since that last attack should, under a quick estimate, cover for the loss within the next month and a half. Our shipments are staying on schedule, and those other enterprises are being accepted more and more widely in legitimate areas like drug rehab centers and even hospitals. How you managed to drum up those dummy corporations with actual FDA approval I'll never know."

"Great news, Bigsby. Yep, I have my moments," Henry said—trying to keep his friend's spirits buoyed—and scratched an itch on his chin. He wasn't really one to honk his own horn, but he was worth BILLIONS. Regardless, there were a lot of people benefiting from nirv now, so why were the Executioners so up in his crawl? Did they like seeing people suffer?

All those people ... Henry scowled. He didn't understand nor would ever be able to understand how terrorists thought. Fanatics.

"Excellent, my friend." Harvardson nodded and continued his efforts to get the accountant to relax. "You and Smithers have been doing a great job. I'm sure Morrison couldn't have done any better."

"Thank you." Bigsby allowed a smile to cross his lips, something Harvardson rarely saw. "I'll double my efforts."

"I know you will, but, do you mind? I need to be alone for a while."

"All right, is there anything else you wanted me to check on ... book discrepancies?" Bigsby was walking toward the doors. His right foot slid a bit from the initial movement and then adjusted.

Henry knew Bigsby's bionics were sensitive subjects, ever since the man had actually gotten angry when Henry had told the CFO that he'd pay for new robotics. Harvardson had no idea how the man had lost the leg and part of his right eye, and had thought it wise to never ask. That had been six years ago, and he hadn't seen Bigsby angry since.

"No, I'm sure you've mulled over them enough already without my endorsement," Harvardson disagreed, shaking his head. "Get some rest for a bit. I'll call if I need you, and Smithers probably won't need anything for now."

He heard the numbers-man groan, as if the CFO had nothing else in his life but work. But that was not entirely true, since

Harvardson often heard Hammerson talking to Smithers about the books they read.

Henry sat down in his chair and watched the steel and oak doors close. Then he turned and gazed out the window and looked at the forest of pine trees growing all around his fortress.

He tried to remember the last time he'd read a good book. It wasn't that he hated reading. He just enjoyed doing other things. "But it would probably be better than just staring at these trees for hours on end, wondering if the Executioners are going to find out where we are."

He rested his face in his palms and thought about all the people who worked here. What would happen if they—

"My God, they killed nearly everyone at the new plant," he whispered to himself in disbelief. "How could they do that?"

He tried to hold back the tears that came. But failed.

Ka-Coooooooooooom!

Henry jerked and woke himself up. He looked around his office, noticing that the suits of armor were shaking ...

He yawned and rubbed his eyes. His mouth was dry, and his head ached. His forehead had fallen onto his forearms while he'd slept, and his neck was now tight and sore. He hadn't believed he'd been so tired. But when had he slept last?

"Mr. Harvardson? Henry? Henry!" Bigsby shouted and pounded on the door, making Harvardson jump. The taps were loud, and more than Henry expected. Was the man so strong? "Henry, are you all right?"

"Yeah," Harvardson said through the door and hit a button on his desk, causing the heavy doors to swing open. Hammerson was there, immediately clawing his way into the office. A Harlow rifle was in his hands, sweat covered his cheeks along with the pits of his shirt, and steam appeared to have collected on the man's glasses again. Fear and a visual picture of determination rested on the CFO's face, but Harvardson laughed at the sight anyway. "Bigsby, what are you doing? Put that thing away before you shoot yourself ... or *me*."

"Sorry, Henry"—Bigsby offered a rare smirk to Henry's joke—"but one of our plants just exploded, and we're not taking any chances. It could've been a problem with the monitoring equip—"

"The Executioners?" Harvardson's mouth was still dry, and the sleep in his eyes and the cobwebs in his head weren't helping him think. "How big was the explosion? How did it go up?"

"It completely engulfed the processing unit, but was kept within the external containment shields." Bigsby pressed a finger to his ear, carefully listening to the earpiece there. It only took Henry another moment to realize that his accountant had actually beaten his security detail here, which he noticed were running up as Bigsby listened to his comlink.

"We still can't find anything wrong with the primary or sub-systems," the CFO said and shrugged, as if he was already dismissing what he was about to say. "As unlikely as it might sound, it might have exploded on its own."

Henry blinked his eyes one last time and drummed his fingers on his desk before he got to his feet. "Well, better send damage control units throughout the rest of the base anyway, get the defensive teams in their positions, and make sure both crews are heavily armed. We don't want anyone being caught with their pants down if this happens to be an attack."

Harvardson turned, moved to the rear left corner of his office while Bigsby relayed the messages over the communication systems and directed the security team. Henry passed a lamp, an old one he had bought while he had been in Asia. It was a simple design: a stick encircled by rectangular, spike-like chain link. He had bought it on a whim about nine years ago, but he still told himself that he should move it away from the Swedish vase.

Great ... our world might be coming down and I'm worried about the feng shui of my office, he grumbled to himself, while he opened the door to his gun safe. He pulled out an S&R pistol and Mark-4 rifle from their rests, and grabbed some extra magazines to be on the safe side. He clipped the pistol onto his belt and slung the assault rifle over his shoulder.

"OK, let's go to the command center," he said and motioned to his CFO and the other men and women, pointing toward the doors. "Smithers may find something eventually, and I'd like to be in there when he does."

He passed through the doors, with Bigsby and the others at his heels, and ran down the hallway. It was decorated with statues and paintings from the Good Book. The art had been purchased by the previous owner of the fortress, who had sold it to Henry twenty years ago but had left the works behind. Harvardson had always admired these figures of the Past—these ancient statues from the Old Age meant more to him than simple art.

After running through the hallway, they made a series of turns, making sure not to run into anyone coming from the other direction. About a hundred feet separated his office and Central Command. He liked the close proximity but also enjoyed a little distance from the perpetual anxiety created by Operations.

They ran up to a door, and he quickly threw a hand on the plate beside it. "Alpha mega, Harvard-Two," he managed without a stammer, even though he was breathing heavily and in worse shape than he thought.

Briefly wondering if the voice print understood him at all, the door popped open. It opened to a very large room filled with people, computers and the like. Everyone in the room seemed to be running from this way to that, with Henry trying to make sense of the confusion as a bystander. He failed miserably.

He looked around and saw that many of them were running to the lanky man in corner. The guy was dressed in denim jeans and a white, gray-striped, long-sleeved shirt.

"Smithers, what's going on here?" he asked as he walked toward him. A lot of those in the room turned around too, including the man being addressed. However, the hysteria immediately overwhelmed the brief calm, and the room soon exploded back into chaos.

"Well, Henry." The tall man moved through the room while people streamed around him. He stroked a hand through short, gray hair and looked at Henry with tired eyes.

"I guess you heard the explosion?" a half-joke crossed Smithers' lips, sarcasm Henry had grown accustomed to over the years. "It seems Plant Four hit critical mass in its number three reactor about eight minutes ago"—Henry threw a quick glance over to Bigsby, feeling his cheeks tighten with a little anger toward his CFO, but Lindle was still talking—"... something obviously went wrong with the containment assembly, but we still don't know the initial cause of its overload."

Smithers turned to one of the monitors, a seismic display, then said: "It detonated with about two megatons of energy, but the outer shields managed to protect the other manufacturing plants."

"Great," Harvardson said and tapped his fingers on a work station he was near. He noticed that the Mark-4 rifle was feeling a little heavy now. And the collar around his neck was a bit tighter too.

"Is anything on the scanners? That was our biggest plant for Christ's sake! I haven't seen anything like that before, and—"

"But the defensive systems haven't found squat," Smithers interjected. "Hell, we weren't even looking at the monitors when the thing blew. It happened that fast, without warning." Lindle had always been a little touchy when it came to his equipment, even when talking to Henry directly. But he never considered the man to be one who talked behind his back.

"Anyway," Smithers answered, calming down a bit, even though the worried look on his face spoke volumes for someone who was generally so even-keeled. "We're still trying to find the problem. But, if it had been an attack, wouldn't bombs be dropping on us right now?" The question was reasonable, and Henry let out a breath, realizing how quickly he'd become a part of the hysteria. He grinned and nodded to his Chief of Operations. Lindle had been under Henry's employ for a long time—nine years before Bigsby—and certainly didn't hold back, especially about questioning authority in regards to personal safety.

Smithers did have good reason to be outspoken. And Harvardson suddenly felt a pang of guilt. It had been several days since he'd last visited Lindle's family. Henry's godchildren, even though they did wear him out more quickly every time, were more important than all this. Fuck man! Nirv had made him money, and he now had a lot of it.

Hmm, what if the plant did just exploded on its own? he asked, aware that the butterflies in his gut had finally gotten the best of him. *Maybe it's time ... time for something different?*

"Well ... shit ... so be it." Henry looked around smiling, calm as he could be, and noticed a startled brow from Bigsby. Had the CFO counted on a different reaction?

Good. I consider him a friend despite what he's done to keep his distance. Shit, after six years you either become a friend or an enemy, Harvardson smirked. *But, friend or no, he does have a stick up his ass.*

"Well, Lindle," he said, dismissed the security team, and motioned for Bigsby to join him. "Make sure everything's cleaned up. I want to make sure there isn't a vapor trail of nirv scattered across the countryside. Check the status of the other plants again, and continue your diagnostics of our own reactors here. I don't want the same thing happening to us." Henry received a nod from Smithers, who smirked too, probably because he had already done those things.

Henry added, "But keep the defensive stations on alert. I want verbal reports every ten minutes until this is all over.

"And, Bigs"—he motioned toward his numbers-man—"come with me. We need to talk."

"But retire?" His voice echoed in the hallway back to Harvardson's office. Bigsby still couldn't believe his boss was serious. Things were heating up with the Executioners, but to call it quits? Hammerson was both in awe and ... well ... a little disappointed. But he had to admit that Henry was definitely different.

"Yeah." Harvardson nodded the CFO's way again, but with less of the smile this time.

Is the man growing tired of seeing the shock on my face? Bigsby managed to muse as he limped along.

Hammerson watched Henry gaze at one of the statues in the ancient hallway, then seemed to shake off a thought. "We pushed it too far with the Executioners. We need to cut our losses. Besides, the pharmaceuticals I set up are starting to finally show profitability."

"But what about the Executioners?" Bigsby felt his cheeks tighten and the spasm in his right eye. His hand gripped the stock of his rifle for support, as past and present seemed to merge. He did not know how, but it did and his knees felt weak too.

"Yeah, those fricking terrorists," Henry scoffed. "They are a problem, a big one, but Frugal can take care of things from here on out."

"Frugal?" The name sounded familiar, and it only took Bigsby another few steps before he realized it was the name of the person they were working with. *The damn mercs.*

"Nelson Frugal ...He told ..." Bigsby let his mind wander while Henry talked. He thought about what his life would be like if they shut all this down. What would he do? Where would he go?

"... anyway"—Henry was still talking and Bigsby listened more intently—"Frugal mentioned something about how he found a way to get to them, but I'll just let him take care of it. That's what he's here for."

"But what's his cut?" Bigsby's leg throbbed at the knee—right where the bionics had been attached—and his limp seemed to be more pronounced than ever. And his bionic eye wasn't doing much better. *Damn mercs.*

"Well, that's a long story." They reached the end of the hall, and they entered Henry's office. "Frugal was actually the one who got me started making nirv in the first place. He told me it would be the wave of the future and shape worlds, and other fancy, flowery bullshit. He was an old merc, a philanthropist, who wanted to use it for those suffering from post-traumatic stress disorder and mental illnesses in war-torn areas like California and the Himalayas. He didn't want to market it, since it would have taken too long to run it through legitimate channels. Besides, he wanted to charge as little for it as possible, if at all.

"Good lord, that was twenty years ago. Can you believe it? That was long before you came on board, and it was at the height of some of the greatest Rebel-Panterian battles in recent history ..."

Being outlaws, even Bigsby knew about the serious problems with the Rebels, who were more trouble than President

Lyly let on. And the very thought of the government hiring mercenary armies to fight them sickened him. But the world was full of such fools, and he didn't want to believe Henry as one.

"Anyhoo, Frugal recruited me and offered me all of *this*." Henry motioned with his hands and his eyes seemed to glaze over as he sat back behind his desk and thought about the past. "The plants basically run themselves. Hell, Bigs, you know, basically we're just growing cultures of modified bacteria and then refining the product like any pharmaceutical. And Frugal promised me absolute secrecy and security, gave me all the equipment I needed for support functions, and even showed us how to transport shipments without being detected. How could I say no? I took the offer and followed Frugal's instructions, letting him transport it to wherever he wanted.

"For several years we built up inventory. Mercs, disguised as couriers, ran routine schedules, and filled most of the obscure storage facilities we have today. But one day I just stopped hearing from him." Henry looked at Bigsby for a moment and nodded, seeming to know what the accountant was about to ask.

"No, Bigs, I don't know. Honestly, I thought Frugal had fallen off the face of Panteria. Don't get me wrong, I hate clichés, but this was serious. After building up those stockpiles of nirv, he just disappeared, about a year before you started working for me.

"But the money kept coming in for us to make it. So, in accordance with my contract, I continued production and kept adding warehouses. And, keeping true to his wishes, we distribute at no charge via Frugal's network. Well, okay, for the rest of the world, we charge but give it to charities. Sue me! They need it!"

"Uh ..." Bigsby was about to object to that. He always knew that they had money coming in from investors; however, the other sources of income didn't seem to adhere to those wishes.

"I know. I know," Henry laughed. "I took a technicality out of the contract. Frugal never told me that I couldn't seek derivatives through legitimate channels, so I sought multiple FDA approvals, using different corporations for each variation of nirv's molecular structure.

"Besides, it had been years since I'd heard from him, and I thought that I was never going to hear from him again ..." Henry grinned sheepishly, and gestured with an "oopsy" shrug. "I almost shit my pants when Frugal suddenly contacted me and told me that we should increase market share after the Executioners had taken out those other drug czars ...

"He still doesn't understand why they started to target us to begin with. Sure we made it worse by possibly killing one of them in that fake warehouse with the Kepler bombs. But they drew first blood by killing Diego!"

"But how much of it does he really need and why did he want us to increase production so much?" Bigsby had a complete count of all the warehouses. There was a shit-ton of them.

"Who knows," Henry joked and tapped his fingers on the desk. "Hell, I can't even remember how many there are—"

"Eight hundred and forty-seven in North and Central America," Bigsby reminded him. "And more in the—"

"Yes, yes." Henry seemed to wave him off and drummed his fingers again on the desk. He even hummed a tune from an old sitcom. "Why do we really need to care anymore? I'll just call him, tell him what he needs and leave him men if people want to stay. If anyone wants to leave, I'll make sure they have safer jobs in the cities. Then we'll be off to retire. That is ... well ... unless you would like to become CEO of Axiom Pharmaceuticals in North America? The current CEO, who seldom visits the company, is finally going to retire."

"What now?" Bigsby didn't think he heard right ...

Henry smiled. "It's a private company so the Chairman of the one-person Board will gladly nominate you too. I'll have Morrison's team drum up some new papers and other credentials so you'll pass through Axiom's security without an issue."

"Wait ... Wha ... What?" Bigsby stepped back. Excitement, embarrassment and anger seemed to exist for him simultaneously. That was the biggest company making an FDA-approved version of nirv.

"That's right, Bigs. Lindle has a family, and he'll probably want to spend it with them." Henry began to fiddle with the buttons on his computer terminal. "Besides, I've seen what you've done over the years, even though you've tried to not bring attention to yourself. Needless-to-say, just give me the word and I'll give you the job. But, mind you, I'll still have need for an accountant on my little island in the Mediterranean. Do you like Piña Coladas?"

"I ... uh ... what?" Bigsby stammered, still shocked from what he was hearing. "Over ... over Axiom?"

"It'll be tough work, but I don't know who would do a better job or trust. This is my way of thanking you. I know it can be frustrating at times, but it will pay well and it's safe.

"The Executioners won't be able to find a link between nirv and the legit businesses, since there are none. Fuck dude, rumor on the street is that nirv is just a bastardized version of Axial-corticalsterol-1 anyway ..."—Henry grinned like a cat who ate the canary—"And I was the one who started that! Besides, Frugal will probably take care of them. I've seen his equipment. And, well, if he doesn't, it doesn't matter."

"But can Frugal be trusted? What if they torture him and he gives us up?" Hammerson's right eye twitched. Did Henry notice this again? "He's a merc. They're all pussies. Why else did he force all of us to use those mind wipes?"

Henry was looking at Bigsby. The man had stopped his typing, but his fingers continued to tap beside the keys. Concern, the best Hammerson could interpret it, was obviously present. Eyes moved up and down, finally resting in direct line with Bigsby's own.

"Bigs?" The question was inevitable, but Harvardson had put it off until now. Bigsby had always appreciated that. "Why do you hate them so much? What did mercenaries do to you?"

BOOOM!

A flash came through the windows, so bright that it nearly blinded him. And, upon hearing an explosion that seemed to rock the entire world, Bigsby covered his head and fell to the floor.

"Bigsby?" Somehow ignoring the explosion, Henry jumped from the chair and ran to his friend after Hammerson collapsed. His comlink beeped, and he hit it. "Stand by, Lindle. Something's wrong with Bigs." The channel was closed, and Henry fell to his knees. "Bigsby, are you okay?"

"Not again ... not again," the CFO stuttered and shook. He was in the fetal position, lying on his side. His cheeks were pink, lips were white, and his eyes were like saucers. "Stop it. Stop."

There was another explosion, and Bigsby curled up even tighter. "It can't be ... uh ... ah-err." Then the man lost the power of speech.

"It's OK, Bigs." Henry laid a hand on the man's shoulder. The man was shaking beneath Harvardson's grip, while the rifle Bigsby had strapped to his side was under his quivering form, which Henry hoped wasn't doing too much damage.

"Come on, Mr. Hammerson." Henry tried again, this time testing Bigsby's pulse. It was erratic, but soon began to slow a bit after Harvardson squeezed his friend's shoulder a little harder.

After another minute, Bigsby stopped shaking, and Henry knew it had been nothing he'd done. The guy had just had a seizure, and Harvardson rested on one knee, trying to figure out what experience had caused his friend to suffer from such a form of epilepsy.

He'd heard about such traumatic cases, but had never seen one. Had he done the right thing by just leaving the man alone, shaking and mumbling? "Bigsby?"

"What happened?" Hammerson grunted eventually, his speech blurred by the electrical discord in his head.

"Take it easy. You just had an epileptic attack—" Harvardson tried to balk himself. "Do you know ..."

Bigsby shook his head, smiled, and then frowned. "I remember thinking of Marie, and—"

"Who?"

"No one ..." Bigsby tried to play it off, but it was too late.

"Come on, Bigs," Henry insisted. He hated pulling rank, but this was his friend's health they were talking about ... "Is she your lover, friend or—"

"Wife," Hammerson finished for him. "She's long dead ... about a decade ... more or less. But I don't keep count anymore."

"Is she the reason you hate the mercs?" Henry was just throwing out questions, but a man's wife? The institution was still sacred, and it would give just cause for anyone. Was this one Bigsby's too?

"Yes and no." Tears fell from the man's eyes. "Did you ever hear of Joshua Liodnoer?"

Henry remembered the name all too well, and he was glad he had competent people working with him, unlike the unfortunate Liodnoer. "Of course, what about him?"

Bigsby rested on his rump, arms around his knees. "Well, I used to work for him, during the height of his success ... In short, I was married then. Her name was Marie, Joshua's sister. She was beautiful, attractive, witty and obviously more than I should have ever deserved." Bigsby shook his head, apparently switching memories while thinking of faraway times.

"I covered up that part of my past. However, I used to work for my best friend Joshua in Los'An-Diego city, before California was sealed off from the rest of the world. It was underground work. We mainly supplied drugs to those who were sick, hungry, or, otherwise, outcasts from the image of perfection the Feds so adamantly tried to create. We were no angels: we also sold many of those pharmaceuticals for extra cash and favors ...

"However, we had heard the rumor about the government's renewed occupation of the area and the decree of martial law. So Joshua decided to move house, since he didn't want to have his base of operations caught behind those lines.

"I initially objected to the move, but he'd told me that I worried too much and that Marie and I needed a change of scenery anyway. He told me there was nothing to fear. Maybe Marie and I should start thinking about having kids ...

"There was one problem." Bigsby's lips tightened, then relaxed, but Henry knew his friend had buried this anger for a very long time. "He hired mercs for the job. They were all in their twenties and early thirties. I was just a kid then too, but they were so immature and they tried to take over the new base. They had to have it their way or not at all. And this was the reason why my wife and best friend were killed on the day the Night Rangers attacked the new headquarters.

"The mercs were fucking idiots!" Bigsby's face suddenly held the most violent mask Harvardson had seen on any man. "They had left obvious trails to our new location. And their skills and defenses were useless when it came down to fighting the most powerful rebel force of the time.

"We were wiped out in a matter of minutes. My wife was crushed underneath a ton of concrete and steel. Joshua was captured and executed on the spot for drug trafficking, even though our operations weren't nearly as bad as disperal or other drugs. I escaped only because I had sworn to Joshua that I would lead survivors to safety, even though I just wanted to crawl beneath the rubble and die next to my wife.

"Henry, mercs ruined my life. I thought I'd never be able to trust my employer or anyone again. My bionic leg and eye are constant reminders of that. Mercs are pretentious pricks and yu should never get in bed with them." Bigsby quieted and sat in silence—demeanor and presence changed before Henry's eyes.

There were no more explosions. Only two had gone off. Henry had turned off his receiver, but another loyalty tugged at him, which was the safety for *ALL* of his people.

"Don't worry, Bigs. We're not going to be working with them anymore," Harvardson tried to reassure him, despite anticipating another explosion. "It will be different this time. I promise. But now"—he pulled Bigsby to his feet with a huff—"we've got to find out what's happening."

They moved out of his office and walked down the corridor of ancient statues. Henry looked at his friend, making sure the man was not going to pass out or snap.

"You okay? Come on. Trust me, Bigs. Everything's going—"

KA-CRACK!

The hall imploded, and they were thrown to the stone floor. Henry blinked his eyes and looked at the engravings on the narrow ceiling. He'd known they were up there, but he'd never realized they were so beautiful.

"Are you okay?" Bigsby's words trembled. Fear was definitely in the man's voice, but anger and even confidence were present too. Then calm suddenly came over his friend, and Henry wondered if helplessness had made this inevitable in Bigsby's mind. "That was a missile strike," the man said.

"Really?" Henry figured as much but he didn't want to believe it. It had been a long time since hearing one.

"Trust me, Henry." A hand rested on Harvardson's shoulder. "I know what one sounds like as I'm sure you do."

Henry only nodded his head, reaching for the hand Bigsby gave him, and was pulled to his feet.

"Well," Bigsby said, grumbling and yanking the Harlow rifle from his own shoulder. "I guess retirement does sound pretty good now. I don't think I could do a Nine-to-Nine at a real job after this anyway." The CFO then slammed the weapon's firing mechanism into position. He turned on its fluctuating em-scanners, and uncharacteristically—at least to Henry—switched on the railgun. With that, the rifle barrel's pulse-field kicked on and made the weapon hum in a disquieting tone, before it fell silent, waiting to be fired. And, noticing the man's twisted smile, Henry realized that luck had not played much part in the man's survival from Liodnoer's fallen empire.

"Great," Harvardson said and motioned with his hand, sending them into a sprint to the control room. "I'll make arrangements."

With that, explosions soon began to bellow throughout the compound, making the complex vibrate with perceived life. Bigsby was lapping at Henry's heels all the way up to the command center. Adrenaline and the second trip had made it easier, but this time the PID plate stuttered when it had asked for verification. Also, the heavy door of the computer room had practically swayed unbalanced when another kiloton-force explosion rocked the base's electromagnetic shielding.

"Smithers!" Henry had to actually strain to hear the explosions when they entered the command center. People were shouting at each other and computers screamed with protocol violations. The external warning systems were blinking with red lights and wailing with the songs of harpies. He looked for Lindle again and found him. "What's going on? How many?"

"I don't know." Lindle ran over to the two of them, almost knocking someone down. "We can't pick up anything on the scanners. We can hardly track the missiles they're firing at us, for fuck's sake." Smithers hit a table next to him, spilling someone's coffee. "Dammit, Henry, who the hell did we piss off?"

A series of explosions above them shattered a number of computer screens on the walls. People screamed. His own eye twitched—much like how Bigsby's did—when Henry remembered an old thought, one where these explosions sounded all too familiar. "Do you know what's keeping them cloaked?"

"Fuck, who knows?" Lindle shook his head and rubbed a hand through his hair. "I don't know. There are so many different ways: electromagnetic disruption, absorption, diffraction, electronic signal distortion."

"But didn't Frugal give us means to combat that stuff?"

"He did," Smithers grunted, overcoming the combination of explosions, other voices and the alarm systems. "But the Executioners might not be using common tech."

"What? Are they ghosts?" Henry shook his head. His legs were tired and he braced himself on a nearby workstation. "Come on, Lindle, we're not thinking here. Don't cloaking devices give off some type of energy signature, a detectable wave?" He looked at his computer tech. The face was blank. Nothing.

"There's gotta be something. Christ, we'll shoot our missiles blind if we have to," Harvardson shouted, since the explosions were getting more repetitive and constant. "Jesus"—he looked around—"don't they ever let up?"

Smithers looked Henry's way. The tall man did not have confidence in his voice, but something was up. "Well, the only thing I can think of is to link the navigation and vector systems up to the blast detectors. The computer should be able to figure out what angles the missiles hit—"

"That would be pretty random," Bigsby commented behind Henry. The CFO was obviously paying attention. "The computer's pretty limited, since it still runs on programming, even if it writes a good chunk of its own. Although it appears sentient, it's not really intuitive like organic quantum computers will be."

Organic computers? Henry chuckled to himself, realizing how quantum computers tended to ignore what their developers asked them to do most of the time. He couldn't imagine the idea of adding the complexities of biology to that whole shitty setup. Bigsby read way too much Science Fiction.

Smithers gritted his teeth and looked at the scanner stations. "I know, but do you have any better ideas? Our missiles may not even leave their bunkers if we wait much longer." Lindle looked at the CFO and then in Henry's direction. The COO only shrugged his shoulders, and a discomforting acknowledgement came from Bigsby.

Another explosion, stronger than all others, shook the complex. People and workstations were thrown to the floor.

Henry managed to stay upright, but his wrist hurt from holding onto the table. He watched Smithers and Bigsby rise to their feet too. "I don't care if we'll be shooting at targets scanned three weeks ago," he said. "Maybe the computer will get some of the predictions correct. I just want to get some of those bastards!" Henry felt the muscles in his neck tighten and saw the red flush in the skin of his hands and arms. "We won't if our weapons are off line."

"Right." Lindle ran to a nearby station, punched in some access codes, and typed in the necessary commands, since the computer would have difficulty hearing anything at the moment. It would be a guessing game, but Henry knew the risks of being a businessman.

A few of the remaining scanners soon blurred with activity. The combat systems were now being crammed with information. And the power from the fusion reactors was boosted to accommodate for the arsenal about to be unleashed from Harvardson's fortress.

Hundreds of explosions slammed against the defensive shields. But they were holding for now, as long as their internal components withstood the kiloton and megaton force shockwaves being pelted against them. Some calimar lights flashed and burned out from the shake. More workstations crashed to the floor. And above all the screams and noise, Henry heard Smithers' voice.

"Fire!" Lindle shouted again in confidence and rage. "Fifteen percent of the defenses ... Launch."

"Oh my God," Henry whispered, seeing what Smithers was talking about. Three hundred tracer images dotted a tactical screen. "How?"

The room became quiet. The external explosions paused, and Henry watched the tactical screens light up from the base's defensive grids. Guided missiles, cannons, lasers and antimatter hover mines were slung out in a hellish sight. Henry heard Hammerson breathing softly behind him. He looked back, finding Bigsby pale but seemingly calm enough.

Harvardson wondered what image of Death the man was seeing, while he watched the base's defenses encroach ... and pass their targets. They finally exploded fifteen miles away.

The three hundred tracers continued toward the base. Their paths slowly began to deviate as the combat computer's margin for error began to increase. Slowly, the bleeps began to fade from sight, which made Henry turn to Lindle.

An image of a ghost seemed to coincide with Smithers' form. Lindle was speechless, his eyes were dilated and his face was whiter than Bigsby's. However, the Chief of Operations stood with his lips drawn tightly around his teeth, and Henry compared the man to a caged tiger about to kill or be killed.

"Smithers, prepare my shuttle," Henry said and strapped the Mark-4 rifle over his shoulder again. He moved and rested a hand on Lindle's shoulder. "Set up the auto-defensive systems, and sound the evacuation. We don't have too many people here, so the cloaked transports can get out of here within the next ten minutes. I want you to time the self-destruct codes for ten minutes after—AND I mean ONLY after all of our people leave. They want a villain? We'll give them one by destroying this sector with them in it. Take that, Mr. Bond!"

He thought about how that movie franchise had jumped the shark by including a nefarious "Panterian Guard" that supposedly ruled the world, while the Average Joe just went about his business. Well, the series had had a good 1000-year run, even if the surviving family endlessly tied those films up in litigation.

He smiled at that brief tangent and then stressed his next words: "Lindle, I want to see you in a couple of days. Do you hear me?"

"Right." Lindle nodded, a half-smile resting on the man's lips. The evacuation sirens were already whining.

"Don't worry." Henry slammed his palm on the self-destruct PID-plate as soon as Lindle typed the proper codes. "They'll be fine, should be on one of the first transports. But make sure." The plate beeped. "Computer, this is Henry. Omega-carmen. Mors-venit. Unbreakable."

He pulled his hand from the plate, gave one last nod to Lindle, and motioned to Bigsby. He never figured that they'd ever blow this place up. But Frugal was a strange cat. If the guy wanted to set up a self-destruct like a silly spy movie, Henry could only protest so much.

"Well, Bigs," he said while they ran out of the main door in the direction of the lower hangars. "We would have gotten you a watch, but we really didn't anticipate this. Nonetheless"—three more production plants exploded and drummed the hallway—"welcome to retirement, my boy."

Harvardson had elected to take the stairs and walkways, and Bigsby knew it was best. They only had to go down anyway. The giant, spiral staircase to the launches was shock-absorbent, and designed to make a safe escape. Occasionally, though, explosions caused both of them to lose their balance, but neither of them had fallen yet.

Sweat poured from his brow and covered his shirt, even soaking the front of his pants. But Bigsby couldn't explain the energy running through him. His cheek twitched and his right leg still made its awkward rhythm. He ignored both and ran behind his friend. He also ignored the fog blurring his glasses while he thought about what he was doing. He couldn't quite picture himself earlier in the control room, and not at all when he'd helped Henry up after the third explosion in the main hallway. Really, he had no reason for the energy, the thirst for life. Those things, he believed, had left him long ago. So why was he still trying to survive? What forced him to run behind Henry Harvardson to protect the man? Why did he care?

He grimaced, holding the electromagnetic rifle in one hand, the other on the railing. *Right now there are only actions, damn the explanations,* he told himself when his feet finally hit level ground and a narrow hallway soon enveloped them.

The length of the hallway to the hangar was illuminated. The path was mainly concrete, steel and plastic polymer. Bigsby had seen titanium reinforcements ignite from an explosion before, and he knew Harvardson's precautions had been good ones. Fewer fire-control teams running through already congested hallways were the better, and vacuum seals were very expensive for the outlaw.

"Not much farther," Henry shouted up ahead by only a few paces. Then the man dropped his rifle, letting it crash to the composite floor. "It's only thirty more yards."

Bigsby stopped, just passing the rifle, and went back for it. He was indeed breathing hard, but he really did not feel the aches just yet. At any rate, Harvardson needed it just in case they had unexpected company. The Executioners had proven such so far, and the pistol on Henry's hip wouldn't cut it.

"Henry, wait," he shouted. "You—"

KA-CRACK!

"Fuck me ..." Henry pushed himself up after being knocked to the ground. He was covered with dust and dirt. Much of the ceiling had cracked and it moaned even now. He wondered what was left of his home after such an explosion. He figured it had been an antimatter pulse—a big one—and probably a direct hit. He hoped the warhead had missed the structures, but there was no way of knowing down here.

Damn them. He rubbed his head thinking of the Executioners.

"Bigsby?" Henry finally asked, while also trying to cough out the dust in his lungs. A lot of it was beginning to fall and was already being sucked away by the circulation systems, allowing him to see down the corridor. It was still lit, although many of the lights had been cracked or had fallen with parts of the ceiling. Wires and conduits hung like vines and stalactites attached to the mounds of rubble shaken loose from the explosion. Power re-route systems prevented currents to flow in the torn lattice now, so Henry did not fear walking around them.

"Bigsby?" he asked again. "Where are you? Are you OK? Bigs?" His eyes traveled back down the corridor. The dust had finally cleared, allowing him to see several more mounds of dirt stretched in the distance. He saw part of a Harlow rifle barrel ... and part of the Mark-4 he had just thrown down ...

A hand ...

He took a deep breath, trying to calm his heart. "Oh ... no ..."

He ran to the hand that was covered by dust, plastic and concrete. Henry's hands were shaking, but he managed to grab hold of the account's grip and pull Bigsby out ... out of his shallow grave.

"No ... no ... no ..." he cried and pulled the man into his arms ... He closed his eyes when a series of explosions rocked the world again ... only to realize that *those* were from his imagination ... from very old memories ...

Between ragged breaths Henry opened his eyes and tried to feel for some type of pulse, tried see if his friend might still be breathing ...

"No ... no ... come on, Bigs! Please! You have ... you have ..." Henry sobbed.

Bigsby's face was white, covered with dust, and blood had clotted on the backside of his head, which was no longer shaped like it was supposed to ... The man's glasses had cracked and were twisted and smashed. The man's eyes were closed and his cheeks were covered in blood and gore. He'd been crushed ...

"Oh ... God ... God ... sorry ... sorry ..." Henry fell to his rump and kept Bigsby in his arms. He'd wanted to keep him safe. He'd wanted to give him back his life.

"I lost my family too, Bigs," he whispered, shaking the dust out of his hair, nose, ears and everywhere. The dust burned his throat.

"No ... not a wife ... kids ... but I have loved. He was a sweet man. Killed ... murdered by rebels in California," he moaned and just held Bigsby close. "I guess our past guides our future, eh?"

Behind him, he heard footsteps, quick ones. His heart raced, but he sat unmoving with his friend in his arms. If the Executioners had found him—

"Come on, Mr. Harvardson," someone said, and hands quickly grabbed his shoulders, pulling him forcefully away and making him lose his grip on Bigsby. "We have to get you out of here."

"No! No! Not without *him*," he protested and pointed, while turning to see to whom he was talking. He noticed pilot insignia over both of their right breast pockets. "We have to give him a proper burial. He deserves that much. He—"

"No, Henry!" one of the pilots yelled. "The whole plant's going to blow up in about five minutes because of that damned self-destruct. It malfunctioned! Who knows how many of our people are going to die. So we don't have time to carry him or you." They began to pull him away. His feet kicked and his body resisted, but they were too strong.

"No! Let me go back then! I'll stop it! I have to save them!" Henry shouted.

"No!" they both yelled. "There isn't time! We have to go now!"

"No! No! I can't let them all die!" he shouted into the corridor and still tried to break free.

"Please, sir!" one of the pilots stammered. "We have to get you out of here. Please ..."

Despite his grief for Bigsby and the others, he realized that both men were scared shitless but were doing their best to hold it together. And he knew that they would die trying to save him, even if he broke away and ran ...

He hadn't looked up to see their faces. He had no idea who they were, despite their loyalty, even though he tried to get to know everyone—everyone!—who worked for him. He knew that he was just as responsible for these two men as anyone. They needed to make it out of here. So he pushed down the hurt and the anguish and got himself together.

"Okay. Okay. I'm sorry. Thank you," he said, patted them on the shoulders and began walking after they stopped briefly for him to catch his breath. "Are you sure that there aren't any others that could come this way? We should wait if that's the case."

"No, sir," the one with *Jenkins* on his lapel said. "I'm sorry about earlier. We're new, but we have a lot of friends up there. Boris got us the job."

"Ah," Henry said, trying to put up a good front despite tears that kept pouring from his eyes. "He keeps a good schedule. He's in Paris right now. He has the sweetest little girls."

The other pilot, a Falconi, looked at him in shock, and then slowly smiled. "I wished that we could have worked longer here for you, sir. We heard good things."

"And," Jenkins groaned. "We're ... umm ... sorry about Hammerson. He was a good man, sir."

"Thank you ... But please call me *Henry*."

His shuttle came into view. It resembled an elongated egg, with several sensor and weapon modules located on the underside of the craft. Two modified, fighter-craft repulsars opposed each other on either side of the craft. They hummed with energy. Even though the ship looked simple enough, its twin engines would almost ensure his escape by speed alone, regardless of the cloaking devices littered all over its hull.

"After you, Henry." The pilots helped him into the craft and strapped him into one of the four passenger seats before entering the cockpit themselves. As they guided the craft into the launch tube, the hum that came from the reactor cores increased—

Henry watched his life suddenly pull away from him, as the craft accelerated into orbit.

"Goodbye, my friends. Goodbye, Bigsby." Henry rested his head against the inner hull, ignoring the monitors telling him where they were going.

In thirty minutes, the Executioners had quickly ended this chapter of his life. Additionally, he'd lost someone he considered a dear friend ... and probably so many more ...

He could only hope that Lindle and his family had gotten out in time. But what type of thread had the Norns woven for anyone? His own was littered with kinks and frays. And despite the tears that wouldn't stop, he thought about Bigsby ... and ... and wondered if he had seen a smile on Hammerson's face.

Maybe ... Maybe ... Henry, despite his life, desperately wanted to believe that good people were reunited with their loved ones after they moved on from this plane of existence ...

"Take care of her this time, Bigs."

Henry closed his eyes and cried for those he had lost.

CHAPTER EIGHT

We love too much, hate in the same extreme.

(The Odyssey, Bk. XIV)

—**Homer, Greek Poet (C. 700 B.C.)**

As it was ... it was a perfectly beautiful day, with the sky as blue as ever it could be. It was mid-autumn, and the Mediterranean still had several months left before the Season of Storms would begin to form. Naturally, an occasional crashing wave warned Henry of the upcoming danger to his coastal home. But the ancient castle had been re-enforced so that it would protect him and his people from the elements, no matter how strong the winds would be this year.

Henry didn't mind the idea of the storms anyway. When he was a kid, his mom used to sing such lovely songs ...

Harvardson smiled whimsically when he thought about her ...

He took a sip from the strawberry margarita, while he scrolled through the PDL for any updates about the people who were still lost or missing. As he put his drink down, his hand brushed up against an antique novel that Bigsby had given to him on his birthday. Over the years, the accountant had given him several books, which Henry had simply shipped out here ... possibly ... maybe getting to read them when he retired someday ...

Six novels later ... between all the updates he was trying to get and directing search parties and trying to find missing people ... or ... more horrifyingly ... confirming the dead ...

Six novels... he laughed to himself sardonically. He'd barely slept in over a week. Reading had helped to occupy his time when the info wasn't coming in. He couldn't bear watching anything on the networks, since California and other rebel actions were too much in the news lately.

But six novels? he mused. The one he was reading now was about a psychotic sea captain who wanted nothing more than to kill a whale ...

He tried to make some type of connection between that bastard's pain and the resolution he sought. He tried to imagine a world in which he had tried to broker a peace with the Executioners ... and imagined what would have happened if they had actually accepted it ...

And then he wondered if he was the captain or the whale. Or was it either? From a certain point of view ...

"Henry?" a strong voice, a higher tenor asked.

"Yes, Pat?" Henry turned, already knowing who it was, despite the period of time he hadn't heard the voice while the security officer had been on leave. "What's up?"

"Well, we got something." Patrick Morrison looked over the serenity of the Mediterranean, shrugged and smiled timidly. The man's wife of fourteen years had been killed from an attack by an army squad in California five months ago. Despite being in a relatively safe area, a stray missile had taken four lives, including Pat's son and two daughters. The security chief had rushed back to work for Henry out of guilt, since he'd been out of contact and not been there to help protect the base when the Executioners had come knocking. Obviously, Henry had protested, figuring the guy still needed more time. But Morrison had insisted, saying he needed to get on with his life. Harvardson understood completely—he himself had done so often enough.

"We've been using the new equipment that Frugal gave us as amends," Morrison said hesitantly. Henry was still angry about the use of the self-destruct mechanisms Frugal had incorporated into the base. But no one figured that the Executioners would have deliberately triggered them early. Even Morrison was still blaming himself for how the terrorists had managed to break the safe codes, thereby speeding up the explosions.

Harvardson did notice that Morrison stood a little straighter, and even smiled. "Henry, I think I have good news. It looks like Smithers' car is heading this way."

Henry grabbed the book and PDL and hopped to his feet. "Great! What direction?" He looked north then south then—the sun's reflection on the sea nearly blinding him. "Has he sent the signal yet?"

"No, Henry, he's not within the safe zone. It'll be another two minutes, but I'll have to remind you that if it's not him ..."

"I know," Henry sighed, nodding to his friend. "Better set up the outer and inner defenses just in case. I think a lot of our people have had enough excitement within the last two months, including myself." Harvardson bit his lip and rubbed the back of his neck. Although the apartments and other living areas had been relatively safe, only a handful of people in the main buildings had been able to evacuate before the reactors went critical. But thankfully, his godchildren and Smithers' wife had made it to the safe house alive. He had just wanted to make sure Smithers got back safely first, before he went for a—

"Sure thing." Pat nodded as though he had already done them. In fact, it seemed the Director of Security and Defense had only one thing left to do.

"OK," Henry said with a defeated look. "Where do you want me?"

Patrick grinned. Possibly he'd thought he was going to have a fight. "I would recommend that you go down to your bunker, near your escape craft."

Henry grimaced as well, not too fond of cages, even when it came to his own safety.

"Okay. Okay," Morrison already interjected. "I think our people can take care of one person, two if there are more in the car."

Harvardson didn't say anything right off. The recent battle with the Executioners had been a disaster to say the least. Morrison, of course, had said the new equipment here would be able to pick up anything, cloaked or not. And although Henry wasn't so confident in the new equipment, he didn't want to be confined to quarters either. "You wouldn't, by chance, need an extra hand in the control tower? I'm good with binoculars."

"Sure thing." Morrison smiled, but Henry now knew what the face of worry looked like, despite what people did to mask it.

Henry drummed his fingers on the sides of the binoculars, trying to see something out there. He knew the monitors beside him could show him what he was looking for a lot better. But he just liked using the field glasses, especially since he could scan the entire horizon for whatever looked interesting. Besides, Morrison would alert him of anything unusual anyway, or anything Henry couldn't see with the hi-powered lenses.

Cool! he cheered to himself when he panned north. Above the ocean, he saw a Palcor eagle and recorded a video when it tucked in its fifteen-foot wings and dove beneath the surface to pull out a large fish. Earlier, he'd already seen some False Kraken surface, along with Stark's orca.

"Are you sure it's him?" Henry asked, especially when Nature seemed to take an intermission. It was just making conversation, more or less, even just for his own benefit ... Morrison sometimes kept to himself, didn't speak much, especially since—

"Yeah," Patrick said, while fiddling with some highly sensitive detection equipment. Henry was glad the man knew what he was doing, since the man just seemed to be pushing buttons. "The external markings and sensory equipment on the HC are generating frictional anomalies and disturbances to the velocity envelops. And the signature of his repulsars and reactors are identical to his personalized transport."

But, Henry smirked. *It doesn't tell me who's in it. But let's see what these new binoculars can do.*

Despite the unbelievable technology that the Executioners had had access to, true cloaking devices weren't all that common, and access to them was strictly controlled by the military. After all, do you want terrorists to actually be able to turn invisible? Fuck no ... look at what the Executioners and the Night Rangers can do ... Therefore, most of the adaptive camouflage that Henry had seen still had a distortive affect as an object moved. And, eventually, such a distortion finally popped up in the distance.

As advertised, the new binoculars helped outline—and highlighted—the distortion. He zoomed in on the craft, but he kept the field of vision wide enough so that he could track of it as it moved side-to-side as the pilot tried to use the horizon and ocean to better conceal it.

"Is he in range?" Henry looked down at the communication systems. Morrison hovered over them too, and a young Comm-Tech gulped and looked in Harvardson's direction.

"No, sir, he—"

"It's, Henry." Harvardson beamed. "You're no longer working for mercenaries, Ted."

"Yes, Henry." The youth smiled too, even though it lacked confidence. Harvardson grinned from something he'd seen too often. "H-he hasn't sent any—wait, here it is." Ted tilted his screen so that Pat and Henry could see it. The passcode the craft sent matched the latest batch.

"That's it." Henry nodded to Morrison. "Better let this bird land to make sure."

"Sure thing." Patrick signaled to Linda at a duties-station. She was already assigning guards for Henry's protection. Her long black hair shimmered in the lights when she nodded his way, and her violet eyes showed confidence. Former mercenary or not, she was beautiful and deadly.

A true Femme Fatale, he thought to himself before biting his lower lip—suddenly feeling foolish for eyeing a woman who was forty years younger than he was. And not even *his* type.

He laughed to himself and followed Pat out of the control room. When they exited the control tower, they met up with the guards—consisting of four men and two women. They walked over to the fifth landing pad, which was located on the north wing of the castle. Each member of the team carried heavy, Mark-4 rifles with medium-plate armor.

Studying the thick plating, Harvardson suddenly wondered if he'd made a mistake by not wearing his own. Despite Pat's vehement recommendations, Henry had left his armor in the control room, even though he'd been simply mimicking the actions of his own Security Director.

They eventually reached the landing pad and stepped onto the deck. Patrick had Henry stand behind the guards, even though sensors had confirmed that there were no external weapons on the car. The pad's landing assists would also prevent the craft from suddenly slamming forward and crushing them.

Beyond the walls of the castle, ocean breakers crashed. Henry felt the wind blowing from the shore, making a rushing sound as it blew around his ears when he turned a certain way. There were a host of other sounds, including the blips from Morrison's handheld equipment, the slight hum from the guards' medium-heavy rifles as they checked the power levels, and the sound of birds.

Looking around, Henry spied the north wall where three doves were sitting. They were milk white, and their eyes glistened in the sunlight. But they immediately flew away when a hovercar rose over the edge of the landing platform and turned off its camouflage. It slipped gingerly toward the waiting party, obviously cautious of the weapons targeting it. As expected, the craft was dark blue, with various black, sensory modules located on various panels. Then, thankfully, as it lowered its landing skids, its forward lights blinked in a familiar pattern. Henry smiled and ran over to the car when it landed. The driver's side door—

"Wait, Henry!" Morrison barked, but Henry was already too close to the craft. He heard the sounds of the guards behind him. "The car's antigravs are working at a higher—"

Ka-crack! Ka-crack! Ka-crack!

Cannon fire made his ears ring. An iron vice suddenly clasped hard around his throat. Above the ringing of his ears, he began to hear screams and groans and final gasps. He tried to see, but the grip around his neck was too tight, forcing his eyes to close.

"Oh, pardon me," a terrible tenor with a familiar accent whispered into his left ear. "By all means, open your eyes and take a look at your future." The grip on his throat loosened some while he was turned around.

He wished he hadn't opened his eyes. There was nothing left of his guards—armor plating had been blown apart and they had pretty much been cut in half. Beside them, Morrison was almost unidentifiable, except for an instrument in the grip of a violently shaking hand.

"What do you want?" Henry stammered. It was a stupid question, but what else could he have said?

A massive, 20mm e-cannon—heat radiating from its barrels—flashed in the corner of his eye. The recoil must have been tremendous, and the bursts he'd heard must have been from supersonic pops. That was impressive for such big projectiles.

The grip around his neck grew tighter. It turned him away from the death and toward his attacker, who was a giant standing before him. Thinking he was still asleep on his lounge chair, Henry couldn't believe anyone that big could have moved out of the car and killed his people so quickly.

"Nothing much," the man said. He tossed the cannon onto one of the car's seats, which discolored some when the heat from the barrels got too close. "Just your life."

"Fuck you! Eat this!" Henry pulled his sidearm, shoved his pistol in the man's mouth and emptied his clip—

Crack! Crack! Crack! Crack! Crack! Crack! Crack! Crack! Crack! Crack! Crack!

Henry expected the hand to slide from his neck, expected to be covered in blood ...

"You done?" the man asked as he spit out one of the rounds.

"What the fuck are—" Henry's voice was cut short when the grip tightened on his throat.

"*That* in due time ... But first, we need some privacy." The giant spun Harvardson around and grabbed him around the waist with an arm bigger than Henry's thigh—

"Fuuuuuuck!" Henry screamed, his stomach suddenly upending, when he realized the monster had jumped off the platform. He blinked too, disorientation almost getting the best of him, and momentarily saw sky. Then tree branches soon clawed at his face and arms while he and the monster fell through them.

They landed, and the giant ran, deftly avoiding the trunks of the large trees nearby his castle. Most of this vegetation had sprouted up from a growth zone on the North African Coast, which was a hundred miles away from Harvardson's island fort—

An electronic scream suddenly began to blare just as Henry was about to shout for help. He wondered if Smithers' old car was now putting off a series of distortion pulses too, making tracking equipment temporarily ineffective. Then he heard explosions and rifle fire. But the alarm persisted, despite what his people did to silence it.

"Now that should keep them busy for quite a while," the giant whispered once they were far enough away from the castle. "I boosted the shielding quite a bit and I doubt that they'll try to hit it with anything too big with it locked onto your castle."

"Great," Henry managed to say. "What the hell do you think you're going to accomplish? Why didn't you just kill me? Unless you enjoy torture?"

He smirked, but his stomach felt queasy. Regardless, he was still going to make this bastard work for—

"No, I don't enjoy it." The monster shook his head, and for a moment even seemed disgusted. "Torture that was politically administered in the past was never proven to gain the truth. It's often wielded by hate and answered in desperation. However, I'm an exception. I'll tell you that some have resisted successfully, but I swear to God that you will tell me what I want to know. This I am determined."

Henry shuddered. He couldn't help it. He just did. A pair of ruby sunglasses hid the man's eyes. The man's cheeks were strong, the hair was cut short, and the stubble of a dark beard rested around taut lips.

"I don't know what you're after. You've taken everything from me," Henry spat. "But I'll probably be a slobbering idiot in a few seconds, so eat shit!"

"You mean by this?" The man pulled out a thin wire, blood still on it. "This was in one of your people. I'm surprised that it wasn't set to kill them. We found out how to disable it with a special transmission awhile back."

Hearing that, Harvardson began kicking the monster in the chest. Frugal had wanted to activate a "kill switch." But Henry had pulled the "partner clause" and prevented it. "You mean you killed all those people at those bases to make a point? You motherfuckers, you could have just left them alone."

The man before him seemed to pause ... seemingly bewildered for a second ... before reforming a scowl.

"It's my sin to bear," the monster breathed out. "Your other fortress' computer didn't have the info I needed. It's taken me eight days to find you. And we're going to play one final game to end this hunt."

"You might as well kill me now," Harvardson shouted, his body shaking with both fear and rage. "I won't run to satisfy your debauchery."

The villain laughed, "No, I'm not that sadistic, but we are going to play a game of truth."

"What?" Henry shook his head. "I have nothing to tell." An old memory suddenly flashed in his mind. He thought about his mother, of an incident like this one concerning her. He'd watched her die when he was very young, under the hands of a government agent. Of course, with such an onrush of memories, Henry almost broke down ... But ... but the face of the man before him caused his pride to take control of him and he spat venom instead: "In fact, shove it! You know I am already guilty of your sick brand of morals. Kill me already!"

"You don't understand. I will ... wait ... what ... what's *this*?" Henry noticed the man look down toward his left breast pocket in shock. The man's attention zeroed in on the shirt pin he had recently gotten for his retirement.

"It's from my partner ..." Henry coughed from the tightness of the grip on his throat. Henry wasn't actually proud of the pin. He'd put it on as a reminder of his shame and of how it had all gone wrong. But it was also a simple reminder of his former life and what he had tried to do ... During these last two decades, he'd been trying to help people ... people whom the government didn't seem to care about.

"You poor damn fool." The monster frowned. "Such good pawns we make, eh?"

Henry didn't understand what the man meant. He could only guess this giant was an Executioner. But how many enemies had he made over the years? Hell, Frugal might have even ended the partnership, necessitating Harvardson's *complete* retirement.

"Anyway," the words from the giant came out in a groan. "I don't have much time. Your time's just as limited, so I'll start this game. I'm sure you'll catch on after my example.

"My name is Jameson Saint John. I am the Leader of the Executioners. I also escaped from a secret, government army of the FGGO, who reports to the Panterian Guard. No, they aren't the silly, made-up, megalomaniacal groups in those Bond movies, or the secretive agencies that hire or recruit superheroes in those Tera Hart movies. Fuck, you probably think these groups are just the mercenary squads that were hired by Congress in Phijeyoton. Needless-to-say, a history lesson for you isn't necessary, and would be a waste of time.

"So I am a Nagi, a human suffering from Nagephon, unlike what lies have told you about such human lineage. I became a Rebel the day my wife died at a battle between my group and the Night Rangers." The ruby visors did nothing except gaze toward Henry, but a cheek twitched beneath them. "I'm a genetic chimera ... homage to and an amalgamation of comic-book heroes that FGGO scientists either coaxed out of my own DNA or simply added to the pot. For example, I have a skeleton that has been re-enforced by an adamant-alloy, which is a derivative of the strongest material on Panteria. It allows me to carry heavy loads and leap extraordinary distances. I'm pretty much invulnerable, can fly and can lift incalculable weight. Hmm ... no heat vision though ... Also, in my forearms, I have three, adamant Kurgon blades. With which I'm going to kill you."

The ... *Kurgon* Beast stood with his left hand around Henry's throat. Jim brought his right hand up near his own face—

Between his knuckles, three crystal-looking blades slowly slid out and distorted the man's lips, cheeks and nose.

"Now it's your turn," Jim said, as the two outside blades slid back into his arm. "But please note that I have a power that can detect the fluctuations of your natural energy and lets me know if you're lying. There is also a penalty point for lying to me—"

The remaining blade flashed, and it sank easily into Henry's shoulder. He screamed, and his eyes watered from the searing pain. But he still managed to spit in the Rebel's face.

"Fighting against me is useless," Jim smirked. "I would have given you a truth serum, but I wanted you to be conscious. I think you would want it this way. So start wherever you'd like. This is your last confession."

Henry couldn't help but let the tears of pain fall from his eyes, and he knew he couldn't keep the words from coming. Naturally, he wouldn't betray any of his surviving people. But apart from that, he really didn't have any secrets anymore.

He started when he was a child, when he lived in the ruins of a city just outside of San Francisco. He talked about his mother and how she had been killed. He then elaborated on his introduction into the drug market. He'd smuggled both medicines and illegal drugs back then—helping the sick and making people forget about what the government and rebels were doing to their homes.

He didn't know the significance of what he was saying, of course. But he figured the giant would ask him more specific questions in time. Besides, he only wanted Death to come now, even if it meant a quicker trip to Hell.

Am I truly damned? he asked. He couldn't bring himself to answer, even when he thought about a series of statues that had been destroyed over a week ago. In his heart he knew those men had been more than sculptured marble. In his heart, he knew that they couldn't have approved of all the things he'd done in his life ... things he had done to rebels, government agents, and any of those terrible bastards, who had killed families and innocent people for the sake of war. However, despite it all, looking into the eyes of the monster before him now, he just hoped that he had made a difference.

Jim St. John landed the hovercar on the deck of HBII. Before turning off its reactor core, he wondered what he was going to do with it. He'd probably destroy it, or, better yet, just toss it into the sun. The thought of it being here sort of sickened him, and he wondered if he should have just flown here on his own and left it where it was.

He smirked at that. Sure, comic books and movies depicted superheroes flying all over the world with nothing but their costumes, but HCs made it easier to carry your luggage. Naturally, he could have had someone just pick him up, but he had wanted the privacy. Needed the privacy and the alone time.

He eventually stepped out of the car, and he was immediately surrounded by people, all wishing him a warm reception home. Arthor was first to take his hand, quickly apologizing for Anna, who was having some problems with the new medical equipment and couldn't make it. Jennifer, who he could tell seemed angry with him, stepped up and gave him a quick but warm hug anyway. John gave him a strong handshake. Other Crystalians were here too in great numbers, all wishing Jim a happy return.

"All right, all right, already," he barked. He'd been gone, but at what price? Still, it was good to feel appreciated and missed, even though he thought about a couple of friends he so wanted to be here too. "I don't mean to pry, but don't you all have better things you could be—

"Why are you guys looking at me like that?" he asked irritably, noticing the way they were all clumped together. Everyone in the huge crowd had these big, goofy smiles and certainly seemed full of mischief. *Is this time for such foolery?*

"We have a surprise for you," Arthor explained, smiling broadly. Then his wing curled tightly—

"Logan!" Jim laughed and gawked at the man, who sported an all too familiar grin. He quickly gave his friend an informal handshake and a hug.

"Glad to see you TOO!" McMillian yelped when Jim got carried away. "Hey! Hey! Easy! I just got these ribs fixed!"

Jim set the man down and held his shoulders warmly. "But I thought you were dead."

"That's obvious." People laughed when the weapons specialist gestured with his hands and face. "I think you guys ended up having a funeral for a wild boar that got caught up in the explosions. And shit, I nearly broke my ass trying to hop up on that damned pedestal you put the *Blade* on."

"But how? Where were you?" Jim smiled, despite what he had just done to another living being. And what he had just learned.

"Well, I would have wrote and all. But I was kinda out of it. You see, Tracie—"

"Who?" Jim had often exaggerated his questions and his perplexity for someone's benefit. But he quickly reminded himself that *she* wasn't here.

"Tracie," Logan repeated. "If it hadn't been for her, I probably would still have been there for you guys to find me. Of course, I would've been dead. Anyhoo, she helped me with my condition, healed my body and gave me back my memories."

Logan gestured with his right arm. The crowd moved apart, and a beautiful woman approached them. She was about five-eight, had black hair, glowing skin, and the most piercing, blue-green eyes.

"Hello, I'm Tracie," she introduced herself. "It's finally nice to meet the person behind the Executioners. I've heard so much about you, and I'm honored to be in your presence. You've done so much here with the base, the resistance, and the building of a wonderful man." She looked at Logan, who smiled back.

"And I would like to thank you for it," she continued. She tugged on his field coat, prompting him to bend down so that she could place a soft kiss on his cheek. Its warmth comforted him some, but he got a weird vibe from her, even though his life-detection power wasn't blaring alarm. However, he shrugged it off for now, knowing that Logan wouldn't have brought anyone here without the necessary precautions.

"I'm glad to meet you too." He grinned and shook her hand again. "But I must say that the base was already here, and Logan has always been a better man than me. So how's your stay been so far? How long have you guys been here?"

"Just over four days, and I've had a wonderful time. Thank you. I never thought it would be anything like this. Modesty should not take its hand in this effort, Jim. You have done a wonderful job. And, with your permission, I'd like to stay."

"By all means, please do." Jim nodded, trusting Logan's judgment. "We'll make all the necessary arrangements. We are always accepting of new friends. An apartment will be accommodated for your—"

"Jim, we have to talk about that," Logan interrupted. "Tracie's been staying with me. And ... umm ... if it's okay, we'd like to be married soon." Hearing that, the crowd cheered with approval.

"What? Absolutely," Jim laughed, hugging them both. "We'll set it up whenever you're ready. Congratulations!" And the three of them were instantly encompassed by a gleeful crowd.

Eventually, Jim pealed himself away. Really, he wasn't in the mood for celebration just yet. Henry's story about nirv was beginning to worry him—so much that he hardly felt the tap on his shoulder.

"Yes?" He turned, lowering his head at the same time. He saw Logan staring up at him. "Shouldn't you be with your fiancée?"

"She knows why I'm here," the man said. "I needed to tell you this. It's important."

"What is it?"

"Well, Tracie"—Logan blinked, looked away, and then stared back in Jim's eyes—"she used to work for Infiltration, and—"

"Infiltration?" Jim then lowered his voice, knowing how good Infiltrators could hear. "Logan, do you really trust her? Do you need us to—"

The former CIA man immediately raised his hands and grinned. "No, no, it's not *that*. Of course I do. This is about nirv. She used to guard the stuff in a facility under the guise of being a GZ Monitor. Well ... I mean ... she really was a GZ Monitor ... but she was still also working as an agent for an affiliate of Infiltration ... but ... then ... not really? It's pretty complicated. Anyway, she ... well ... the warehouse she was keeping track of was also nearby the booby-trapped base that blew me up. So I guess ... I mean ... it was most likely created by the government. They're up to—"

"Logan, go back to her." Jim interrupted him. "This is your time to be happy. Don't spoil it just yet."

"But—"

"I know, man. I know ... we had suspected that since Jennifer's arrival, remember? Anyway, this last mission was to confirm it. I found the man who had been contracted by the government to make it. But do you know what they're going to use it for?"

Logan lowered his head, tapping his right foot softly. "No, by then, Tracie wasn't really even in Infiltration's command structure ... something ... something about being ... banished? She'd only been assigned to watch one of the facilities. She didn't even know about the one that had been booby trapped. So, damn, I guess not."

"Good God," Jim sighed, suddenly feeling tons of sympathy for their new citizen. "If she was banished, she has had to deal with a lot of shit. I'm glad she found you."

"Thanks, Jim."—Logan nodded approvingly—"but I'm the lucky one. So ... what now?"

Jim rested a hand on his friend's shoulder. "As for nirv? We'll all need to sit down. She'll be a good resource to help us figure it all out ... This is just too big to be benevolent ... Puppeteer government agencies are only altruistic if it benefits them. But, shit, it's not even physically addictive, and it wouldn't do well to control a person's mind ... let alone one of a Nagi ..."

"Maybe they have some other plan for it," Logan offered. "Arthor couldn't come up with anything, nor John. Tracie is offering whatever help she can. Otherwise, we've held off telling the rest of the Governing Council, because we wanted to talk with you first. We fear the worst."

"True," Jim agreed. "Considering the expense and construction, it's certainly not just a simple hallucinogen. But I have no idea what it could be. They have over a thousand warehouses hidden all over the world. The manufacturer, Harvardson, told me that even though he was told that it was for humanitarian reasons—for PTSD or other psychological disorders in war-torn areas—the push into the general public hadn't happened until recently ..."

Jim motioned to Logan to head back over to the crowd and save Tracie, who was starting to turn a bright red from all the attention. "There's a lot to discuss, Logan, but let's give the Crystalians some time to enjoy your guys' engagement. Go and enjoy the rest of the day with Tracie and the others. Then we should all get some dinner to catch up, okay?"

"Yeah ..." Logan frowned but eventually let his broad, infectious smile form on his face when he looked over at the woman he was going to marry. "Okay. Good. Tracie is looking forward to getting to know you. You sure made one hell of an impression on the FEMET kids back then."

"Well, of course, I did. It's *me*," Jim allowed himself a chuckle and gave Logan a quick hug before his friend walked back over to his fiancée—actually doing a little dance to the claps and cheers of the crowd ...

Jim's smile eased from his face while he walked the parameter of the hangar ... making it look like he was doing a little inspection so that no one would worry.

"Ah fuck ... fuck ... fuck," he sighed and then looked up at the ceiling of Hangar Bay Two, carefully eyeing the several pairs of large doors that sealed the Executioners away from the rest of Panteria.

For a moment, he wished, actually wished that the ceiling was the extent of their world ...

How wonderful would that be? he wished quietly, but knew that the Executioners had been created just to fuck with *this* type of bullshit.

He shook his head and reached into his coat pocket. He noticed that there was no blood on the material of his coat, even after the incidents with Henry and Smithers.

St. John closed his eyes and said a quick prayer for those two men. They had been good people, at least better than Jim could ever hope to be. Even under torture, Harvardson's Chief of

Operations, Lindle Smithers, had given nothing away about his former life: absolutely nothing about his coworkers ... especially his boss. Adding to that, Smithers had had a family and a kind heart. The man had two daughters ... so young ... Harvardson had been their godfather and treated them like his own grandchildren ...

Good men ... good enough for this world anyway ... and Jim had escalated this war and had brought ruin upon them ... Then he'd chased Harvardson down just in the minute hope that the man had known something about Rebecca ...

Harvardson hadn't known anything about Rebecca either, Jim sighed, worried about what had become of her. *Henry said that he'd turned the matter over to Frugal ... Nelson Frugal.*

Jim's fingers fumbled around and finally found what they were searching for. He pulled a piece of jewelry from his pocket—the same shirt pin Harvardson had been wearing. It was the size of an Old Age quarter. Its features burned into his skull and brought back memories he always tried to forget, but failed to do so.

There was no other reason why Henry would have been given this, except as a warning. They knew the Executioners would find the man. Hell, they probably had set him up for a fall.

The Governor of Crystal Mountain looked at the black, gold eagle seeming to jut out from the rest of the ornament. Its wings were stretched out wide, and its feet were raised as though they appeared like tiny nostrils, which were part of a mask. Skull and crossbones, the ancient symbol of the Jolly Rogers, rested behind the eagle-shaped mask. However, instead of bones, swords with bone handles pointed downward behind the partially hidden skull. And a Latin phrase rested between the crossed swords and under the skull ...

Jim closed his eyes, thinking about Fate ... the Norns ... those fucking bitches ...

Shit, why can't we be like those unknowing bastards out there? Why can't we be part of the mindless? not knowing truth from lie or reality from dream? However, he knew that he once had been such a person. And he dared not think about what he would have been like today if Lisa had not freed him.

Jim looked down at the pin again, and he quietly read what was inscribed on it: "Domini Absconditi Mortis."

The words were easy to read, clear enough, and the meaning was just as clear. It was a motto, a familiar phrase Jim had heard often after General Eric van Anderson had taken over the Agency.

"Masters of Secret Death," Jim repeated, this time in English. "Who else would have been behind this? It had to be Infiltration."

EPILOGUE

When I hear the word "culture" I reach for my revolver.

(Schlegeter)

—Hanns Johst, German writer (1933 A.D.)

"Nelson, I'm sorry," Henry Harvardson had said. "I should have brokered some type of truce. I never could have imagined what they were capable of. They have an army. A good one. Be careful."

Grand General Jeffery Neilson McDonald—AKA Nelson Frugal—remembered the last thing Henry had said to him. That had been a week ago, and about two weeks earlier the Executioners had destroyed his nirv production facility. It had been a well-guarded and well-armed complex with six production plants, multiple buildings for admin, storage, labs, housing, and a fortress at its center.

Jeff had to admit that the Executioners had been very vigilant and thorough. They still hadn't claimed any responsibility for what they had done. They never did—only relying on rumor and speculation that they were involved with anything. Hell, some government agencies—Puppet and Puppeteer alike—still didn't believe the Executioners existed. They were just bogeymen to bring fright to the unjust and unlawful.

Jeff knew they existed. Henry's warning even surprised him though. *That* in itself meant something.

Thankfully, the Executioners hadn't even scratched the surface on all the storage sites that Henry had set up for him. It wasn't like Jeff was hiding it from the Executioners. Fuck, they hadn't even existed when he'd first contracted Henry to start building it *en masse*.

He realized, however, that the Executioners had finally popped up on the Guard's radar. Overall, the Guard didn't mind vigilantes and other do-gooders—those types tended to inspire people and keep some bad people in line. But, nevertheless, such activities were also limited to a very small sandbox, as far as the Guard was concerned. Naturally, the Executioners had been suspected of Anderson's assassination, but the investigations had been inconclusive. So, the Guard had been monitoring scuttlebutt on the street, and following the expedience of how quickly the Executioners had taken out the first group of drug czars, and, of course, Henry's operation.

Now, with the Puppeteer Government's efforts to curb riots and all-out turf wars behind the scenes—assisting the Puppet Government as needed—the Guard had asked Infiltration, the Blood Raiders and other agencies for strategies and solutions to deal with this new group of instigators. With their "holier than thou" war on drugs, the Executioners had caused some chaos. The Guard didn't like chaos, even though Jeff knew that they caused a lot of it. Still, they were the Guard and they ruled the Solar System. The Executioners didn't and they had fucked up.

The Blood Raiders—the pompous, egotistical assholes that they were—presented a blunt and overly simplistic resolution. For the most part, they had gained significant influence in dealing with such matters. They had capitalized on the devastation that the AOM had suffered years ago, and had maneuvered in and filled the void. Now, they were the primary agency to engage stigs with large numbers of combatants. Their plan was simple: WAR!

The other agencies, smaller and *specialized*, recommended finding the Executioners' base and/or bases of operation and hit them with antimatter. Simple enough.

McDonald grimaced. The Executioners had actually been doing some good. Of course until they had started fucking with his plans.

He'd submitted his own proposal to the Guard, citing his experience and his recent intelligence about the Executioners.

He also had a few aces in the hole, which he'd utilize as needed.

The Executioners had an army.

Well, fuck, he *had* one too.

—<><><>—

To Be Continued in ...

Panteria Chronicles: Tarnished

ABOUT THE AUTHOR

L.B. Sisk works as a Director of Marketing for a robotics company, which supplies analytical systems for clients in medical, environmental and government laboratories. Sure, you'd think developing marketing collateral for sophisticated robots would be fun; however, when they're boring and benefit Humanity ... Blah. Blah. Blah. Therefore, by night, he aspires to share his twisted imagination with like-minded folk. He lives in the Portland, Oregon, which, according to some vagabond he met in Barstow, CA, is a beautiful, fantasyland of unlimited strip clubs and craft breweries. What more could you ask for?

Please find out more at:

www.lbsisk.com

Made in the USA
Charleston, SC
23 November 2016